I0721335

Knights of the Octagon:
Benefactor

Colleen Snyder

Thanks To:

My WordWeavers Critique group, Page 37: Merilyn Howton, Donnie Stevens, Bobby Bixler, Mary Claire Branton, Marilyn Brandon, and Ane Mulligan.

Also my ACFW Scribes Critique group, Group 260: E Marie Ullrey and Jane Baker.

You make me a better writer every time we talk. Thank you!

MONDAY—WEEK ONE

Roiling water spit Micah up from the bottom of the river. Seconds later, frothing rapids buried him again. Submerged tree limbs clutched at his shoulders, raking across his back. Half-exposed boulders arrested his descent. The river's power jerked him and hurled him further down the canyon. There was no thought of saving himself, no glimmer of a plan to escape the raging flood.

He gasped at air when his head wrenched above the liquid death before the water dragged him under. Over and over, the torture repeated. Breathe. Smash into something. Lose your breath. Sink under the waves. Get thrown in the air. Breathe. Sunlight and shadow. Daylight and darkness. Life and death.

A last curl ejected him onto a shoal of weathered stones. His body washed on the rocks. Battered. Crushed. Beaten. But still. Gloriously still.

Micah drew in long gulps of air. He forced his bruised and cracked ribs to expand and contract, drawing in oxygen. He closed his eyes. "Tav. Luke. Jeremiah." Each name a prayer. Finally, he whispered the only Name that mattered. "God. Help us. All of us. Please. Save my friends." Consciousness raced away.

* * *

Micah woke, his body convulsing with the cold. Something heavy was being dragged near him. Micah's head spun from the thrashing the river gave him. He couldn't focus his eyes. The dragging stopped. A weight dropped beside him. Footsteps crunched on the gravel. Walked away.

More dragging. Coming closer. Lighter. Faster. Micah tried to force his eyes open, his brain to make sense of what he heard.

A still, water-logged figure lay beside him. With a muffled thud, another burden dropped across the way. A dark blur of willow branches, reeds, and ferns knelt beside the second lump on the shore. The figure began bouncing up and down on the lump's chest.

CPR?

Too many blows to the head. A bush doing chest compressions? Micah swept his hands across his face, trying to understand what his brain thought he saw. Yet the vision remained. A shrub was doing CPR on the figure on the ground. Micah tried to sit. His muscles refused to respond. He choked, then called out, "What?"

No answer. The rescue-bush didn't turn or stop. The figure kept working, feverishly pumping. The object on the ground coughed, spit, coughed, rolled over, and moaned.

Tav. The voice belonged to Tav. Which meant the water-logged figure closest to Micah was Jeremiah...or... Micah heard his friend wheezing. Snoring. Yeah, that would be Jeremiah.

Micah rested back. He closed his eyes. They were alive. They survived. He whispered, "Thank You, Lord."

Micah heard more movement. Their rescuer shuffled around for several more moments, then grew quiet. Warmth radiated on Micah's left side. He opened his eyes again.

A fire burned in a rock pit. The rescue-bush disappeared. Whoever he might be, he'd given life twice. Once in the CPR, and now in the fire to keep them from hypothermia. Micah sighed and closed his eyes again. "Thank You, Lord, for sending Your angel. Send him back so we can thank him properly, please." He chuckled as he drifted off. "Angels in the bushes."

A hard thought jolted him awake.

Luke.

* * *

Luke tore at the scrub pine blocking his path. Tears of anger, frustration, and loss poured over his face. "I've got to find Tav! I've got to find my brother!" He fell to his knees and screamed at the sky. "God! Why did you let this happen? Help me. I've got to find him."

A rafting trip. The Knights of the Octagon's last hurrah before Luke went to college. Tav, his older brother by two years. Tav's two best friends and classmates, Micah and Jeremiah. Followed by Luke. Knights of the Octagon. That's what they'd called themselves ever since they were kids. Octagon because no one owned a round table, and Knights of the Oval sounded weird.

"Stupid game. Look where it got us." He lifted his head and bellowed, "Tav!"

There was no answer. There wouldn't be. Couldn't be. Their four-man raft hit a gnarly set of rapids and dumped them all. Luke was thrown toward shore. Micah, Tav, and Jeremiah all disappeared under the torrent. He'd seen their heads bob up, go under, bob up, go under….

And he didn't see them again. He'd pulled himself to the trail running alongside the river. He would outpace them to the bottom. Be there to pull them to safety. They would all have a laugh, blame each other, hike out. Sure, they'd lost their cell phones, their GPS, their gear. But they would survive. Together. They would.

Except the trail moved inland, and the river divided. Luke couldn't know which way his brother went.

Luke stood and slashed at the foliage in front of him. "No! I have to find him. I will find him. Tav!"

Something smacked Luke on his shoulder. He whirled around to look behind. Nothing. No one. Muscle spasm? Shoulder pull? He faced front again and started beating a path forward.

Something hit him again. Luke spun around. Definitely not a muscle spasm. But nothing in view. Something plopped to his right. Luke eyed the direction the noise came from. Shrubs blocked his view. But a bush swayed. Did something stalk him?

Too little oxygen to the brain. He must be imagining. Luke backed away carefully, one step at a time. He turned to resume his path.

A rock hit him in the back. He swung around. His hands curled into tight fists. "Knock it off! What do you want?"

A bush jiggled a few yards away. Then another yard further. And another. Luke yelled, "Go away! I've got to find my brother!" He turned back, only to be pelted by small stones. Luke raised his arms over his head and howled. "Stop! I'll kill you if I catch you!"

He was yelling at the bushes. Trees. Nothing. But again, the bushes jerked. Something moved away. The motion stopped. Waited? Why? For what? Luke turned his head enough to watch the shrub out of the corner of his eye. He pretended to step away. The bush shook violently. Luke faced the motion. What was with this plant? "You want me to follow you?"

Branches a yard further ahead dipped. Up and down. Nodding.

Luke narrowed his eyes to peer into the distance. Nothing. He could see nothing. But bears don't throw rocks, and they don't tempt you to follow them to their lair. Whatever this might be, the thing knew which direction they wanted to go and wanted Luke to follow. In his desperation, he didn't care. Alien or Bigfoot, if the bush knew Tav's location, Luke would follow. Luke called, "I'm looking for my brother and his friends. Do you know where they are?"

Another nod from a sapling further up the way. Luke's

"guide" wanted to maintain distance between him and them. Out of sight? Why?

What mattered? If they knew where to find Tav, he'd follow them anywhere. Luke limped forward. "I'm coming. I'm coming."

* * *

Evening neared when the guide made a mistake, allowing Luke to glimpse what he followed. A shadow between two trees moved unnaturally against the gentle wind blowing. Luke got an impression of tree branches, ferns, vines…a little over four feet tall…two feet around? *A child in a ghillie suit? How? Why?* And how did they know where Tav and the others ended up? Luke hobbled hard to catch up, trying to come alongside the guide. But the little guy moved faster and stayed just beyond Luke's reach.

Until they topped a rise. Luke heard a thump and saw his guide roll over and over down the hill. Still between bushes, so Luke couldn't nail down a profile. But the small ball tumbled to the bottom of the slope. The thing lay still for a few seconds, crawled to its feet—if it had feet—and crept into the darkness between the trees.

Luke chuckled. "You okay, guy?" He slid down the side of the incline and reached the bottom. "You okay? You out there?"

No answer. Luke waited for a sign, a signal, something. Anything. "Now what?" Did the bush bring him this far only to abandon him?

The smell of wood burning caught his attention. A fire. Luke followed his nose to a clearing beside the river. The deep gloom made identifying shapes almost impossible. But three lumps or logs lay prone around a small campfire. Covered in silver, survival-type covers. Luke approached the first one. He held his breath, lifted one end of the shroud….

Boots. Feet. Wrong end.

Did it have a wrong end?

Luke stepped to the top of the figure and pulled down the

cover.

Jeremiah Acosta grabbed the blanket back. "Mine." The four-day growth of black beard shrouded Jeremiah's face. He muttered more than spoke. Still sleeping.

Air rushed from Luke's lungs. He spun, pulled a cover back to reveal a second man.

Tav. Blond touseled hair concealed most of his eyes. In contrast to Jeremiah's plenty, Tav's sparse beard scattered across his bruised face. Luke sank down beside his brother. "Thank You, God."

Micah's weary voice drifted across the clearing. "Good to have you with us, Luke. I was worried about you."

Luke turned and climbed over to sit beside Micah.

His friend sat and passed his hand across his face. Micah motioned to a bundle near the fire. "There's a blanket for you, too. Someone knew you were coming."

"Someone?" Luke eyed Micah carefully. His meager brown beard barely covered the cuts, and his eyes looked exhausted.

Micah exhaled. "Yeah. We can talk about it in the morning. I need sleep."

Luke squeezed his friend's shoulder. "Yeah. We all do. We'll talk tomorrow."

Micah eased back to a prone position and covered up with the wrap. Luke moved to get his own blanket. He sat near his brother, lay down, and closed his eyes. He whispered, "I mean it. Thank you. I owe you."

He slept.

TUESDAY

Micah opened his eyes and sat up slowly. Morning trickled through the trees, bringing light and life back to the cove. He looked across the still-smoldering campfire at the long, lanky figure of Luke Vannose lying next to his brother. The two remained fiercely protective of each other even into their twenties. Who protected who this time?

Did it matter? Luke found them. Micah raised his face to the sky. "Thank You." He crawled from under his blanket and stirred the fire, bringing the warmth back to life. A pile of pre-broken tree limbs sat stacked outside the circle. He smiled. "Thanks for the wood, too. Send our rescuer back, please. I want to shake his hand. If he has them."

He moved as little as possible, afraid to test his body and find out if anything was beyond bruised. Sitting in front of the fire, he decided warming himself would be enough for the first hour. Once his muscles stopped shivering, he'd test them properly.

Luke stirred. He sat and blinked his eyes as if to clear them. He seemed dazed. Micah could relate. He called, "Yeah, we're all here."

Tav groaned. Luke spun to face his brother. Tav jacked to a sitting position. "I hurt everywhere. My chest feels like someone pounded on it." He rubbed his hand across his eyes.

Before Micah could open his mouth, Jeremiah turned

over and joined the meeting. "What happened? Where are we?" His hand clasped the silver covering. "Where did these blankets come from? We didn't have them on the raft, did we?"

Micah led the discussion. "What does everyone remember? I know we came around the bend, and the bottom dropped out of the river. Then I landed in the water."

Luke agreed. "Yeah. We all did. Except the river carried you three farther downstream than me. I got lucky and ended up on the bank." He scooted closer to the fire.

Tav continued to rub his head. "I remember the drop and a lot of water." He gazed at Jeremiah. "You?"

"What you said. Nothing much beyond that." The big man mirrored Luke's action. Closer to the fire would be warmer.

Tav turned to his brother. "You followed the river to find us?"

Luke hesitated, then dropped his gaze. "Uh, not exactly. I, uh, got twisted around. The river splits. I didn't know which way you guys went."

Tav insisted, "But you found us. Good work on your part." He glanced around at the blankets. "Still doesn't explain all this."

Luke continued to stammer. "No. I didn't find you. A guide showed up. Someone led me to you."

Tav sat a little straighter. "A guide? Who?"

"I don't know. I, uh, never got a real good look at him. It."

Tav's eyes narrowed. "What do you mean, 'It?' What are you talking about?"

Jeremiah joined the interrogation. "Yeah. What are you talking about?" The big man leaned forward to peer at Luke, his green eyes narrowing.

Micah raised his eyebrows at Luke. The younger man picked up a stick and tossed it into the fire. "Okay. There was this thing." His voice sounded embarrassed. "A short thing. Like a haystack. Or a bear in a ghillie suit. I don't know. The guy wanted me to follow him. That's all I knew. So I did. The thing proved very insistent." He grimaced. "And throws a mean rock."

Micah cocked his head. "How tall?" Maybe Luke saw their rescuer?

Luke motioned with his hand. "Four foot? Maybe a little more."

Tav sniped, "I'll bet you didn't get a good look. I bet you didn't see anything. When we get back to civilization, I'm going to get you a good doctor. You got hit in the head one too many times." He reached up and patted Luke on the shoulder.

Micah shook his head. "He's not crazy."

Jeremiah and Tav turned on Micah. "What? How would you know?"

"Because I saw the same thing. Only bigger."

Jeremiah groaned and lay back down. "He's got brain damage, too."

Micah jerked on his blanket. "Where do you think these came from? Jere, you said yourself we didn't have them in the raft."

Tav stared at the blanket and back at Micah. "No. No, we did not."

Micah pointed to Tav. "Someone—or something—pulled you and Jeremiah out of the water. I washed on shore, but a savior pulled you two out." Micah tapped Tav on the chest. "You hurt because the thing did CPR on you. You weren't breathing, man. He saved your life."

Tav lay a hand on his chest. He stared into the blue and orange flames dancing in the logs. "You didn't start the fire, did you?"

"Nope. He did." Micah pointed to the supply of logs. "And the wood wasn't there last night. Someone is looking out for us. We owe our lives to whatever is under that pile of brush."

Luke frowned. "What I saw wouldn't be big enough to haul Tav this far, much less Jere."

Micah shrugged his shoulders. "Maybe. Maybe there's two of them. Maybe there's a whole herd of them. I don't know. I only know I'm grateful. And when I see them, I'm going to thank them."

Tav stared at the ground for several moments. "Resolved. We thank whatever they are."

Jeremiah snorted. "And question motives later."

Tav ordered, "All in."

All four men raised one hand with a thumbs-up. "Carried." He sat forward. "Who's got what on them? Knives? Multi-tools? Anything?"

The body search revealed three pocketknives, one survival knife (Jeremiah), and one waterlogged compass. Not much to bet their survival on. But they would have to make do.

Luke and Jeremiah walked down to the river. Micah and Tav remained behind to explore the area. Micah noticed Tav didn't try to rise until Luke walked out of ear and eyeshot. Only then did he lean forward and stretch out his right leg. He grimaced as he did. Micah inhaled sharply. "The knee?"

Tav nodded, disgusted. "Yeah. The knee."

Micah knew the knee well. They all did. They lived through the trauma with him when he tore the ligaments his junior year in high school. Stayed with him as he fought and cried and worked and sweated and groaned and rehabbed…only to tear the same knee the following year. Micah remembered how Tav's dad rejected him immediately after. Mr. Vaughn wanted a son who would be an NFL quarterback. If Tav couldn't be one, what good was he?

Micah studied his friend. "How bad?" He dreaded the answer.

Tav rubbed his leg. "Maybe not torn. Maybe bruised. I don't think I can put any weight on it right now." He glanced at Micah. "Don't tell Luke."

"How are you gonna hide this from him? He's gonna know as soon as you stand." Micah tried to hide the mirth in his tone.

"I'll hide it one minute at a time. I don't need him being my mother hen again. I can deal with the knee." Tav threw a rock. The projectile carried some heat as it sailed across the clearing.

Micah swallowed a sigh. Brothers. *Wonder what having a brother would feel like? Or anyone who stayed around and cared what happened to me?* Micah abandoned the thought. More important things to think about. Survival. Food. Getting out of the canyon. Old business could stay in the past. That his brother walked out for a pack of cigarettes and never came back when Micah was only ten meant nothing—Micah slashed the thought hard. No. Not here. Not now.

Tav raised his chin to point. "Look. Three trees back from the wood pile."

Micah peered into the forest. A shadowy four-foot mound peeked around a trunk. Ducked back. Peeked again. Ducked back. Peeked.

Micah studied the shaggy creature a minute. He quashed a niggling fear and called, "You can come in if you like. We want to thank you for saving our lives."

The haystack stepped out three paces. Three deliberate, measured, marched paces. The mound stopped, did an about-face, stepped three paces back toward the tree. The haystack stopped. Its head turned to look over its shoulder. Shaggy took three measured steps backward, stopped, stepped with exaggerated paces forward.

Micah glanced at Tav. Tav stared at the visitor, admitting, "I got nothing."

Micah thought hard. He tilted his head and called, "You want me to follow you?"

The haystack jumped up and down with what Micah took to be excitement. Micah rose to his feet. "Sure. Why not? You've helped us this far."

Tav held out a hand and cautioned, "You're following a guide you know nothing about. You want to rethink this?"

Micah studied the diminutive shrub. "I think it's safe. The thing brought Luke to us, right?"

Tav dipped his head to the side. "So Luke said. I still think he needs a shrink."

"Maybe we all will after this is over. Until such time, I'm

following." Micah moved toward the waiting bush. "I'm coming."

The figure stayed far enough ahead to remain out of reach of Micah's grab. But the little shrub turned back every now and again to make sure Micah stayed behind him. Micah followed him through the woods, probably farther downstream than Luke and Jeremiah. After twenty minutes, the little guide stepped into the sunshine. A grassy appendage waved to the shore, ducked back into shadow, and disappeared.

Micah studied the river's edge. Their camping gear was neatly stacked by the water. Some of their camping gear, anyhow. Lanterns (slightly battered). Waterlogged clothing. Flint. The food box. Micah checked inside and found the rations they brought safely intact. He crowed as he pulled out his coffee pot. "Yes! Safe!"

No sleeping bags, though. The first aid kit was lost, too. Yeah, well, they'd survive. Micah noticed some additional items. Items different than the ones they packed. A hatchet. Rope. Fishing tackle. Pack shovel. Backpacks. Micah guessed the haystacks had been scouring the riverside for lost gear for a while. Successfully, it seemed. And now they wanted to share?

Micah called out, "Thank you. You keep saving us. I hope we can repay you somehow." He raised his hand skyward and added, "Thank You. 'For just the right time,' right?" He smiled. God was good.

He gathered as much paraphernalia as he could carry and followed the river back to the camp. Luke and Jeremiah waited. Jeremiah met him and relieved Micah of his load. "Where did you find this?" Suspicion laced the man's tone.

"Our short haystack led me to their stash. There's more. Further down the shore."

Luke climbed to his feet. "Show me."

Micah motioned with his head. "Follow the river. It's about fifteen minutes."

Luke repeated. "Show me." Intensity laced his tone.

Okay, I get it. You want to talk. Gotcha. "Let's go."

They walked downstream. Micah broke the silence. "So, what's the question?"

"Tav hurt his knee, didn't he?" Luke kicked at rocks.

"Did you ask him?"

"You know I did. And you know his answer. That's why I'm asking you."

Micah couldn't miss the frustration in Luke's voice. "Yeah. I don't know how bad. Maybe a day of rest will help."

"With all this stuff, we could probably give him more than a day. I don't want him to damage the knee permanently."

"We'll put the thought to a vote."

Luke shook his head. "We'll split. Jere always votes with Tav. I'll vote against him, and you'll be the peacemaker."

"We'll have to throw stones for a winner. You know the rules."

Luke grimaced. "I think we're past all those made-up rules, Mick. We're adults. Knight's rules worked when we were younger, but we should be able to handle this without relying on kid's games."

Micah considered his words. "I never saw what we did as a game, Luke. I thought we made life choices." *They gave me a reason to choose life. Without Tav and the Knights, I wouldn't have made it through the dark.*

Luke scowled and gave him the side-eye. "Now you're going to vote against me?"

"I'm going to vote for the well-being of my friend and your brother. That's my commitment to both of you." Micah kept his voice patient.

"Well, I think…" Luke trailed off and pointed. "What is that?"

Micah studied where Luke indicated. The little haystack stood inside the forest but clearly visible. The thing jumped up and spun around, landing one-hundred-twenty-five degrees from where he started. Evidently not good enough. He finished turning the full one-eighty, jumped again.

Still not enough. He tried again. And again. Twigs and branches cycloned around its body, making the little figure look like a vacuum cleaner roller.

Luke and Micah both chuckled. Luke grinned at Micah. "What is he doing?"

Micah considered briefly. "Playing. I think the little guy's playing." Micah watched a minute, then whistled sharply.

The haystack spun to face him, stepped back into the woods, hesitantly moved back to the edge of cover. He came out just enough to be seen but remain safely out of reach.

Micah stayed about five feet from the bush but knelt at eye level with their guest. He visually searched the shrubbery for a face, something to tell him what the thing might be. He saw eyes. Human eyes. Dark. A face covered in mud and dirt. A young face. Micah smiled. "Hi, again. I'm glad to see you. We owe you for helping us out. Did you find all this stuff on your own? Are you alone here?"

The bush made no motion. Luke tapped Micah on the shoulder. "Too many questions, Mick. One at a time."

Micah nodded. "Right. Sorry." He twisted to a sitting position. "Are you alone out here?" The little haystack spun its body back and forth. Micah continued. "I'll take that as a no. Did you find all this stuff by yourself?"

Again, the spinning.

"Do you have a friend who helped you?" The bush bent forward, straightened. "Yes. Is he here?" Spinning. Slow spinning, but the meaning was clear.

Luke tapped Micah again. "Ask him if his friend is bigger than he is."

"You ask him."

"One questioner would be better."

Micah gazed at Luke in confusion but turned back to the shrub. "Is your friend bigger than you?" Again the bow at the middle. Which explained the two sizes. "Is your friend older than you?"

The bush stood still for several moments, making no move to answer.

Luke kept his voice soft. "Maybe that's not something he knows how to calculate."

"Or understand." Micah smiled at the figure. "I'd like you to come back to the camp with us, so you could meet the other guys. Would you join us?"

The shrub bent forward. As it straightened, a wildcat yowled from the hills. The little figure spun and ran off into the woods, leaving Micah confused. Micah stared at Luke. "Did that sound like a call? A summons?"

"Sounded like it."

Micah climbed to his feet. They gathered the remainder of the equipment on the riverbank and returned to the camp.

Jeremiah set up the cookstove while Tav stowed the other gear in an orderly fashion. Jere gawked at the equipment, then grabbed the extra supplies from Luke and Micah. Tav remained seated in the position they'd left him.

Jeremiah nodded. "This'll do. We'll survive."

Tav chuckled, "You doubted us?"

Jeremiah snorted. "I doubted everything about this trip. Since it took us four years to make it happen."

Luke eyed him. "But you came."

"Someone needed to look out for you morons. I don't see any of you getting any smarter."

Tav protested, "It took four years because we waited for Luke to finish high school. Then there was saving the money for tuition to enroll him in college." Tav's eyes narrowed. "Which Mick has helped provide. You promised you'd help, but I don't remember seeing any money coming from you."

Jeremiah snarled. "Because I have a wife and children to support."

Tav sniped, "No, you got suckered into a marriage you never should have been in, and that's why you dropped out of school our senior year."

The big man stared hard at Tav. "And whose fault was that? Where were you guys when Shelly lied to me about being pregnant?"

Tav humphed. "Nursing the bruises you inflicted on us when we tried to tell you the truth. You didn't want to hear it."

Micah rubbed his shoulder reflexively. He remembered

the pain. Jeremiah could pack a punch. And did. Several.

Luke threw his hands into the air. "Are you two still going there?" He pointed to Jeremiah. "We warned you. Shelly played you. You wouldn't listen." He pointed to Tav. "You bailed on the wedding."

Tav grumbled. "It wasn't a wedding. It was an execution."

Luke countered, "Which you still should have attended. All for one and one for all, remember? Knight's honor?" He shot back at Jeremiah, "Where were you when Dad beat me and threw me out of the house because I wouldn't take Tav's place and be the all-everything football star? Tav dropped out of school to go to work to support both of us."

Micah added, "And I dropped out to support my mother. So, we all screwed up. Warner High's brightest and best, and we're all drop-outs. Rehashing the past isn't going to get us back to civilization. Get our minds on where we are, we must. What doing we are." He added a Yoda accent, hoping to lighten the exchange.

It worked. Tav lifted his fist to Jeremiah. Luke put in his fist. Jeremiah did the same, and all three men tapped knuckles. Micah changed the subject. "Up the river or down?"

"Tonight? Neither." Luke. Always protecting Tav.

Micah scowled. "Tomorrow."

"Why then? We have food, water, and fire. Let's rest a few days before we start out."

Jeremiah protested, "So we can run out of supplies before we get to civilization? I vote we pack early tomorrow and head downstream. It's the direction we're headed anyhow."

"Except we don't know which fork of the river we're on. We could hike for days and still never get anywhere near safety. We can wait a day or two to get our bearings."

"How is an extra day going to make the decision any better? The sooner we get started, the less chance I have of losing the kids to Shelly for being a no-show."

Jeremiah's boys, Enoch and Isaac, ages three and two. And one on the way, so Shelly said. Except Micah knew Jeremiah finally grew tired of the games. Shelly moved out after

Isaac was born, leaving Jere as a single father because she got a better offer.

Which blew up in her face. She came back in the spring, pregnant, desperate, and wanting to "make it work." Jeremiah said no. The boys lived in Jere's parents' home with Nana and Papa. Jeremiah lived in the room over the garage. He would be welcome back in the house after he paid off the debts he and Shelly accrued. Micah figured that would be about when Isaac started middle school.

Back at the argument, Luke continued to lobby for a delay. "Tav's knee is messed up. I'm not going—"

Tav jumped in. "My knee is fine. I'll decide whether I can walk or not. I'm not an invalid."

Micah let the others argue, their voices angry and loud. He looked off to the side of the camp and spotted a shadowy figure standing in the open. The little haystack shivered. Not twirled. Didn't splay his twigs in wide circles. Shivered. Frightened? Why didn't he leave? Run away?

Micah glanced from the stranger to his friends and back again. He held up his hand. "Guys, look."

No one paid attention. The voices grew louder.

"Guys, stop. Look."

Still nothing. The little haystack continued to quiver. The tree limbs rustled and shook. Micah demanded, "Knights!"

They ignored him. Micah shouted, "Albatross!"

Three heads turned to stare at him, slack jawed. Micah seized the silence to point at their visitor. "You're scaring him. Shut up, all of you."

Micah stepped slowly toward the small figure. "It's okay, bud. They're not mad at you. They're being stupid. But not mad. It's okay."

The shrub collapsed, melting into an oak leaf-covered puddle with a two-foot mound in the middle. Micah moved closer, keeping his voice soft. "No one here is going to hurt you, ever. I promise. We get mad at each other, but no one will raise a hand to hurt you or anyone else. Okay?"

Micah knelt beside the puddle. He sat back on his

haunches. "You understand? We want to be your friend. You saved us."

The mound sat upright. Climbed to its feet. Stood unmoving in front of him. Micah smiled, making all his moves slow and deliberate. "Right. We're sorry we scared you." He looked over his shoulder. "Aren't we?"

The others nodded. One by one, voices muttered, "Yeah. I'm sorry." "Right. Sorry." "Didn't mean to upset you."

Micah turned back to the shrub. He held out his hand. "Friends?"

The figure brushed aside Micah's hand and stepped into Micah's chest. Micah closed his arms and hugged the shrub. He could feel the human shape under the branches. He wrapped his arms around a child's shoulders and held the boy. Micah released him the second he felt tension in the child. The boy stepped back and stood in front of Micah. Micah made out eyes and a face, but the shadows were too deep to identify colors. He smiled again. "Thank you for letting me get close. Do you have a name?"

The boy twirled back and forth.

Tav hobbled over to stand beside Micah. He addressed their visitor. "I have a name for you. Ben. For Benefactor." He smiled at the child. "A benefactor is someone who looks out for other people. Who helps them when they can't help themselves. You've been our benefactor. So, we'd like to call you Ben. Is that okay with you?"

Ben stood motionless. Considering it. After a moment, he bowed in his stiff way.

In the hills, a big cat purred. Not the scream. A sound of approval? Ben seemed to think so. He jumped up and down, bouncing over and over. Micah laughed. "Glad you like it." He lifted his voice to the watcher in the hills. "You're welcome to come down, too. We're harmless. We won't hurt you, I promise."

Silence. After a few minutes, the plaintive cry of a lonely cat sounded further away in the hills. Ben cocked his head and stared up the mountain. Was he waiting for a summons?

None came. Micah called gently, "Ben." The boy faced him. "Maybe your friend wanted to do something tonight. Maybe he wants you to stay with us. Just for tonight. Would that be okay with you?"

Ben stared up the mountain again. No call came. The boy walked over and sat on Micah's lap. The boy's soft sigh drifted around him. Micah wrapped his arms around the boy again, leaned his cheek on his head. "He'll be back, Ben. He won't abandon you. Neither will we."

Tav cleared his throat. "Um, how about if we fix some dinner? You brought us all this food, so let's see what we can cook, okay?"

Ben jumped and bounced. Micah laughed. "Well, that struck a chord."

Luke echoed, "With me, too. I'm starved."

Ben crossed over and stood in front of Tav. Tav glanced at Micah. Micah shrugged. "Introduce yourself. We're sharing names, remember?"

"Oh, right." Tav bent down. "I'm Tav. It stands for Taylor Alexander Vaughn." He leaned close to the boy and stage whispered, "But nobody calls me that. Ever. Never. Understand?"

Ben nodded in his solemn style. He skipped over to stand before Luke. Luke grinned and put his hand on the boy's head. "I'm Luke." He motioned to Tav. "I'm his brother."

Ben jumped up and down. Luke watched and commented. "I think he knows what a brother is. And likes it."

The boy stalked stiff-legged to stand in front of Jeremiah. His body leaned back as if trying to measure Jere's height. Jere stared down at the figure. "Yeah, I'm the tall one. I'm Jeremiah. Glad to meet you, Ben."

Ben stepped into Jeremiah. Jeremiah reached down and held the boy for a moment. Micah saw the smile in Jere's eyes. And the pain. The boy stepped back, ran to Micah. He sat down again in Micah's lap. Micah grinned at his buds. "I guess we know who ranks where."

Jere sneered. "You've always been more rank than me. I

can't speak for these two." He jerked his head to Tav and Luke.

Tav rolled his eyes.

* * *

After a dinner of "Meals Ready to Eat" and turkey jerky, the men sat back in the glow of the campfire to watch the stars come out. Luke spoke first. "Wonder how long Ben has been out here?"

Tav added, "And why?"

Ben sat snuggled next to Micah. He leaned his head into Micah's chest. Micah could hear the lightest of humming from beneath the camouflage. He raised his eyebrows. "One of these days, we may get an answer."

Jere lowered his voice. "What happens when we start off?"

Micah's insides twisted. Surely Ben had family somewhere. Someone loved him. Cared about him. Wanted to protect him. Unlike Micah, who'd been abandoned by his dad at the age of four. His brother abandoned him at ten. Micah dropped out to care for his mother… He blocked the thoughts from continuing. God accepted Him. Declared He loved him. Enough. God was enough.

Then why—

Micah silenced the question. Enough. Period. He wrested his attention from internal conflicts to the conversation at hand.

Jere continued talking. "Do we know which way to go yet?"

Micah threw in a factoid for consideration. "On the map, the river forked below Keenan. The north side went deep into the mountains, and the south headed to populated areas. I don't know which side of the divide we're on."

Jere dug at a tree root. "So, what do we do? Go back toward where we started, or risk being lost by going further downstream?"

Tav snorted. "More lost than we are now? Tough call."

Jere pitched a stone into the fire. "I say we pack early and head downstream. Gets us that much closer to town and rescue."

Luke returned to his argument, though with less vehemence. "Who needs rescue? We're hiking instead of boating and still have a week of vacation. I vote to hang out another day, maybe two, go back upstream. At least we'll know where we are."

Jere grumbled, "We don't know how far down we are. We could hike upstream for days and not reach the starting point."

Tav looked over at Ben. "Don't suppose he could tell us where we are, do you?" Tav stretched out, getting comfortable for the night.

Micah shook his head. "I doubt it."

Ben nodded.

Micah leaned his head to get better eyes on the boy. "You know where we are?"

Ben nodded again. Micah asked, "Where?"

Ben patted the ground. Micah chuckled. "We're here. Is that what you mean?" The boy nodded and patted the dirt again. Micah glanced at Tav. "There's your answer."

Luke nudged an ember closer to the fire. "That helps."

Tav grinned. "I did ask." He stared into the sky. "Proposed: we table discussion for tonight. Sun's gone down, so it's got to be after nine. Knight's rules. Make no unnecessary decisions after eight. We can take it up in the morning."

Micah watched the grimace appear on Luke's face. The younger man shifted in his spot. "Don't you think we could dispose of the kids' games? We're adults."

Tav stared at his brother. "Kids' games?"

"Come on, Tav. The Knights. They were fine for—"

Tav interrupted him. "—for kids. Which virtue would you like to eliminate? Honesty?"

Luke squirmed. "That's not—"

"Loyalty?"

"Tav, what I meant—"

"Chastity until marriage?"

Jeremiah chuckled. "Blew that one."

Tav barely skipped a beat. "Forgiven. Move on." He continued to address his brother. "Sobriety?"

Micah intoned, "Which is not the same as abstinence."

Luke groaned. "Come on, guys."

Jeremiah joined in. "Clean heart, clean mind, clean tongue."

Luke threw up his hands. "I get it, I get it. It's a lifestyle. One I'm following, okay? But can we get rid of the voting on everything? Can't we decide and leave it there?"

Tav nodded. "Sure. How do you want to settle the decision when we don't all agree? Ro Sham Bo? Draw straws? Two out of three falls?"

Micah jumped to object. "No. Jeremiah would win everything." Even with Micah's wrestling background, he still couldn't take the big man down. Not unless he snuck up on him from behind. Which would hardly be sporting. Successful, but not sporting.

Ben shifted his position to stand in front of Luke. Micah turned his head to watch the youngster. What did he sense? What did he need?

Ben reached out, head-butted Luke in the chest, turned, and plopped in the man's lap. Luke chuckled. "I hear you, bud. I'm not mad. We're all good here. Just trying to figure some things out." He gently and carefully hugged the boy. Ben climbed to his feet and raced back to Micah's side. He snuggled down under Micah's arm. *Protection. Ben needs protection. We'll take care of him until we find his people. That's what You want. Right, Lord? Keep me straight. I know how being off the meds can mess up my thinking. I get lonely. Self-absorbed. Help me stay focused on Truth. Please.*

Tav laughed. "Guess we know who the favorite is. Fatherhood suits you, Mick."

Ben stood again, crossed over, and sat on Tav. He stayed only a moment, moved to stand in front of Jeremiah. He seemed to hesitate, almost as if waiting for permission. Jeremiah moved his arms. "Come on, little man. You can sit on me, too."

Ben fairly hopped onto Jeremiah's lap. He snuggled a

second then retreated to Micah's side. Micah smiled. "He's an equal opportunity snuggler. One for all and all for one."

Tav repeated his declaration. "Proposed. We table discussion of which way to go until tomorrow. Objections?" No one spoke. "All in favor?"

Four voices answered. "Aye."

"Carried. Let's get some sleep."

Micah looked at Ben. "Do you want to sleep in your suit or take it off for the night?" He stopped and asked, "You do have clothes on, right?"

Ben shook his head, nodded. The boy lay down, spreading the branches out to make a clear surface to sleep on. Micah spread his blanket over the boy and lay down beside him. He looked through the tree limbs to the stars above. He sighed.

Luke called out, "Give us a Word, Mick."

Micah paraphrased the Scriptures. "When I look at the sky, the moon and stars You created, who are we that You even care about us? You've numbered the hairs on our heads. You knew us before we were born, and You love us anyhow. Great are you, Lord."

Three voices echoed, "Amen."

* * *

WEDNESDAY

Micah woke to see Jeremiah pulling on his size fifteen boots. The big man wandered into the trees and disappeared. Sunlight cleared the far edge of the ravine. Micah stretched and rose, careful not to wake Ben. He stirred the fire back to life and dug out his beloved coffee pot.

Jere returned and sat opposite Micah. "You gonna fix coffee?

Micah began filling the basket with grounds. "Yep. You gonna insult it?"

"Yep."

"You gonna drink it?"

"Yep."

"I'll fix coffee." Nothing new in the conversation. Micah put the container and its contents in the fire.

The air had a fall bite to it. Micah shivered. Moving around would help. He walked to the trees, walked back, strolled around the clearing, did some jumping jacks. Muscles screamed at the abuse. Maybe not such a good idea. He moved back to the fire and sat down. A breeze rustled through the tops of the pines.

Jere sat and poked the fire. "What's your vote? Upstream or down?"

Micah stared at the river. The rapids splashing along gave him no insights. "Up. I hate doubling back, but I'm afraid of being on the wrong side of the split."

Jere jerked his head to the side. "Yeah. Today or tomorrow?"

"If Tav can go, then today." Micah checked the color of the percolating coffee. Not ready yet.

Tav stirred. He groaned and sat up. "I smell coffee."

Jeremiah grunted. "Coffee now. Mud when Mick says it's ready." He stirred the fire under the pot.

"You can always water it down, Jere." Micah could give it to Jeremiah now before it got to Micah's liking. But the rules stated he who made the coffee got the first cup. However strong he liked.

Crows cackled and knocked. Songbirds added their voices to the choir. Micah breathed deep. Life. Peace. Friends. Did they have to go back?

Yes. This wasn't real life. In real life, he worked from home and cared for Mom and her demon cat. The monster who attacked him from under the furniture every time he passed it. Boots were a form of self-defense. Until Mom complained the boots ruined the carpets. Better to ruin his ankles than the carpets. Carpets cost money.

Micah closed his eyes to shut out the accuser. He lowered his head to avoid answering questions from Tav or the others.

Didn't work. Tav's voice broke the silence. The eldest Vaughn son sat beside Micah and kept his tone quiet. "How long you been off your meds, Mick?"

Micah opened his eyes. "What?"

"You're off your meds. Fighting the demons. I've seen it in your face. How long? And why?"

"Three weeks. Since I told Mother I would be going on this trip. My anti-depressants disappeared the next day. And it was too soon to reorder them. She swears I don't need them anyhow." Micah stirred the coals under the coffee pot and chewed the inside of his mouth. He would not voice aloud the pain inside.

Tav groaned. "Mick! You've got to do something about her."

"Like what, Tav?" Micah felt the frustration boiling. "She's my mother. I'm the only one who will take care of her." He glared into the fire, forcing himself to remain silent.

Tav cut in. "Will. Not can."

Micah snapped his head toward Tav. "Who else is there?"

"Who's taking care of her now?" His friend's tone stayed even. Infuriating. But even.

Micah threw a stone into the bushes. "I took out a loan to pay for home health care."

Tav kicked his foot on the ground. "You moron! Why didn't you ask for help?"

"Because you're working three jobs supporting you and Luke. Jere is still trying to get out of the garage. It was the only way I could make this trip happen." Micah exploded. "I wouldn't let her steal this from me, too. Just like she's stolen…" He trailed off. *Stop. Just stop.*

Tav lowered his voice. "I'm sorry, Mick." Tav breathed, then returned to his questioning. "Ask yourself, if you weren't in the picture, what would she do?"

Micah gritted his teeth. "I'm sure she'd get along fine. She always does. But I *am* in the picture. It's my responsibility to take care of her. You know what the scriptures teach about taking care of widows, right? How I'm worse than an unbeliever if I don't? I don't have a choice."

Tav dropped the argument. The old argument. The forever argument. Which nothing ever resolved.

Micah turned his attention to something more pressing. Tav's knee. "How's the knee?"

"Sore, but I can manage. With a little help."

"What kind of help?"

"A friend to lean on? Until I can find a good stick to use as an assistive device."

The sound of boat motors interrupted the birdsong and the conversation. Micah and Jeremiah jumped to their feet. Jere pointed upriver. "There. Two boats."

Micah looked over his shoulder. "Three more coming from downstream."

Luke crawled to his feet, coming awake at the sounds. "What's going on?"

Micah's heart lurched. *Ben.* He roused the boy. "Ben, wake up, buddy. We've got company coming. Lots of it." He held the boy's eyes. "I need you to help me out, Ben. Can you?"

Ben gave a solemn bob of his head. His camouflage bounced with the motion. Micah snapped a look at Tav. "Hide him? I don't want people to know he's here. Not until we find where he belongs."

Tav hesitated, then agreed. "Yeah."

Micah turned to Ben. He took the boy by the shoulders and looked him in the face. "I want you to go into the bushes and wait, okay? Pretend you're a shrub. Be very still. Got it?"

Ben's head bobbed again. He shuffled off into the low brush and melted into the background.

Tav studied the boats headed for their position. "I don't think this is a rescue." He picked up a stick and hit the ground with it. Just because.

Jere muttered, "What's your first clue?"

"All the boats coming from different directions."

Luke added, "At the same time."

Jeremiah snorted. "And not a one of them says Ranger." He questioned, "Lead?"

Tav pointed. "Mick."

Micah groaned. "Why is it always me?" The weight of having to speak for the group aggravated him.

"Because you're the most diplomatic." Tav glanced at his brother. "You keep your mouth shut."

Luke threw his hands in the air. "What'd I say?" The younger man appeared thoroughly confused.

"Nothing. Let's keep it that way." Jeremiah helped Tav shift to a spot closest to the woods, and they both took seats. Micah and Luke sat on the side nearest the river. Covering all the bases.

The first boat reached the shoals and ran on the shore. A man with a rope jumped out and dragged the craft into the landing, tying it to a bush. Three people climbed out. Micah didn't have time to sort out the bodies. Sorting would come later. The second craft pulled into the shallows. A crewmember threw out an anchor. Three more figures jumped into the water and clambered onto dry land. Boats three, four, and five soon followed and dislodged their occupants. Micah stood to welcome anyone who wanted to be friendly. And deflect anyone who didn't.

An angry twenty-something man with a rifle on his shoulder demanded, "What are you doing here? No one was supposed to be out until nine." He stepped into Micah's personal space, challenging him.

A small mob of newcomers gathered around the rifle-carrying man. Multiple voices demanded explanations. Rifleman glanced around. He shouted, "Where's your boat? Camping before the event isn't allowed."

Before Micah could respond, a stocky, muscled man in his mid-fifties stepped forward. The crowd quieted. The man wore khakis, his silver hair a Marine buzz-cut. He approached Micah and held out his hand. "Morning."

Micah shook the man's hand. Finally. Someone with authority. And decorum. He hoped. "Morning. Coffee?"

"Wouldn't mind it."

Micah poured the man a cup and held it out to him. "Micah."

The man took it. "Quinn." He looked around. "You boys lost out here?"

Micah chuckled. "You could call it that. Rafting. The river took the boat and dumped us. We washed on shore…yesterday?" He eyeballed his buddies, returned to Quinn. "Day before, maybe. We're trying to decide which way to head." He smiled. "We won't have to walk if someone wouldn't mind taking us back to civilization." He narrowed his eyes. "But I don't think you're a search party looking for us, are you?" He made sure to keep focused on Quinn.

Quinn smiled pleasantly. "No, we're not. But I'm sure we can give you a ride back if you can hang out a few more days."

Rifleman protested. "They can't be part of this. We've

already got five teams at this location. That's one more than should be here."

A young woman declared fiercely, "Yeah, Race. And your team was the last to sign up. So you should leave."

Quinn held up his hand, and all the bickering ceased. "I'm the monitor, and it's my job to make sure you follow the rules. No one needs to leave. This is an open competition. Mr. Magary's rules, remember? All you need is a team of four." He grinned at Micah. "And you have four." He took a long swallow of coffee. Quinn held his cup. "Who made the coffee?"

Micah raised his hand. "I did."

Quinn's eyes narrowed. "You're in. That's good java." The man took a seat near the fire. He looked at all the others and said, "Have a seat or unpack your gear. No one leaves the clearing."

Race protested, "But they've been here two days already."

"And they have no clue what the competition is." Quinn's eyes narrowed slightly. "I'm the monitor." He repeated slowly, "Have a seat or unpack your gear. And put the rifle away."

Race stalked back to his boat and climbed aboard. He began throwing gear over the side. Quinn shook his head. "Always one."

Luke moved forward and sat across from Quinn. He questioned, "Did you say Magary's rules? Are you on the Magary search?"

Micah jerked his head over to look at the younger man. "You've heard of this?"

Luke shrugged. "Vaguely. Very vaguely." He leaned forward. The younger man risked a glance at his brother and mouthed, *Sorry*. Tav shrugged.

Quinn took control. "Let me spell it out. Fifty years ago, a man named Warren Magary hid a treasure. A substantial treasure. A box of gold coins. The exact value is unknown, but estimates run from two-hundred-fifty thousand to a million dollars."

Micah used his hand to push his jaw closed. Quinn

grinned. "Yeah. Like that. He created a game to find it, but no one has figured out the instructions. Several groups, which up until now have been investigating individually, decided to put their collective heads together and make a push to find the treasure. There are four possible starting locations based on the clues Mr. Magary left. This clearing is one of them."

Tav and Jeremiah leaned in. Quinn continued. "Mr. Magary insisted on a team of four. Each team was given four cards with three symbols and a compass heading for each symbol. Nothing more. Once you determine the starting point, find the first symbol. Follow the compass heading until you find the next symbol. And so on."

Micah raised both palms in the air. "That doesn't sound too hard."

"Not if you know the starting point and how far to go between symbols or which symbol comes in what order."

Micah let the concept play around in his head. "I see the problem." He sat back slightly.

Quinn nodded. "Thought you might." He held his coffee cup out. Micah topped off the cup.

Tav interjected, "And no one has found the prize in fifty years? Or did someone find the treasure, and no one is saying?"

Jeremiah added, "Or he never hid the money to start with."

Quinn shook his head. "He hid the coins. They've never reappeared, so they're still out there."

Micah noted the abundance of gear some of the teams unloaded. Ground-penetrating radar. Lidar. Metal detectors. He raised his eyebrows at Quinn. "I think we'd be underdressed."

Quinn chuckled. "Doubtful. You have a camp shovel?"

Micah did a quick look, even though he already knew the answer. Like looking at your watch when someone asks you what time it is, and you looked moments before they asked. "Yeah."

"You have everything you need. If you want to join the hunt, you're welcome. Otherwise, I'm sure some of this bunch will be back in the next three days and will happily give you a lift home."

Micah glanced at his fellow knights. Tav dipped his head to the side. He stuck one fist into the circle. The others joined suit. A silent count of four, and all four thumbs went up. Micah smiled at Quinn. "I guess we're in."

Quinn chuckled approval. "I'm impressed. I like you boys." He stood, handed Micah the empty coffee cup, and addressed the crowd on the shore. "You've got twenty minutes to get yourselves sorted, then I'm declaring the game open. Get at it, people."

He turned back to Micah and the Knights. He lowered his voice and his volume. "You want to explain about the shrub? The one who keeps shifting side to side and not with the wind?"

Micah ducked his head to hide the smile. "We call him Ben. Non-verbal kid we found—or who found us—out here. We have no idea where he came from or where he belongs. He's not much on communicating abstracts."

Quinn nodded. "My kind of person. Deal with specifics. Okay, we'll take him with us. Maybe we can find his people. Did you make his disguise?"

"No. We found him that way."

"I see." He didn't turn to look but nodded. "Impressive. One of the best ghillie suits I've seen. Maybe he can give me some pointers." He studied Race, still grousing about the newcomers and still carrying his rifle. After a thought, Quinn said, his voice low, "Don't call the boy in just yet. Let this crowd clear out, and we can talk to him." He raised his eyebrows. "And I wouldn't worry about anyone having a head start. Odds of this bunch navigating their way out of a paper bag aren't high, much less finding the treasure. No discipline."

Tav motioned. "What's with the rifle?"

"Bears, he says. I'm not buying it. I'm also not trusting him farther than I can see him."

The Knights packed their meager gear and waited. After twenty minutes expired, Quinn announced to the assemblage,

"Go. You're on your own."

Race and his team bulled into the forest and slashed at the undergrowth. Two of the groups began comparing notes. Micah guessed they preferred to split a found treasure rather than risk not finding any. There came a great deal of arguing and debating and complaining, but eventually, the groups moved off. Quinn waited a few minutes longer, then directed, "Call your friend in."

Micah walked to Ben's location. He smiled as he reached the boy. "Hey, Ben. Good job staying out of sight. You can come in now. I want you to meet a new friend."

Ben didn't move. Micah laid a hand on the boy's shoulder. He could feel Ben quivering under his disguise. Micah knelt to be at eye level. He made sure to look directly at the boy. "What's wrong, Ben?" *Stupid question.* "Did someone frighten you?"

Ben wrapped his arms around Micah. Micah hugged the boy, then moved him back so he could face him. "Did someone scare you?"

Ben nodded. Once. Emphatically.

Micah looked around. The only one of the newcomers left was Quinn. Micah addressed Ben again. "Is the person who scared you still in the camp?" *Please, don't say Quinn.*

Ben swirled his body in the "no" fashion.

Micah breathed a sigh of relief. "Okay. We'll talk more later. Let's introduce you to a new friend." He held out his hand. Ben took hold. They walked back to the clearing. Micah stopped in front of Quinn. The older man eyed Ben closely.

Micah said, "Ben, this is Quinn. He's a new friend who's come to help us not be lost anymore. Quinn, this is Ben. Short for Benefactor. Since we don't have any other name to call him."

Quinn knelt. His tone was even and respectful. "Hello, Ben. I understand you've been watching out for these guys. I'm honored to meet you. That's one fantastic ghillie suit you're wearing. You will have to teach me how you made it."

Ben bowed low and held the pose for several seconds.

The boy straightened and walked into Quinn's arms for a hug. Quinn chuckled and hugged the boy. "Thank you, Ben, for trusting me."

Ben went back to stand by Micah's side. Quinn noted. "He's adopted you, hasn't he?"

Micah shrugged. "He's sort of an equal-opportunity friend." Micah cocked his head. He knelt beside Ben and signed, "Do you know sign language?"

Ben watched Micah's hands but didn't respond. Micah tried again but got the same non-response. He shrugged and stood. "Thought it might be worth a shot."

Tav suggested, "Maybe we can teach him."

Ben danced and bounced at the word "teach." Micah guessed the thought of whoever scared him passed. *Let the matter go. If he sees them again, we'll deal with whatever comes.*

Quinn dug out a set of long laminated cards. Each one contained three symbols. Some looked like animals, some landscape features, some letters or numbers. Each symbol corresponded to a compass heading. The game monitor passed cards to each of the Knights. "Here are your instructions. Find the symbol, follow the heading. Find the next symbol, follow the heading."

Jeremiah studied the cards. "I get the idea. But how do you know when you've chosen the final correct heading? What signals the treasure?"

Quinn smiled. A long, slow smile. "Only one group has gotten to the third segment. No one has reached the fourth. When someone does, they will be shown where to look."

Tav eyed the older man. "Is that your job?"

Quinn shrugged. "Possibly. I'm here to make sure the lost are found. We get more of those than any other."

"How do you do that?" Micah seemed skeptical.

"Today, we have GPS trackers on each team. If one of them gets lost, we can always find them."

Tav stated the obvious. "Fifty years ago, they didn't have GPS."

"Fifty years ago, people didn't come back. The game has

experienced casualties. Three people have died, and two went missing. Permanently." Quinn stared at the four Knights. "This isn't a picnic hike. This is a million dollars you're after. Take the matter seriously."

Tav held each man's eyes. Micah watched, waited, then nodded. In unison with his fellows. They were in.

Quinn motioned to the clearing. "You're on your own. Until tomorrow. I'll expect coffee in the morning."

Micah chuckled. "I'll supply. Where will you go?"

"I have to check on the others. See if anyone has given up, gotten lost, or decided to cut his partners out of the game. But I'll find you. The GPS is embedded in the cards. Don't lose them." He saluted the group. "Take care, boys. I'll see you tomorrow." He stopped, reached into his boat, and pulled out a first aid kit. "Do you have one?"

Micah shook his head. "Ours went down with the ship." Quinn tossed it to him and disappeared into the brush.

Tav raised his eyebrows at the others. "So, what are we looking for?"

They huddled to look at the cards. After a moment, Jeremiah offered, "The marker can't be organic. Growing, I mean. It can't be a tree that looks like a horse or anything. Fifty years of growth will change the contours. We have to be looking for something else."

Luke added, "But not magnetic, either. Quinn said we wouldn't need a metal detector. Which leaves what?"

Micah thought, then looked around. "A rock formation?"

Tav nodded. "And one large enough, no one is going to come along and knock the formation out of place."

"Whose got card number one?"

A quick check revealed the cards bore no designation. The realization took a minute to sink in. Micah's eyes widened. "So we have to find the symbol without knowing which symbol to look for?"

Jere stated the obvious. "We'll know which one when we see it, right?"

Micah checked his card for the characters as the others

scouted the clearing. Each man checked for anything that might resemble what was on his card. Micah looked for a bird. A prone man. An L. Each with a corresponding compass heading. But in what order? He studied the figures. Micah looked around the area. Nothing. He saw nothing.

Ben pulled the game piece from him. The boy held the card in the air. He turned a complete circle, followed by another, then another. Finally, he stopped. Ben stood stock still, aiming at a point across the river.

Micah shook his head. "No, bud. Not over there. We can't cross the river here." Micah reached for the card, but Ben refused him. Micah tried again. "Ben, the marker can't be over there."

Tav must have heard the discussion and came over. He knelt beside Ben to see what the boy saw. Ben did not point but remained standing, his head fixed in one direction. Tav squinted, turned his face side to side, and asked, "What is the symbol?"

"A bird. But it can't—"

Tav raised his hand to point. "There. The rock formation on the cliff looks like a bird."

Micah acknowledged what they saw. "I see. But the mark can't be across the river."

Tav held out his hand to Ben. "Can I see the card?" Ben gave it to him. Tav called, "Luke, bring me the compass."

Luke and Jeremiah left their search to join Tav. Luke handed his brother the compass. Tav checked the directions and walked to be directly in line with the rock formation. He set the compass to the required heading. The device indicated an area downstream but still on the wrong side of the river. After a moment, he pointed. "There. Look at the top of the hill. Doesn't that look like someone lying down? There's the belly, there's the head."

Everyone peered to see what Tav described. Micah's gut tightened. Tav was right. He could see a figure. The group grabbed their gear and hiked down the shore until they stood opposite the man on the hill. Tav adjusted the compass again.

This time, the heading pointed to a direction on the near side of the water. He ordered, "We need an L. Everyone look sharp."

The group began searching the shore, the rocks, and the trees. Anything could be marked. Or look like a mark. It took an hour before Luke called, "Over here. I see it."

Micah joined the others by Luke's side. The younger man pointed to a boulder. "There. It's carved in. You can just see it."

Tav's face reflected speculation, but Micah nodded. "I see it."

Jeremiah traced it with his hand. "Maybe." He glanced at Tav. "What do you think?"

Tav shrugged. "Not convinced. But I'll bow to the group if everyone else agrees."

Micah leaned down. "Ben, what do you think? Is this the mark?"

Ben took the card, held it up, held it up next to the rock, turned it upside down, turned it sideways…after several seconds, he bowed in his "yes" manner. Micah smiled. "Good man." He held out his hand for the compass. "What's the reading?"

Tav read it off to him. Micah lined it up. Before they could head out, though, he asked Ben, "Do you want to take your cover off? It might make it easier to get through the bushes."

Ben stared at the ground. Micah assured him, "We'll take it with us, buddy. I'll carry it in my pack. If you ever want to put your suit on or see I have it, I'll bring the ghillie suit out for you to inspect. Okay?"

Ben remained still. Finally, he looked up and smiled. He slipped out of the covering. A small, thin boy of about seven, longish blonde hair, his clothes oversized and filthy, appeared from under the bushes. He folded his camouflage and handed it to Micah. Then the boy skipped to the front of the line. Micah stuffed the suit in his backpack. *Lord, may he never have to hide who he is again. Help me protect him.*

Tav picked up a sturdy fallen tree branch to use as a

crutch.

And off they went.

* * *

They walked until the sun settled below the tops of the trees. Tav suggested, "We should make camp. I don't want to be stumbling around in the dark." His limp, better in the morning, became more pronounced as the day wore on.

Jeremiah huffed. "You think the others brought night-vision goggles?"

Micah reminded him, "Quinn said we'd only need the shovel. I don't think all the high-tech toys will make any difference."

Luke added, "Especially since fifty years ago, they didn't have night-vision goggles. Wherever Magary put the treasure, looking at night won't help."

Micah motioned up the hill. "I see a flat area at the top. Let's try there for tonight." He led the way with Ben behind him. A crack of a rifle echoed in the hills. Micah felt fire slash across the top of his shoulder. He went down, grabbing the area and shouting in pain. "Arrrgh!"

Tav yelled, "Down!"

Everyone hit the dirt. No one moved. Micah curled in pain, trying not to writhe in agony. He ground his teeth. *Lord! Don't let me dishonor You! Guard my mouth!*

No more shots came. Jeremiah lifted his head with caution. "You think they're done?"

Luke rose to his feet. "We'll know in a heartbeat." He slipped up to check Micah's shoulder. "Let me see."

Micah moved his hand. Luke examined the wound. "Through and through. And the bullet just caught the top." He put pressure on the wound.

Micah looked behind him. "Get Ben. Help him."

The boy sat curled in a ball, his arms wrapped around his ankles. He rocked back and forth frantically. Tav and Jere surrounded him. "It's okay, buddy. Mick's fine. He's only hurt a little. It's okay."

Ben continued to rock. Jeremiah put his arms around the boy and held him, rocking with him. He laid his head on Ben's and murmured words Micah couldn't hear.

Luke broke out the first aid kit and made short work of bandaging Micah's wound. As he finished taping the dressing, he intoned, "Keep it dry. Stay out of the shower. And mail in the hundred bucks."

Micah sneered at him. "What's in the kit for pain?" He held his arm to keep the shoulder from moving.

Luke rigged a sling for Micah. The younger man checked the contents of the kit and pulled out a white bottle. "Aspirin and Ibuprofen. Grunt candy. That's as strong as it gets."

Micah started to shake his head, then thought better of it. "I think I'll be okay with the aspirin. If I can't sleep, I'll let you know." He didn't stand but continued to eye Jere and Ben. Jere continued to hold the boy, whose rocking slowed. Not stopped, but slowed. He glanced at Tav. "What do you think?"

Tav stared at the ground. "I think he's seen someone get shot before. I would bet the person who scared him was Race with the rifle."

Micah grimaced. "Agreed. I don't know how to ask Ben, though."

"Maybe we don't. First thing we need to find out is who shot at you and why." Tav's eyes searched the woods.

"Were they shooting at me? Or just the group?" Micah would not entertain the idea someone shot at Ben. Not a kid. Not a little kid. No.

Tav jerked his head to the side. "Either way, we need to be sure it doesn't happen again."

Jeremiah looked up from his position with Ben. "How do we do that?" His voice reflected disgust.

Tav kept his tone even. Rational. "We report it to Quinn. Maybe he calls the whole game off for this crowd."

Jeremiah sniffed. "Tough call for the non-offenders." He hugged Ben and whispered in the boy's ear. Ben slowed even further.

"Quinn will have to decide that." Tav gazed at Micah's

shoulder. "You good to finish getting up the hill? With help?"

Micah drew in a long breath. "Yeah. Let's do it."

Luke helped Micah to his feet. His head swam at the sudden altitude change, but he stayed alert. Tav struggled uphill with his crutch for support. Luke supported Micah the remainder of the way. Jeremiah cradled Ben in his arms and carried the traumatized youngster to the flat at the top of the hill.

A grassy clearing welcomed them. It would be soft sleeping tonight. Luke lowered Micah to the ground and set up camp. Tav collapsed nearby. Micah watched Luke dig a pit, find wood for a small fire, and start a cheery blaze. Only large enough to keep the chill off and give them light to see their way around. Jeremiah set Ben down on Micah's good side. Micah put his arm around the boy's shoulders and murmured, "You're safe, Ben. You're with us. We'll never let anything happen to you. You're safe. That's all that matters."

Ben's rocking stopped. His eyes regained their focus. He managed a tiny smile. Micah hugged him. "There's our Ben. Good to have you back, bud." Micah didn't let go of the boy, however. Not yet.

They ate MREs and chewed on jerky. Everyone stretched out and did what guys always do: poked the fire with sticks and tossed rocks into the center of the blaze. After a quiet period, Luke asked, "What if we find the treasure? What will you do with your share?"

Jeremiah huffed. "Gotta find it first."

"Right, but what if we do? What would you do with 250,000 dollars?"

Jeremiah refused to play. "125,000 dollars after taxes."

Luke ground his teeth. "That's still a chunk of money." The blond younger man sat forward.

Tav joined the conversation. "I'd put a down payment on a house. Quit two of my jobs and go to college." Tav pointed at his brother. "And don't start. You're not why I'm working three jobs. Life is." He paused and asked his brother, "What would you do?"

Luke pitched a rock. "Pay you guys back for your support and go to college like we planned."

From across the fire, Jeremiah offered, "Pay off my parents, and move into the house. I'd go to school at night."

"Study what?" Micah sensed Tav wanted to keep the conversation going. Keep them all awake? On guard? Maybe.

Jeremiah stretched his six-eight frame. "Mechanical engineering. You should remember that. It was the only class I never cut."

Tav chuckled. "I remember. But I thought maybe you'd changed your mind in four years. Maybe wanted to do something else. Brain surgery. Marine biology. Male modeling. You know."

Jeremiah threw a pebble across the fire and hit Tav. "Smart guy."

Luke lifted his head. "What about you, Mick?"

Micah stared into the flames. The light blinded his eyes to everything around him. He answered slowly. "Ben saved us. He clearly doesn't have someone looking after him properly. I think I'd make sure he had a place to live."

Tav's voice floated gently from the far side of the fire. "What about your mother?"

Micah "I'd still be working my tax consulting. I could afford help for her. Maybe pay off the house. And if Ben truly has no family, I'll be it."

Reality burst his fantasy. *Pipe dreams. The money won't matter. Mother would never let me spend money on Ben. Never. I'm supposed to care for her first. Right?*

He hugged the small boy beside him. "I'm not going to leave you out here, Ben." He whispered his defiance.

Luke cleared his throat. "Um…we all should help with Ben. All be his family. He saved all our lives, you know. So, he's all of our responsibilities. We should take a cut of the money and create a trust for him. Or something similar."

Jeremiah reminded them, "We need to find his parents. Guardians, someone. Kids don't wander in the forests by themselves. Someone has to be missing him."

"Not someone who cares very much."

A mockingbird called from the trees above them. Across the way, another answered. Micah resisted the urge to cling to Ben and scream, *No way!* Whoever the other person in the ghillie suit was, Ben couldn't go back with them.

What is wrong with you? You can't just claim him as your own. Get over yourself. Have you even thought about what this entails? He's a kid. One who doesn't speak. A huge responsibility. A lot to bite off. Off your meds is no excuse. Lord, help me!

Tav maintained a voice of reason. "We'll talk to Quinn. He seems to have an information network."

Micah ground his teeth. "If Ben's people left him to wander in the hills all this time, they don't deserve him. I can take care of him." *Someone abandoned him. See? He needs me.*

Tav became firm. "That's not how children's services work. You don't even live in the same county." He lay back on the ground, his arms crossed behind his head.

"I don't care. He's staying with me, at least until I know he's safe." Micah couldn't keep the heat from his voice.

Jeremiah cleared his throat. "You need something for pain and a night's sleep, Mick. You're not thinking straight." He stood, retrieved three pills from the medical kit, a cup with some water, and handed them to Micah. "Take it."

Micah didn't argue. When Jere gave a directive, you obeyed. Or risked him sitting on you. Micah took the ibuprofen and the water and swallowed both. He handed the cup back to Jeremiah. "Thanks."

"Go to sleep. You'll think sharper in the morning. We need your brain firing on all cylinders." Jeremiah returned to his place, set the cup with the camping gear, and lay down.

"Right." Micah settled down on the grass. His shoulder burned. The pill would take care of the pain.

What would ease the emptiness in his heart?

* * *

THURSDAY

Micah woke first. He guessed pain pills gave him a better night's sleep than his buddies. He got up and fixed coffee in case Quinn made an appearance. His shoulder still burned, but he would refuse to let Luke redress the wound. Fine. He was fine. No one would mother him.

While the men ate breakfast—more MREs— they compared the cards Quinn gave them. Tav took the lead in the discussion. "We need to start looking for any kind of marker. There's no order for these cards. And no distances to travel."

Jeremiah grumbled, "We could have already missed the next one. How would we even know?"

Tav threw his hands in the air. "The only thing I saw all the way here is trees. And they all looked the same. I saw no special features, no rocks, no anything. If Magary wanted the treasure found, he'd leave good clues people could follow."

Luke offered his opinion. "The fact no one has found the treasure only means people aren't paying attention. We have as much chance of finding the money as anyone else."

Micah added, "If God wants us to have the gold, we'll get it."

Jere packed his bag. "You think God cares who wins a game? Come on." The big man scowled at Micah.

"If He numbers the hairs on our head, He cares. I don't think He picks sides, but He uses the contests to teach us." It was the closest Micah could come to a rational response.

Jere chuckled and turned it on him. "What, like humility, because the teams you like are all so bad?"

Micah huffed. "Maybe." Jeremiah laughed and tossed a small pinecone at him.

Quinn stepped into the clearing. "Morning, gentlemen. Coffee ready?" No one heard him coming.

Micah rustled out a cup and handed it to the man. "Waiting on you."

The older man sat on the ground. Quinn swallowed a mouthful of the brew before motioning to Micah's shoulder. "What'd you do?" Ben hopped over to jump in Quinn's lap, hugged the monitor, and returned to Micah's side.

Micah breathed out slowly. "Got shot. Or shot at."

Quinn's eyes flared, then narrowed. "Say again?" Seemed the man could be caught off-guard.

"Someone shot a rifle yesterday afternoon. Came from over the hill. I got grazed. No one else got hurt." Micah hugged the boy beside him. "He reacted badly to it. We think it's something he's experienced before."

Quinn looked at the hill. "Show me where the shooter was."

Tav faced uphill and pointed to the bluff above them. "Seemed like he fired from there."

"He? Did you see the shooter?" Quinn stood, left his coffee, and walked to the top of the hill. He examined the ridgeline before he came back down.

"No, but five'll get you ten it was Race." Disgust tainted Micah's voice. He poured more java into Quinn's cup.

Quinn sneered. "Sorry to disappoint your jump to conviction, but Race wasn't anywhere near here. Not yesterday, and not today." The man retook his seat on the ground.

Micah started to demand how Quinn could know but remembered Quinn's job title. He should know.

Luke apparently read Micah's mind. "How can you be sure?"

Knight's mind trick. We all think alike. At this point, we probably all smell alike.

"Because we extracted Race yesterday. He said he couldn't work with his partners. Refused to work with them. Strange they couldn't figure out their issues before they came." He swallowed more of his coffee.

Luke frowned. "I'll apologize next time I meet him."

Quinn humphed. "I wouldn't. Square it with the Maker and move on."

Tav cleared his throat. "What about the rest of Race's team?"

"One went home. We let the other two continue. They'll have to connect with someone along the way, but they're still eligible. Don't want to penalize someone because they had a jerk for a partner."

Tav scratched his neck. "What about the other teams? Are they still in the hunt?" He tried to look uninterested but failed.

Quinn smiled. "I can't tell you. I can only tell you about your team. I'll say you are on track. But that's all I'm gonna say."

Tav grinned at the group. "Alright, Knights!" He high-fived Jere, Luke, Ben, and Micah.

Quinn poured more coffee into his cup. "But it still leaves us with a problem of who is shooting around here. This isn't a designated hunting area, and it's not hunting season."

Micah shifted in his seat. "Poachers?"

"Might be. I'll put the word out. We'll send some drones to look for anyone out here who shouldn't be." Quinn smiled at Ben. "We do have our young friend here, too. Have you asked him about it?"

Tav shook his head. "No. He was pretty shaken up, and we weren't sure how to ask him without upsetting him more."

Quinn nodded. "Understood." He held out his hand to Ben. "Buddy, I want to ask you a favor, okay? I need some help."

Micah ground his teeth. He didn't appreciate Quinn interrogating Ben. Ben walked over to stand beside Quinn, his expression one of waiting.

Quinn smiled at Ben. As much as Micah wanted to hate what Quinn was doing, the man's face held a genuinely warm countenance. "When we started at the river, you saw someone who scared you. Is that true?"

Ben's face grew solemn. He nodded once.

Quinn lay a hand on Ben's shoulder. "Can you draw me a picture of what the person looked like?"

Ben cocked his head to one side, then the other. He smiled wide and nodded. He picked up a stick and began drawing in the loose dirt.

Micah expected Ben to draw stick figures. But the portrait Ben drew proved anything but rudimentary. A full-featured face took shape in the soil. Deep eyes. High-bridged nose. Full mouth. Lips slightly apart. Front teeth with a slight gap between them.

Jere muttered something. Tav glared at him. "That'll cost you five bucks to the obscenity jar."

"If I had my wallet, I'd give you ten." Jeremiah bent to look closer at Ben's drawing.

Quinn retrieved his phone and took several shots of the portrait. He squeezed Ben's shoulder. "Thank you, Ben. This will help me. When I find her, I'll ask her why she made you afraid. We'll get to the bottom of this, I promise."

Micah hesitated. Maybe he shouldn't mention anything. Maybe he should. He squatted down beside Ben. "Buddy, was that the first time you saw this person?"

Ben shook his head with an emphatic "no."

Micah pursed his lips, then asked, "Was your brother with you when you saw her?"

A solemn nod followed.

Should he push one step further? "Were you in your house?"

Ben began to quiver again. Micah surrounded the boy in his arms. "It's okay, Ben. It's okay. You're safe. You're with us.

You're safe."

Quinn picked up a chunk of wood and placed it in Ben's hand. "Feel the wood, Ben? Can you feel it? You're in the forest with the wood, bud. Feel it."

Ben's shaking slowed. He stared at the burl in his hand. Micah let the boy go from his embrace. Ben rotated the wood. His fingers brushed against the texture. Touched the roughness to his cheek. Rubbed the chip between his hands. Finally, he looked at Quinn and smiled.

Micah exhaled. He shook his head. Quinn directed Ben to Tav's keeping and motioned for Micah to step away. He eyed the boy but asked, "What brother?"

"Ben's not big enough to have dragged Tav and Jeremiah out of the river. Someone taller and stronger did. We heard him in the hills calling to Ben, acting like a wildcat. Maybe a game they play. I took a chance asking if they were together when he saw the person."

"Smart move." He made as if to slap Micah on the shoulder but stopped. He held Micah in his gaze. "You sure you're okay? You don't need medevacked out, do you?"

Micah shook his head. "No. I'm fine. I'm not leaving my team."

"I'll keep a check on you anyhow." He laughed. "Gotta protect my barista." Quinn stepped back to the group. "You've done well for the first leg. Keep it up. I'll check in with you later." He stooped over and hugged Ben. "You keep these boys safe, you hear?"

Ben's face shone with joy. He hugged Quinn back. The older man disappeared into the trees from where he'd come.

Tav muttered, "Hi, ho, Silver."

Luke stared at him. "What?"

Jeremiah growled. "Never mind. Since we haven't missed anything yet, I want to keep hunting."

Over Micah's protests, they redistributed his share of the supplies, leaving him with nothing to put pressure on his bad shoulder. Ben was even allowed to carry Micah's backpack. The boy strutted and preened. Jeremiah suggested, "Put some weight in it. That'll settle him soon enough."

Adding coffee, the coffee pot, and some MREs brought Ben back to earth. They retired Micah's card to concentrate on the remainder of the markers: a snowman, horse, octopus, anvil, fish, boot, and the letters X, G, and Y. The group continued on the trail. Tav's knee seemed better with the night's rest. He leaned on his walking stick and managed to climb the hill without other assistance.

They walked another two hours before they reached the top of a ridge. The trail stopped overlooking a steep gorge.

Tav checked up and down the area, but the trail disappeared. Micah's gut dropped. How could this be a dead end? Did they screw up their calculations? Miss the compass heading?

Luke cautioned, "Wait. Wait. Look at the rocks."

A cairn of stones piled near the edge of the cliff. Three boulders rested at the bottom, side by side, supporting the remainder of the structure. The stack resembled an upside-down V.

Jeremiah shrugged. "So? We're not looking for a pyramid."

Luke pointed. "But check out the three stones on the bottom. Look at them sideways."

Micah cocked his head to try to identify what Luke saw. After a moment, he asked, "You mean how they are graduated in size? Each one slightly smaller?"

Luke pointed at Micah. "Bingo. Like a snowman."

Tav studied the structure for several minutes. "Maybe." He limped to the pile of rocks and ran his hand along the boulders. His eyes narrowed. "Jere, come here."

Jeremiah walked beside him. "What?"

"Feel along here. In the head. You feel any indentations?"

Jeremiah brushed at the smallest of the rocks. He frowned, then brushed it again. Finally, he raised his eyes to Tav. "Three holes. Eyes and nose."

Luke cocked his head. "No mouth?"

Jere shrugged. "Maybe he's speechless."

Micah groaned and rolled his eyes. Ben rolled his head. Tav grinned at him. "Smart guy." He pulled out the game card and the compass. "Alright. Last time we used all three symbols to locate the direction we'd go. Let's see where this one directs."

The heading pointed out across the canyon. Four sets of eyes followed the imaginary line looking for a horse or the letter X.

Leaves crunching in the forest stopped the search. Micah and the others swung around to see who approached.

A group of four advanced along the cliff line. Tav muttered, "Lead?"

Jere and Luke both echoed, "You." Luke added, "Mick's hurt."

Tav frowned. "Great. Call the B team."

No time to complain further. The group arrived. Two men, two women. Married couples? They appeared older, in their mid-forties. One couple was of mixed heritage; a dark-complected man and an Asian woman. The other two were Caucasians like the Knights themselves. Light skin, light hair, brown eyes. Tan, weathered faces. Being outdoors wasn't something new to them. Micah glanced at Tav to see how he would greet the newcomers.

Tav waited until the new group raised their heads long enough to acknowledge the Knights' presence. Tav raised one hand. "Hello."

The dark-complected man waved back. "Howdy. Didn't think we'd cross paths with another group. Not once we left the beach. I'm Nance."

Tav offered a handshake. A round-robin exchange of names and greetings followed. Ben stayed glued to Micah's side. He stared at the ground expressionless. Micah kept his arm around the boy.

Once acquainted, Win, Nance's partner, asked, "And who is this young man?"

Before Tav could speak, Micah jumped in. "Ben. He's my brother. He doesn't do well with crowds. Or people he doesn't know."

Sissy, the Caucasian woman, stepped up to Ben. She smiled wide and said, "Oh, that doesn't matter. I've never met a stranger." She knelt and held her hand out to Ben. "Hi, Ben. I'm Sissy. Now you know me, and I'm not a stranger."

Ben didn't raise his head or make eye contact. He didn't move at all. Micah interceded. "Ben is shy."

Sissy ignored Micah. Her tone, however, let him know what she thought of him. "I know how to deal with children." She continued to hold her hand out. "Ben, when I reach out to you, you're supposed to take my hand and shake it in return. It's the polite thing to do."

Ben remained frozen.

Micah shifted in front of Ben. "We're not forcing Ben to do anything he isn't comfortable with. Thank you for your concern." Micah stole a look at Sissy's face. Was she the woman Ben drew? The similarities were close. Striking, even. What did it mean? Sissy scared Ben. But why? And when had Ben seen her before?

Sissy glanced at Micah. "What's wrong with him?"

Tav took over the conversation. "There's nothing wrong with him. He doesn't talk."

Sissy glared at Tav. "Let me guess. He's *special*." She stood and rejoined her team. The contempt in her voice raised Micah's hackles. He started to speak, then stopped. Tav was the lead. Tav would take care of it.

Tav kept his tone even. "God designed us all special. It manifests in different ways. Ben may not talk, but he saved our lives. So yeah, we think he's special." He turned from Sissy to face Nance. "How is your search going?"

Nance chuckled. "About like yours, seeing how we're all in the same place."

"Good point." Tav surveyed the countryside. "Where are you headed next?"

"Same as you. South down the ridge. It's the heading we're following."

Win smiled. "It's so strange. We've backtracked ten miles,

I'm sure. But that's the way we needed to go."

Doug, Sissy's partner, stared Tav and the group up and down. "Funny, we never crossed paths with you before this. If we're all going the same way." His voice darkened. "If we all have the same directions."

Tav shrugged. "We're moving slower. Mick injured his shoulder, so we're taking our time." He asked, "How'd you four get hooked into this search?"

Win laughed. "Drew names."

Tav eyed her sideways. "What?"

Nance nodded. "We were part of a network of players trying to find the treasure. About fifty of us. But when the trip opened, about thirty could actually come. We drew names to see which partners we'd have and who would start at what point."

Tav raised his eyebrows. "Are you dividing the treasure amongst all of you, then?"

Sissy snarled. "No. Whoever finds it keeps it. Sorry for everyone else's luck."

Doug studied the ridge. "What do you know about the monitor, Quinn?"

Micah kept his eyes focused on the ground in front of him. Tav responded, "He seems straight. He let us join the game. Why?"

Doug kicked the dirt. "He stopped by our camp last night. Wouldn't tell us if we were going the right way or not. He told us one team got airlifted out, but that's all he said."

"It's probably the rules of the game. He's here to monitor, not guide."

"I think he knows more than he says. I'd bet he's a party to the location of the treasure." Doug's eyes narrowed, and his tone darkened.

Tav eyed Doug sideways. "What are you suggesting?"

"He knows where the treasure is. Or was. He found the money and hid all those coins for himself. He pretends to help the teams, but he's really keeping them away from exposing him." Doug lifted his head, defying anyone to gainsay him. At least that's what Micah read in the treasure hunter's body language.

Tav rubbed his chin. "Interesting idea. But why bother? Why not declare he found it and call the game over?"

"Money."

Micah looked at Win and Nance. He tried to decipher if this was Doug's fable or a joint fantasy. Hard to tell.

Doug continued outlining his case. "People are still writing about the game and the treasure. I'm sure Magary gets a cut anytime something new is published. And we pay good money to arrange these searches."

Tav's eyes opened wide. "You have to pay to play the game?"

Nance jumped into the conversation. "No, not like that. It costs in supplies and gear and transportation to come out here. Magary doesn't get anything from those rentals." He glared at Doug, but Micah could tell the man tried to be careful not to let his partner see.

Doug's voice sneered. "Yet. I bet it'll come. Magary's group will offer special trips, all gear provided, at a premium price, to come out and search for the treasure that doesn't exist anymore."

Tav spread his hands wide. "No one says you have to be here. No one is forced to go on a search." Tav's face held as much personableness as Micah knew the man had.

Nance's eyes lit up with amusement. He hid the expression quickly before Doug could see him, however. Doug still grumbled, "Tell the wife."

Sissy glared at Doug. "I told you I'd find another partner for this trip. You didn't believe me. All we do is search the mountains. You didn't trust me. You thought I came out here to find a playmate. Well, mister, now you see what it's like. I'm looking for a real goldmine for my future. Since you're not providing one."

Lord, thank You Tav has the lead on this one. I would not know how to answer any of these complaints.

Nance took his wife's hand. "I'm sure you gentlemen

don't need to hear our doubts and discussions."

Tav held up a hand. "Did any of you hear a gunshot yesterday?"

Sissy's face reflected shock. "Gunshots? Out here? Who would be shooting in the woods? Especially with people in them?"

Doug's eyes narrowed. "Of course, there weren't any gunshots. The monitor would have warned us. He hasn't said a word about it."

Nance eyed Tav. "Did you hear something?" A raven flew overhead, expressing discontent over the people on his ridge. A second raven called back, probably agreeing with him.

Tav nodded. "Yeah, we did. Yesterday afternoon. Sounded close, too."

Only way for the shot to be closer is if it killed me. Micah rubbed his shoulder.

Nance exchanged glances with Win. "We thought we heard something, but we couldn't be certain. And it only happened once."

Tav agreed. "Yeah, we only heard the one shot as well. It might have been an accident. Quinn didn't hear it from wherever he was."

Nance shrugged. "I don't know." He motioned down the trail. "Are you headed out now?"

Tav shook his head. "No. We'll need to get Ben settled first." He smiled at Nance. "But we'll probably cross paths again."

Win smiled. "On the race to reach the treasure." She laughed. "And I will fight you for it." She bared her claws in a mock attack.

Tav laughed with her. "I believe you. Be careful."

The intruder group walked down the edge of the ravine. Doug's voice drifted up the hill. "Did you notice how only two of the guys talked?"

Sissy huffed. "Maybe they're all special. They certainly wouldn't let me get close to the boy with them. I still want to know what's wrong with him."

Micah sighed and shook his head. He tapped fists with Tav. "Great job." He dropped his gaze to Ben.

The boy stood frozen. His eyes stayed fixed on the ground. He barely breathed. Micah knelt and tried to catch the boy's face. "Ben, it's okay, buddy. She's gone. They're all gone."

Ben didn't respond. He continued to stare at the ground. Tav knelt as well. "Ben, the bad people are gone. It's just us, Ben. You're safe."

Luke and Jeremiah joined the group but didn't say anything. Tav tried again. "Hey, bud. We need you to come back to us. Can you do that? Can you look at Mick and me?"

In a flash, Ben took off, running down the hill. The motion caught the Knights flat-footed. Micah yelled, "Ben!" But the boy didn't turn or react in any way. He raced away, dodging into the brush, and disappeared.

Luke jumped to follow Ben, yelling to Tav, "Stay here!" Micah and Jeremiah sprinted after Luke.

Tav called out, "Marco Polo. Talk to each other. If you can't hear, you're too far."

The group split. One north. One east. One west. Ben wouldn't go south. The scary people went south.

Micah began half-breaking small tree limbs and brush to mark his path. Urgency drove him. *You have to find him. You have to find him. You can't lose him.*

A nagging feeling struck him. *Lord, please. Help us find Ben. Show us where he went. Help us bring him back. He's too little to be out here without help. Show us. Please.*

He didn't bother trying to explain further. The Lord already knew.

"Marco."

The call came from Tav. Micah answered, "Polo."

Two more "Polos" sounded from a distance.

Micah cried, "Marco."

Three "Polos."

"Ben. Where are you, buddy? Come back, Ben. We need you. We won't let anyone hurt you."

"Marco" sounded from the left.

"Polo" came from the right. Micah echoed, "Polo." "Polo," hollered from behind him on the ridge.

Still no Ben.

Micah looked for footprints. Broken branches. Turned down grass. Anything which would mark the boy's passing. But he saw nothing.

"Marco." The chant became softer. Harder to hear. Micah pressed on. He wouldn't stop until Ben was back. Even if it meant losing himself.

Lose myself. For a kid? Yeah, for a kid. A kid who saved all our lives. He's worth it.

He heard the "Polos" in the extreme distance. He repeated it back. And cried out, "Ben! Buddy, it's Micah. Come on, please. Come out of hiding. We want to help you. Ben."

He stripped tree limbs. He twisted grass. He marked his trail. He would not stop....

An hour went by. Micah could no longer hear his fellow Knights. He didn't care. All that mattered was Ben. And getting him back.

Not even a sparrow falls to the ground without God knowing. Ben is worth more than a sparrow. Trust Me.

Micah's tears ran hot. "I'll trust You when I find him. I need to find him. I have to take care of him."

Who put the stars in their places?

Micah stopped. "But he's out there by himself. Alone. Scared. I have to find him. It's up to me."

Where were you when I formed the earth?

Micah closed his eyes. "But God, he needs me."

What does "I will lead you and guide you. I will never leave you alone" mean?

"He doesn't know You." Micah leaned against a tree to catch his breath. And let his heart stop pounding.

I formed you in your mother's womb. I formed him. I know him. I know where he is. He is not alone. Ever.

Micah sank to his knees. "But I want to find him. I want to bring him back."

My strength is demonstrated through your weakness.

Micah hung his head. "But Lord…"

You have so little faith. So little belief.

Micah sobbed. "Help my unbelief. Bring him back to us."

Go back to your friends. Go.

"Does this mean they found him?" Micah opened his eyes and looked up. His soul jumped. "He's back?"

Go back.

"But is Ben back?"

Obedience is greater than anything you can do.

Micah sat back on his haunches. "You want me to go back without him. And trust You no matter what. Lord, that's hard. That's so hard."

You love because I loved first. I love Ben.

Micah nodded. "I know. I know. But I want to love him, too."

Silence.

"Will You bring him back?"

Silence.

"Will You take care of him?"

I care for the sparrows of the air and the lilies of the field. Will I not care for you?

Micah bowed his head. "Lord, wherever Ben is, I know You are with him. I know You love him. I know he is safer with You than he will ever be with me. Take care of him. And if I don't see him again…" Tears threatened to destroy him. "Your will be done. You are God. I am not. You are love. I know it. Take care of him."

Micah rose and followed his trail through the woods, up the hill, and back to shouting range. He heard a desperate "Marco!" being yelled by three voices. His shoulders dropped. He closed his eyes.

"Polo."

He climbed the hill and rejoined his team.

Tav grabbed him and shook him despite his wounded shoulder. "You're supposed to stay in range! You know the rules. We don't lose one man to find another! We don't trade lives, ever!" Tav's lambasting continued.

Jeremiah glowered but said nothing. Luke held his tongue. Tav must have drawn the censure duty.

Micah waited until Tav finished to offer his one defense. "But he's still out there."

Tav dropped his anger. "I know, Mick. I know. But we can't lose everyone. We'll look again. We'll keep looking. But as a team, not one by one."

The team set out again. Tav accompanied them, leaning on his makeshift cane. They stayed closer together, searching the area in the middle of the field. They looked under every bush. Beside every tree. And they stayed in sight of each other.

Twenty minutes of searching and Luke yelled, "Found him!"

Micah rushed to Luke's position.

Ben sat under a pine tree covered by branches. He held the lower limbs to provide cover and camouflage.

The Knights knelt at eye level. Ben stared at the ground, unmoving. Micah barely whispered, "Ben. It's us. The guys you saved. We need you, buddy. We need you to stay with us and show us the way. You're part of the team. Remember? Quinn told you to take care of us. We need you."

Tav waved his hand by his side. Micah stopped speaking. Tav put both his hands on Ben's shoulders. "You're a Knight of the Octagon, Ben. We stay together. We care about each other. We love each other. We don't go off on our own. We're not leaving until you're ready to come with us. Got it?"

It took several minutes before Ben raised his head. Tav smiled. "Thanks, Ben. You're safe, buddy. Just us. Mick and me and Luke and Jeremiah. Just us. No one else."

Ben thawed, melted, and became human once again. Micah hugged him. "Glad to have you back." He waited, then asked, "Was Sissy the scary lady from the beach?"

Ben trembled, unable or unwilling to answer.

Luke muttered, "Ask about Win."

Tav frowned. "She didn't act like a threat. She—"

Luke repeated with more force, "Ask him about Win."

Tav turned back to Ben. "Did Win scare you?"

Ben nodded. The once-only solemn nod from the waist.

Tav exchanged glances with Micah and Luke. Jeremiah muttered. Tav snapped, "Obscenity jar. Watch it, Jere. We've got a kid here. You don't talk like that around your kids, do you?"

Jeremiah hung his head. "Sometimes."

Luke huffed. "No wonder your folks make you live over the garage. You don't need to be teaching your kids foul language. They'll hear it soon enough, but they don't need it from you."

Jeremiah snapped, "You know so much about parenting. Your parents are such great role models." He glared at Luke, his hands in fists at his side.

Micah intervened. "At least you both have parents. As in two. Can we focus on what's in front of us? Win was the scary woman Ben saw before. Where is still unknown. We won't help him by arguing between ourselves."

A moment, then Jeremiah and Tav touched fists. Luke and Jeremiah followed. Jeremiah asked, "So what do we do now?"

Micah thought hard. "Ben, did you draw a picture of Win for Quinn?"

Ben spun his body in the "no" response.

Micah didn't have to look to know his brothers in Knighthood shared his same confusion. He tried again. "Was Win *a* scary woman?"

That got the solemn nod.

"Did you see her someplace before the beach?"

Nod.

"Did you see her at the cabin?"

Nod.

Micah stopped. He wanted to push the questions but stopped. Maybe now wasn't the time. He didn't want to lose Ben again to fear. He raised his hands, palms up, at the group. "I don't know how to push this without scaring him. Maybe we should give him a break."

Tav put his arm around Ben's shoulders. "What do you suggest?"

"We keep following the clues. We found the snowman. Let's see if we can find the equine and the X."

The group returned to where they were before being so rudely interrupted. Lined up the snowman with the compass direction. Which again indicated across the ravine. Micah knelt beside Ben. "We're looking for a pony, bud. Do you see any?"

Ben pointed. Micah peered into the ravine. Three horses grazed in a meadow. "Not a real one. Something which looks like a horse."

Ben continued to point. Micah stared again but saw the same three horses. "Not those, Ben. They have to be—"

Jeremiah called, "He's right."

Micah whirled on Jere. "It can't be. There's no way—"

Tav interrupted. "One of them is a statue, Mick."

"What? How?" Micah squinted his eyes. A palomino hadn't moved. The other two did. "Are you sure?"

"Yeah. I saw it before Win's group came but didn't think anything of it. The horse hasn't moved since they arrived."

Jere added, "Or left. There's our second symbol."

Luke called out the heading, and Tav adjusted the compass. It pointed north up the ravine. Jeremiah called out, "Look for the X."

Micah added, "A permanent one."

Luke corrected, "An old one. At least fifty years."

Micah grumbled. "Yeah, right." Nothing growing would work. Too much chance of changing.

The search led them deeper into the woods than Micah thought possible. Forty minutes down, and he was ready to throw in the towel. His head pounded, and his shoulder burned. He should have Luke look at it. Or Tav. Or Jere. Anyone but Ben. No sense adding to the little guy's trauma. Maybe he shouldn't show anyone.

Luke pointed in the air. "Up there. Look."

Five sets of eyes lifted to where Luke indicated. An ancient oak twisted and crossed its limbs. Probably from storm damage. But the result appeared to be a definite X. No question. So, the symbol *could* be organic. Swell.

Placing the compass in line with the tree, they read their next instruction. Down the hill, but veering away from the river. North, not south. Opposite Sissy's group and glad of it.

They shouldered their packs (except Micah) and marched on.

* * *

After two hours of marching (give or take a degree in the sky), the Knights took a break. They came to a stream. According to their calculations, they needed to cross it to continue their search. Jere dropped his backpack and suggested, "I'm tired of MREs. I say we spend some time fishing. Gotta be better than the turkey jerky."

Tav spoke, "Proposed—"

Jeremiah cut him off. "Proposed nothing. I'm fishing." He dug out the fishing pole and tackle the "shrubs" had scavenged. Jere moved a few feet down the trail beside the stream and got his line in the water. He sat down to wait for a nibble.

Ben's eyes widened as he watched Jeremiah. He glanced from Micah to Jere to Micah to Jere... Micah nodded. "Go join Jeremiah. Let him teach you how to catch fish."

Luke grumbled, "Like he knows."

Jeremiah called over his shoulder, "I heard you."

"I wanted you to. What do you know about catching fish?"

Jeremiah turned to face Luke. "I'll tell you what, college boy. We'll make it a competition. You eat what you catch. The rest of us will eat what I catch."

Luke grinned. "You're on, big man. Give me a turn with your pole."

Jeremiah gasped. "My pole? I don't think so, punk. You find your own equipment."

Micah sank against a tree trunk. Tav joined him. Luke protested. "Not fair."

"So? I've got to fish for four people. You've only got to catch for one. Go figure it out."

Ben again turned his focus back and forth, but this time from Jeremiah to Luke. The studious look on his face made Micah wonder if the boy worried the two argued. He assured him, "They're having fun, Ben. They're not fighting."

Ben nodded one time emphatically. He went back to watching Jeremiah. Luke moved off down the creek.

Tav let out a long sigh. "What are we doing out here, Mick?"

Micah chuckled. He tried to stretch his injured shoulder. The breeze cooled his body. He hadn't realized he was sweating. And now felt chilled. He scrunched in closer to the tree to gather some warmth from the sunshine.

Tav seemed unaffected by the wind. He continued his rhetorical questioning. "I mean, honestly. What are we doing?"

Micah closed his eyes. "Looking for treasure."

"As if we don't have enough?"

"What treasure?" Micah opened his eyes, aghast. "You're working three jobs. You and Luke are living in a one-bedroom apartment. Luke sleeps on the couch. Jeremiah is sleeping above the garage in his parents' house." *I'm working my anatomy to the bone, taking care of my mother in* her *house with* her *money, so she says. Everyday. All the time. Outloud.* He closed his eyes again.

Tav's voice lilted. "Ah, yes, but we have each other. Isn't that enough?"

Micah opened his eyes. "No."

Tav grinned. "You're right. I know the chance of us finding this prize is slim to none. We'll spend a week out here running around in the bush, then go back to our lives of quiet desperation."

Jeremiah quipped, "Start now with the quiet. You're scaring the fish."

Tav lowered his eyes. Micah closed his. It made the headache less. Sort of. A little.

He barely unwound before four chunks of dust kicked up, followed almost instantaneously by four gunshots. Jeremiah knocked Ben to the ground and spun on top of him. Micah and Tav scrambled for cover behind any shelter they could find. Tav raised his head enough to locate Luke further down the stream. The younger man flattened himself on the rocks, trying to look invisible. Everyone lay perfectly still. No one breathed.

Thirty seconds went by.

Sixty.

Ninety.

Two minutes. Tav lifted his head. "You think it's safe?"

Fear swamped Micah's attempt to rise. Remembered pain from the last gunshot paralyzed him. He closed his eyes and lay still, unable to move.

Luke called from his position, "You go first." Luke was the most exposed and, thus, the least willing to try his luck. Micah didn't blame him.

Tav grabbed a handful of dirt and threw it into the air. Another rifle round smashed into the ground a few feet from where Tav and Micah lay. Micah screamed silently, *Please, God. Please. Protect me. Protect Ben. Protect the others.*

Shame washed through him. His first thought was for himself? He wasn't a Knight. He was a fraud. A coward. A—

There is no condemnation for those in Christ. No means none. King David knew fear. All the apostles knew fear. And they weren't being shot at. Peace.

They waited another lifetime. Tav slipped out of his shirt, put it on a stick, and slowly raised it above the ground.

Nothing.

Tav waved it back and forth.

Still nothing.

Tav called, "Opinions?" He stayed glued to the ground.

Jeremiah lifted up from sheltering Ben. He rose far enough to be visible. Nothing. He stood and picked up Ben, holding the boy close. Micah breathed out slowly. He shifted on the ground. Tav rose beside Micah. He tapped Micah on the shoulder as he passed by. Micah curled into a sitting position. Luke crawled more than walked back to the group.

Only after coming under the shelter of the trees did he rise to his feet. Jeremiah carried Ben to the trees and sat down beside Micah. Luke joined the group. Jeremiah rocked back and forth to soothe the petrified boy.

Tav cleared his throat. "MREs might not be so bad after all."

* * *

The Knights waited another hour before setting out again. They waded across the stream. Jeremiah carried the semi-catatonic Ben. Micah walked and prayed, *God, help him. Help Ben to come back to us. I should be praising You, I know. Thanking You for being You. But I can't. Not now. I need You to help us. You want honesty? You're getting it. Help us. If You don't want us on this hunt, make it clear.*

Could being shot at be a sign they should quit? Or a test to see if they would persevere? And what about Ben? If they quit, what would happen to him?

Coward or not, Micah would protect Ben. Ben would know love for as long as Micah could provide it. He would.

They walked until the sun slipped below the tallest trees. Jeremiah set Ben down gently. The boy sat unmoving. Unseeing. Micah dropped beside him and put his good arm around him. "It's going to be okay, Ben. It is. You're safe with us. Whatever happened, you're safe. You'll always be safe." Micah lay his head on top of Ben's. He whispered, "We'll take care of you."

Luke shed his backpack. He tilted his head, then called, "What are the next symbols? Who's got the cards?"

Tav pulled out the game pieces. "There's an octopus, an anvil, and the letter G. The other card has a fish, a boot, and a Y."

"There. The tree." An ancient oak fell some time ago. Its roots splayed into the air. "Could it be the octopus?"

Jeremiah examined the tree. "If an octopus only has six legs." He dropped his pack and began gathering firewood.

Tav helped with the scrounging for kindling. "Leave the

62

hunt 'til morning. If the octopus has been there fifty years, it'll be there in the morning. Let's get this ground cleared, and fire started."

Micah watched his fellow Knights work. His job was Ben. How could he help him? Quinn handed the boy a piece of wood. Maybe...

Micah picked a palm-sized stone and placed it in Ben's hand. He turned it in the boy's fist. "Feel the stone, Ben? Can you feel how round and smooth it is? The stone is real, Ben. The stone is here with you and me. It's not in the shadows. It's here. Feel it?"

Ben's fingers twitched. Twitched again. Touched the stone. Fingered it oh, so lightly. Rubbed it. Micah crooned, "That's it, Ben. You've got it. It's a rock. A smooth rock. And it's in your hand." Micah clasped Ben's hand. "And your hand is in mine. Micah. You know me. We're with Tav and Luke and Jeremiah, the big guy. We're all here, and we're all safe. No one is going to hurt you. You got this, Ben."

Ben's eyes regained focus. He stared at the rock. Lifted his face. Looked at Micah. He laid the stone down. Put a hand on Micah's face. Micah smiled. "It's me. Whiskers and all."

Ben rubbed his hand against Micah's scruffy beard. Micah chuckled. "You should have seen the first time we all tried shaving. It was a disaster. We looked like we'd been attacked by a herd of kittens."

Ben leaned against Micah's chest. He lowered his face. "Mew. Mew."

Barely a whisper. Micah grinned. "You're right, Ben. Kittens say 'mew.'" He hugged the boy tight. "You're something else, buddy."

He called out, "Guys. Ben speaks!"

Tav dropped his bundle of sticks and hobbled over to kneel beside Micah. He eyed Ben. "He did? What'd he say?"

Jeremiah and Luke joined them. Micah leaned into Ben's head. "Tell 'em, Ben. What did the kittens say?"

Ben repeated his whisper. "Mew. Mew."

Everyone cheered. A quiet cheer, but still a salute.

Jeremiah glanced at Micah. "What kittens?"

"The ones who scratched our faces the first time we tried shaving."

Jeremiah lifted his chin. "Ah, those kittens." He shook his head but patted Ben on the leg. "Thanks for sharing, Ben."

The group ate a quiet dinner. No one complained about the fare. Once the meal was finished and legs stretched out around the fire, Luke questioned, "You think they actually wanted to hit us or only aimed for intimidation?"

Tav hummed. "I'd say intimidation. If they wanted to hit us, the shots would have been closer."

Micah closed his eyes. Voices became a drone. The heat in his shoulder and face grew while his body shivered. Ben snuggled beside him.

Coward. You're still shaking. No one else is. Coward. You're as worthless as your mother says.

"Mick!"

Micah raised his eyes. Tav stood over him, concern in his eyes. "What?"

"Where have you been, man? We've been talking to you for five minutes, and you haven't answered."

Micah snapped. "Not true. I heard every word you said. None of it made any difference, so I ignored it."

Luke's voice stayed even. "Truth, Mick. We called questions to you, and you didn't answer a word."

Micah jumped to his feet. "You want to know where I've been? I'm shaking in my boots! I'm a coward. Okay? I admit it. When the shooting started, I only thought about saving my own skin. No one else."

Tav raised an eyebrow. "Yeah, so? I hid right there beside you."

Luke added, "And I tried to be one with the rocks. We all panicked. We all dove for cover."

Micah pointed. "Jere didn't. He thought about Ben! That's who I'm supposed to be caring for. I'm the one who wants to be his guardian. I'm the one he looks up to. And I only thought about myself!"

Anger and shame coursed through his body. He yelled his frustration. "I'm worthless!"

Tav yelled over him, "Stand down, Knight!"

Micah lashed out. "Who are you to tell me—"

Tav repeated but in a calmer voice. "Stand down, Mick. You're sick."

Micah shook his head. Bad move. Vertigo made him stagger. "No, I'm not. I'm fine."

Jeremiah stood to his feet. "No, you're not. Luke, get the first aid kit. Tav, make sure the coffee pot's clean and boil some water. And put some salt in it."

Jere continued to give orders. "Take your shirt off, Mick."

Micah seethed, "I'm fine. There's nothing wrong with me."

Jere held out his hand. "Give me the shirt, or I'll take it from you. And you'll lose that battle. Come on, Mick. You're not thinking straight. You're sick."

"I'm not sick."

"Either give me the shirt, or I'll hang the GPS card from the highest tree, and Quinn will come wondering who is suspended in midair. And then I'll have you medevacked home."

Micah stripped off his shirt. It stuck to the bandage, and he jerked it loose. Jeremiah led him to a rock and made him sit down. They waited until the water boiled. The big man saturated a cloth and soaked the old bandage loose. Jeremiah pulled it off carefully.

Tav gagged. Luke joined him. They both stumbled to the treeline and lost their dinner. Jeremiah shook his head in disgust. "Amateurs. Nothing grosses me out. I got kids."

The wound was green and gray and yellow and ugly. Jeremiah covered the gash with the cloth and ordered, "Hold this there." He pulled antiseptic from the first aid kit, along with gauze bandages. He put his knife in the center of the fire.

Micah's voice trembled. It matched the way his body shivered. "What are you going to do?"

"Lance it, clean it, bandage it. You want something to bite

on, or you want to do bear calls?" Jere moved his knife around, turning the blade side to side.

Micah gritted his teeth. It wouldn't be enough. "Give me a stick."

Tav and Luke, both white as sheets, rejoined the operating area. Tav's voice shook. "What can I do?" He stood out of sight range of the wound.

Jeremiah stared at him. "I don't know. What can you do? If you're going to hurl when we get started, I don't need you." His voice came down hard.

Luke spit. "There's nothing left. Tell us what to do." He shuffled his feet.

Jeremiah's voice took a gentler tone. "One of you take Ben for a walk."

Luke and Tav Ro Sham Bo'ed to see who would leave and who would stay. Luke threw rock. Tav threw scissors. Luke held his hand out to Ben. "Come on, bud. Let's see if we can find some more firewood."

Ben grabbed one of the game markers before he took Luke's hand. The boy patted Micah on his good shoulder, then walked into the woods waving the card in the air.

Jeremiah wrapped a sturdy stick in gauze and handed it to Micah. "Bite on this. It'll save your teeth."

Tav stepped closer. "Where do you want me?"

Jere motioned to Micah's wound. "When I lance this, I need you to get in there and express all the junk. You follow me?"

Tav's Adam's apple moved up and down in a gulp. "I got it."

Jere warned, "Don't let me down, Tav. Mick's life could depend on you."

Tav nodded. "I got it." He positioned close behind Micah.

Micah breathed out. "I trust you, Taylor." He grinned weakly.

Tav sneered at him. "Just for that, I'm giving Jere the dull knife."

Jeremiah snorted. "If you two comedians are finished,

we'll do this." Micah put the stick and cloth in his mouth and bit down. Jeremiah pulled the glowing knife from the fire and dipped it in the water. He sliced open the wound.

Micah screamed into the wad in his mouth. A big cat screamed in the woods. Pain exploded through his shoulder. Micah wanted to pass out. Begged to pass out. Prayed to pass out. But didn't. Again and again, the pain escalated, erupting in his shoulder. He shrieked. He burned. He existed as the fifth man in the fire. The flames seared his being. Over and over, he cried, but only muffled grunts came out.

Finally, the words he needed to hear. "We're done, Mick. You did good, Knight. I'll get you something to help you rest tonight."

Breathless, Micah spit the stick and gauze out. He stared at Jere and panted, "Why didn't you give me something before you operated?"

Jere shrugged. "What fun would that be?" He pulled out the drugs from the kit and handed four of them to Micah. "I didn't want to waste them. And they wouldn't have helped, anyhow."

Micah sagged. "You're probably right." He glanced at Tav. "How'd you do?"

Tav looked whiter than the gauze Mick tossed in the fire. "Oh, peachy. Just peachy."

Jere called, "Luke, Ben, you can come back now. Mick's done yelling."

Micah watched Ben and Luke return to the campfire. He studied Ben. "Did I hear a cat scream? Ben's cat?"

Luke nodded. "Yeah. He's prowling around on the perimeter. Maybe checking on Ben."

Tav leaned his head to the side. "I wonder why he doesn't take the boy home?"

A voice from the woods spoke. "Maybe there's no home to take him."

Ben jumped to his feet and headed for the voice. He jerked to a halt as the voice commanded, "Wait. Stay where you are."

Ben stopped but stared into the darkness. Micah read confusion on the boy's face.

The voice said, "You call him Ben. It's a good name for him. Folks called him Eugene. He never liked it. Ben is better."

Ben nodded once. A solemn bow.

Tav waved to the fire. "You know we won't bother you. Why don't you come in and tell us what's going on?"

"No. You'll want to stop me, and I won't let you."

Three Knights fell silent. Tav took the lead. "Stop you from doing what?"

"Killing the one who killed Uncle Petey."

Tav sat down, facing the unseen speaker. "Tell me about it."

"Nothing to tell. We were at home. Some dealers came by with a shipment for Uncle Petey." Sarcasm ran deep in the voice. Micah tried to place the age and could only come up with older than Ben but younger than Luke. Fourteen? Fifteen, maybe?

The speaker continued. "Ben and I always had to hide under the floorboards when Uncle Petey's doing his deals. We watched him pull out some gold coins and try to pay for the shipment with them. The dealer wanted to know where Uncle Petey got the gold. Petey said he found a stash with a boatload of them.

"One of the dealers was this woman; she's the only one me and Ben saw clearly. She said the coins were fake. Worthless. Uncle Petey got mad and said they wanted to cheat him out of his gold. There was a lot of cussing. Shots got fired. Uncle Petey got hit and died. One of the men said maybe Petey's gold was fake, but he knew about some real gold in the area. He planned on coming back to look for it."

Tav kept his voice low. "When was this?"

"Hard to keep track of time. But had to be a month or two ago."

"You and Ben have been out here by yourselves for two months?"

"I know how to take care of myself. And I can care for

Ben. He's no trouble. People think he's stupid 'cuz he doesn't talk. But he's not stupid."

Tav kept his voice low. "I'm sorry about your uncle."

"He wasn't blood kin. County lady left us with him. But he did care for us. Made us go to school. Most days. We helped him around the place. Ben carried drugs for him sometimes. No one suspected a dumb kid of doing nothing illegal. Petey didn't deserve to die. I'm gonna make sure that lady who killed him pays for murdering him."

Micah thought for a minute. "The woman who brought you to Petey and the woman who came with the dealers. Were they the same woman?

"Different. I don't care about the county woman. It's the drug dealer woman I'm gonna make face justice. I'll see to it."

Tav lowered his head. "Then what? What happens to you? What happens to Ben? If you kill someone, they'll put you in jail. Who watches out for Ben?"

The voice didn't answer. Tav waited. "You still there?"

No answer.

Ben tilted his head. He stared at the woods, stared at Tav. Tav raised both hands, palm up. "I don't know, Ben. He'll be back. He will."

"Who will be back?"

Five heads looked behind to see Quinn come in from the tree line. He gazed around the camp. "Boys, you look like death warmed over." He pointed to Jeremiah. "Except you. And Ben. What's going on?"

Tav reversed direction to face Quinn. "Who said anything was going on?"

Quinn took a seat. "Someone kept swinging the GPS marker back and forth. Like they waved it around. I thought it might have been a distress signal. From the looks on the three of your faces, I guessed right." Micah knew the monitor wasn't referring to Jere or Ben, either.

Jeremiah wiped his knife on the grass, poured the boiling water over it, and wiped it on his shirt sleeve. "Mick's wound got infected. Tav and Luke had some...problems with the surgery."

"And you didn't?"

Jere repeated his mantra. "I got kids. Nothing can gross me out."

Quinn smiled. "Hear, hear." He eyed Ben. "Did you tell me the boys needed help?"

Ben nodded once. Definitively.

Quinn chuckled. "Smart kid." He held his arms out. Ben moved to Quinn's side and hugged the man. He returned to sit beside Micah.

Tav emptied the pot, put some clean water in, and set it to boil. "We got shot at again today."

Quinn's eyes narrowed, and his head bobbed. "I heard the rifle reports. Didn't know where they came from or who they aimed at."

Tav's voice carried disgust. "Getting tired of being used for target practice."

"Understood. The drones we sent didn't locate anything. You have any ideas?"

Tav exchanged looks with Jeremiah and Luke. Micah felt too woozy to render an opinion. Jere and Luke both nodded. Tav reported, "We ran into a group of people. One of them, Win Osborn, scared Ben. But she wasn't the woman from the beach he drew."

Micah wanted to add his suspicion about Sissy, but withheld comment. His judgment wasn't to be trusted at this point.

Tav continued, "Win didn't recognize Ben that we know of. But he recognized her." Tav paused, added, "Ben has a friend or brother out here. He told us about a county worker who used to come to the house. We think it could have been Win. But the woman at the beach had to be someone else. She showed up at Ben and his brother's cabin as part of a drug deal. It went bad. Ben's guardian got shot and killed."

Quinn gave Tav the side-eye. "Let me guess. He wants revenge."

"Something along that line, yeah."

Quinn growled. "They always do. How old?"

"The boy or the woman?"

Quinn waved a hand. "The boy, the boy. I know how old the woman is. I've got Ben's picture of her." His eyes narrowed. "A picture that could look like several people. No jumping to conclusions, right, gentlemen?"

Tav continued in the lead role. "My guess is the boy is in his mid-teens. Maybe a little older. But not much."

Quinn gazed around the group. "Anyone see him?"

"Just heard the voice." Micah forced his mind to focus. "Ben could tell you what he looks like."

Quinn smirked. "Now, why didn't I think of that? Ben, can you draw me a picture of what your brother looks like? The one who can scream like a cat?"

Jeremiah muttered under his breath, "In heat."

Tav tossed a woodchip at him.

Ben set about drawing in the dirt. A sudden thought hit Micah. It would probably be the last coherent one, but he said, "Ben, draw Jeremiah, too." Micah added, "For accuracy's sake."

Quinn stuck out his lower lip. "I like the way you think. No one can say he didn't know who he drew then."

Jeremiah added, "It's not the whole story. There are some gold coins involved. Seems the guardian, Uncle Petey, tried to pay with gold coins. The woman said they were fake. Petey begged to differ. Thus, the argument and the shooting."

Micah slipped down to a prone position. The best he could manage was a mumble. "Night, Mary Ellen."

Tav chuckled. "Goodnight, John Boy."

Micah closed his eyes. Darkness kept him, but he continued to hear everything anyone said. Except no one said anything. Micah guessed they watched Ben sketch.

He guessed right. Jeremiah humphed. "I'm not so good-looking."

Quinn chuckled. "Eye of the beholder, sir."

Tav cleared his throat. "You notice he drew you without the beard? And still got you dead-on."

Silence.
Luke gave a low whistle.
Micah's consciousness faded.

* * *

FRIDAY

Micah woke in the morning with the bird song. Ravens cawed. A crying hawk let his displeasure be known. Wrens and sparrows chirruped and cheeped and generally raised a ruckus. Who said the woods were quiet? He tested his shoulder. It pained him to touch it. *So don't touch it.* He slipped his shirt on, visited the trees, returned, and stirred the fire. He gazed around at the silvery-shrouded lumps and noticed an extra body.

Quinn. The monitor must have chosen to spend the night with their camp. Having the man around suited Micah. Now when the shooting started, Quinn would witness it. And hopefully, stop it.

Micah added fuel to the fire and set the coffee on. He wandered over to where Ben sketched his drawings in the dirt. Jeremiah's face stared back at him. Perfect likeness. Down to the cleft in his chin. The cleft hidden beneath the bushy beard Jere sported after a week of not shaving. The cleft Ben never saw. Or had he?

Had Ben and his brother spied on the Knights ever since they arrived? Is that when Ben saw Jeremiah clean-shaven? How could he ask Ben and get an answer Micah could understand?

Micah moved to examine the second sketch. Ben's brother bore no likeness to Ben. Guessing from the face, the young man might be fifteen. Sixteen at most. Maybe less. High cheekbones. Shallow cheeks. Small eyes. Ben drew him angry. Maybe his most common expression?

The smell of coffee brewing brought the dead to life. Quinn moved out from under his survival blanket. He rubbed a hand across his face. "Coffee ready yet?"

Micah smiled. "Not yet. Soon."

Quinn muttered something, climbed to his feet, and disappeared into the trees. Tav rose next and wandered in the opposite direction. Luke and Jere awakened, followed by Ben. By the time everyone returned from their morning constitutional, the coffee reached full strength. Micah poured cups for Quinn and Jeremiah, then poured one for himself. Tav passed his cup to Luke. They might be a cup low, but they could still share.

Tav passed around protein bars for breakfast. Luke tore the wrapper. "Just once something other than MREs and protein bars would be nice."

Quinn chuckled. "You have a whole forest to get food. Rabbit, squirrel, wild turkey, quail, snake…"

Luke shook his head. "I know how to clean a fish. I'm not a survivalist."

Tav voiced his agreement. "Yeah, we're city boys. Scouts was a long time ago."

"College boys." Quinn's voice dripped disdain.

Micah chuckled. "High school dropouts, you mean."

Quinn's head came up sharply. "What? Who?"

Tav pointed to Jere, Micah, and himself. "All of us. Luke's the only one who graduated."

Luke added, "Because you three threatened me with bodily injury if I didn't."

Micah drawled, "Yeah, well, one of us has to be a success. You drew the short straw."

Quinn rose from his seat and poured more coffee into his cup. He swallowed a mouthful and crossed to sit beside his pack. "I never got your full names. I should put it in the records." He smiled. Or smirked. Micah read it both ways.

"Luke Vaughn."

"Tav Vaughn."

"Jeremiah Acosta."

"Micah Andres."

Quinn cocked his head. "A-N-D-R-E-S?"

"Yeah." Quinn eyed him close. Closer than Micah felt necessary. "There a problem?"

Quinn waved him off. "No, no. Name sounded familiar."

Micah indicated the drawing of Ben's brother. "Can you do anything with the face?"

"Yeah. I'm running it through the missing person's database as we speak."

"Did you take Ben's picture, too?" Micah's hands shook. Did Ben belong somewhere? Or was he abandoned by the system and needed a guardian? Could Micah be his guardian?

A soft breeze made Micah shiver. Jeremiah pushed off from his seat on a downed tree and approached Micah. "I need to check your shoulder. See how it is this morning."

Micah opened his mouth. Jere cut him off. "Save it, Mick. I don't want to hear, 'It's fine.' You said that last night, and you almost died from sepsis. Take the shirt off, and let's see the wound."

Micah sighed but slipped out of his shirt. Jeremiah eased the bandages off. The area was red and purple but not yellow or green. Definite improvement. Jeremiah replaced the dressings. "You're good. For now."

Micah settled his shirt again. "Thanks, Jere. I appreciate you saving my life."

Jere sneered. "Don't mention it. Ever. To anyone."

As the group packed and readied for the next leg of the journey, Micah studied Quinn. "I have to ask. Who are you? I know, the monitor. But you're more. I mean, running pictures through the missing person's database? Having GPS trackers on everyone? This isn't just about finding coins for a game, is it?"

Quinn grinned, but his eyes hardened. "Let's leave the occupation as we understand it for now. We might revisit the topic if we need to."

Tav grumbled. "That sounded clear as mud."

Quinn picked up his pack. "Happy to serve." He lost the smile. "And keep the overnight visit between us. I don't need people claiming I have favorites. Or did anything to influence a winner in the game. I treat you all the same." He chuckled. "Except you do have the best coffee. Which makes you my favorites." He gave Ben a hug. "Plus, you have this guy here."

Ben hugged Quinn in return, then danced in front of him. Happy dance.

Quinn moved into the woods and disappeared. Luke raised his eyebrows. "Shouldn't he swash a Z somewhere?"

Tav closed his eyes momentarily and shook his head. "Let's look at the symbols. You saw the octopus."

The cards came out. Octopus, check. Heading? Check. But nothing they found looked like an anvil or the letter G. They needed to follow the heading.

Jere groused. "Twice, we saw all the marks from the same spot. Why would it change now?"

Micah suggested, "Because we're closing in on the treasure? Quinn said only a few made it to the third leg of the hunt. Maybe this is why. The pattern of the game changed."

"Could be." Jere put Micah's pack on Ben, settled the shoulder pads, and swatted Ben on the head. "Okay, soldier. We're ready to go."

Ben smiled and marched around the small clearing. Tav, Luke, Jere, and Micah followed the compass heading. Luke picked up a stick to beat back the bushes. "Maybe we will get lucky and cross the stream again. We could get a second chance of catching fish."

Jere harumphed. "You still have to catch your own, college boy."

Luke snorted. "I've been thinking about fishing. I could spearfish. Or try scooping them out by hand."

"Sure you can." Jere voiced his disbelief. "You do that. We'll see who eats and who goes hungry."

Together the group moved on.

* * *

Based on the position of the sun, it was four hours later when the group came into a clearing. Tav called "Break." Four packs dropped. Everyone found a comfortable place to relax, drink water, and snack on a protein bar.

Micah pulled out the game cards. He studied the compass directions. After a thought, he picked up a stick and drew a circle. He marked the river at the bottom. Micah traced in the first direction they went. He couldn't be sure of the distances. It didn't matter. All that mattered was the direction they headed.

Tav wandered over. "What's up, Mick?"

Micah indicated the headings. "Look at this. With what we've got, we could end near where we started."

Tav stared at the map Micah drew in the dirt. He checked the compass and shook his head. "We could be on the same heading, but not the same distance. We could be a long way from the river by now. Even if we're told to cut back, we'd still be miles from the bank we washed up on."

Micah shrugged and erased his map. "I suppose. This game has got to be the strangest thing we've ever done."

Jere raised his head. "And we've done some strange things in our day."

Luke chuckled. "Yeah, remember—"

He got no further. A crash from the forest stopped him. All eyes swung around to see who or what would come rumbling out of the woods. The group jumped to their feet, ready to fight or run. Tav stepped forward, his eyes narrow and on alert.

Cursing followed the crashing. A woman's voice. Micah could see figures battling their way through the undergrowth. Funny they hadn't found the trail Micah and his partners traveled. Being in this area, you'd think they would be walking the same path. But you'd think wrong.

Ben caught Micah around his middle, curled behind him, and held him tight. Micah put a hand on Ben's back to comfort the boy. As much as he could.

Two women emerged from the woods, slashing at shrubs, kicking tree roots, and knocking down anything in their way. As they made their way into the circle, one cursed roundly. "Great. Company. Fantastic."

Micah watched each of his brothers-in-arms lower a hand surreptitiously to their side. Micah breathed the silent four count, put out four fingers. Jere and Tav did the same. Luke threw two. The fours won.

Luke stepped up. "Welcome to our clearing." He smiled. "What brings you to our fine forest?"

Both women wore camo pants and shirts. Black ball caps. One stood a few inches taller than the other. The shorter woman, with deep purple hair pulled into a ponytail threaded through the back of her hat, glared with hard eyes around at the Knights. Nineteen, maybe? Twenty at most, but definitely over eighteen. Micah kept his musings to himself.

The taller woman, with short silver hair sticking below her cap, smiled at Luke and extended her hand. "Glad to see survivors of this cursed chase. I'm Grace." She jerked her head sideways. "This is Chay. She of the sailor's mouth. You probably heard her coming."

Chay let a few choice words fly. Grace raised an eyebrow. "I rest my case."

Luke waved a hand. "Make yourselves comfortable. I'm Luke." He pointed around the clearing. "Jeremiah. Tav, my brother. Micah. Behind him is his little brother Ben."

Ben peeked his head around Micah to sneak a glance at Grace. He avoided looking at Chay. He slipped back, peered around again.

Grace smiled. "Why, hello, young man."

Ben snuck out again, stepped away from Micah. He walked over and stood in front of Grace. He bowed low. Grace chuckled. "I'm not royalty, Ben. You don't have to bow to me."

Ben straightened, stepped in, and hugged the woman. She reached down and hugged him as well. Her voice broke.

"Thanks, Ben. That's the best hug I've had in a very long time." She lifted her face. Her eyes glistened.

Luke said softly, "He's a good judge of character. Doesn't talk, but doesn't need to much."

Grace hugged the boy again. "We could use more people like you in the world, Ben."

Chay cursed again. "Can we move on? We're on a quest, not a 'let's make friends' outing. I want to find this treasure and go home." She inserted a few words to describe the prize Micah decided to erase from his memory. No garbage in.

Ben skipped back to Micah's side and sat. Micah joined him on the ground. Ben picked up a stick and began drawing in the dirt. Micah watched to see what might appear.

Luke gave Grace a sideways glance. "Where's the rest of your team? I thought you needed four."

Grace nodded. She sat cross-legged on the ground. "We had four. Lou and Ferris were friends from long past. We'd planned this trip for almost a year. Plotted every point, knew every direction. Then Lou died of cancer. Ferris brought on Race, his son. I never liked Race, but what can I say? Old friend, sudden death. Race seemed a convenient replacement. Kind of a sleaze, but you know. You'll put up with anything for an old friend.

"Until the first day we were out, Race decided he was the leader. Wouldn't take no for an answer. We couldn't agree on left or right, up or down. So they demanded to be released. I knew Ferris' heart wasn't in it when we started. I gave him every opportunity to step out, but he insisted it was what Lou 'would have wanted.' But when it came down to it, he quit. When the monitor, Quinn, came, we discussed being allowed to remain in the hunt. He gave no objections, so we're still poking around in the forest with Smoky Bear. I promised Little Miss Sunshine we'd try one more day, then call it quits."

How much did Miss Sunshine contribute to the early exit? Micah kept those thoughts to himself.

Grace cocked her head. "Weren't you the guys who joined at the last moment? The ones stranded on the shoals?"

Luke grinned. "That's us. We're still poking around as well. Probably just as lost as we were at the river." He sat opposite Grace. "What got you into this craziness?"

Chay leaned against a tree. "She's always after something. Puzzle solver. Thinks if there's a riddle, she should be able to solve it. This makes the what, fifth search we've been on?"

Grace shrugged. "It keeps my brain young." She stretched. "The rest of me is aging, but my brain is still going strong."

Micah noticed the strong resemblance between the two women. He guessed mother-daughter. But would never suggest such a thing. Consequences for wrong guesses could be severe. Ben continued drawing. Animals.

Luke wisely didn't go there, either. "Have you seen many of the other groups since you left the river?" He picked a blade of grass and chewed on it.

Grace shook her head. "None. Well, we passed one set of idiots two days ago. They spent so much time arguing they never saw us. We didn't bother saluting them, either."

"Have you heard any gunshots?"

Chay expressed an opinion. "Yeah, we heard them. Couldn't tell what direction they came from. I thought it might be Race, but he's gone. So it must be someone else. Poachers, maybe?"

Luke shrugged. "I don't know. We spoke to the monitor about it, but he doesn't have any information."

Again, Chay voiced her opinion before continuing, "I don't know what the man does. Other than appear and disappear. Some kind of ninja. Scares me." Her statement sprayed expletives.

"Clean the mouth! There's a child here." Grace's voice carried a no-nonsense tone.

Chay grimaced. "Sorry."

"Is it any wonder Ben didn't come over to you? There's no reason for a mouth that foul."

Chay's eyes narrowed. "Oh, I don't know. I wonder where I learned it?"

"Yeah, and I unlearned it. You can, too, you know." Grace's voice softened.

"We don't need to share family history with strangers, okay?"

So family. Micah would let them declare the relationships, though.

Grace gazed around the clearing. "Do your buddies speak, or are they silent like Ben?"

Luke chuckled. "No, we all talk."

To prove the point, Jeremiah quipped, "Too much sometimes."

Luke explained, "We find it easier if only one speaks initially. Less confusion and speaking over each other."

Grace stuck out her lower lip. "Impressive. How do you decide who talks?"

Luke shrugged. "We take turns."

Micah hid the smirk. *No, we vote on it. You got picked. We figured you handle women better. You're more "disarming" than the rest of us.*

Luke motioned over his shoulder. "Which way are you heading from here? What's your direction?"

Chay sneered, "Tell us yours first."

Luke didn't look around for support. But his left hand tapped the ground as if nervous. Micah watched Tav wiggle his left foot. Saw Jere shrug his left shoulder. Make it unanimous, or dissent? Micah cracked his neck to the left.

Luke dipped his head. "We're following thirty-five north. You?"

Grace checked her card. "Ninety East."

Chay grimaced. "I knew we went the wrong way."

Luke corrected her. "Maybe we are. That's the way the game goes. The markers are easy to misidentify."

Chay's face drew down into darkness. "If we even have the right directions. We could be running around in this cursed forest for nothing."

Grace smiled. "Think of it as spending quality time with your mother. Doesn't it count for something?"

"We could have spent quality time at the beach. Or at home on the porch. But no, we have to play Wilderness Explorers and nearly get eaten by bears and cougars, and who knows what else is out here."

Ben added a snake to his menagerie. Micah swallowed his chuckle.

Grace tilted her head to the side. "Those drawings are fantastic. He is quite the artist."

Ben raised his head and smiled at Grace. He began another sketch. A person this time. The eyes wrinkled at the corners, but not from age. A young woman began to take shape. Micah went still inside. He knew who Ben drew.

Within minutes a smiling face peered from the dirt. Chay leaned forward to examine the drawing. She slapped her hand over her mouth. Her eyes widened as she shifted from the portrait to Grace and back again. "Oh. My." She shook her head. "He nailed you. Absolutely perfect. But maybe ten years ago. How?"

Ben started another drawing. He lowered his head in concentration, scratching, erasing, sketching… He worked hard. Fast. But clean. Finally, he sat back and held Chay's eyes.

Grace peered at the face in the dirt. "It's you."

Chay's voice cracked. "It was me. Before all…" She trailed off. Turned her head away. Dropped her gaze to the ground.

Ben stood, walked over to Chay, and stood before her. He bowed to her as he did Grace. Chay reached out her hand and took Ben's. She pulled the boy to herself. Ben wrapped his arms around her. Chay buried her head in his shoulder. He waited until she released him, then skipped to sit beside Micah.

Tav cleared his throat. "Rolling thunder. Now."

Micah groaned. Jere echoed. Tav repeated, "Now."

The four Knights moved to a position of sitting in a square, paired off facing each other. Ben stayed beside Micah and watched. Tav said quietly, "The Raven."

Luke chipped, "Night Before."

Micah threw in his contribution. "Psalm 136."

Jere added, "Current reading list. Green Eggs."

Rolling thunder. Tav's favorite invention. A way for us to talk to each other in American Sign Language but not have anyone else know what we're saying. We each sign a few stanzas of a poem. Two can talk while the other two keep signing. Switch off and keep talking. The lyrics are muscle-memory by now. Except Green Eggs. That'll be interesting to watch.

They all did a simultaneous one-time run-through. Tav called two numbers. "One, two." Tav and Jeremiah would talk. Luke and Micah would keep their poems going. Tav would announce the switch, and the round-robin discussion would continue.

Tav called, "Go." Eight hands began signing.

Once upon a midnight dreary…

Sam I am. Do you like green eggs and ham?

Oh, give thanks to the Lord, for He is good.

'Twas the night before Christmas, and all through the house.

Tav and Jere broke from "The Raven" and "Green Eggs and Ham" into an actual discussion. Micah followed most of the dialog. Tav wanted to invite the women to walk with the Knights.

Jeremiah objected. *We're splitting the treasure four ways as it is. Dividing it six ways means we get less.*

It's not ours to start with. And who says we can find it without extra help?

They're lost.

So are we.

No, we're on track.

We think.

Tav said, "Two, four."

Micah didn't follow the conversation as close. Jeremiah would tell Luke what Tav wanted to do and Jeremiah's objections.

"Three, four."

After telling Micah what Jeremiah told him, Luke explained his thoughts. Micah and Tav shared Micah's opinions. Tav and Jeremiah compared notes.

The final call came for the vote. Four fists went into the circle. The silent four count and four thumbs went up.

Grace and Chay watched closely while the Knights talked among themselves. When Micah and his brothers-in-arms stopped signing, Grace asked, "What were you doing there? How is it you all know sign language?"

Luke continued as spokesman. "We got a new kid in junior high school who was deaf. Tav wanted to be able to talk to him, so we all learned. Came in handy other times, too. Just now, we wanted to throw around an idea. Would you like to join us? If a four-person team works, maybe a six-person team would be even better."

Grace raised her eyebrows at Chay. Chay's eyes narrowed. "Why would you want to split the money with anyone?"

"The money's not ours. We didn't have any of it to start with. If we get any treasure, it's more than before. And a win all around."

He smiled. "And there's those bears and cougars. Safety in numbers."

Grace asked, "If we were two guys instead of two women?"

Luke shrugged. "Same offer. Look, we got dumped by the river. If we come home with anything more than our lives, we've received more than we deserve. So what do you say?"

Grace wagged her head back and forth. "I can see your point. Okay, last question. How long have you been on your current heading?"

"Since this morning. Sun-up."

Chay rolled her eyes. "I'm in."

Luke's eyes widened. "How long have you been on yours?"

"Two days." Grace laughed. "Count my vote as yes." She side-eyed Luke. "How do we know we'll be safe with you?"

Tav stood at attention. He intoned, "We are Knights of the Octagon."

Jeremiah muttered the second refrain. "Because no one had a round table, and Knights of the Oval sounded weird."

Tav grimaced. "More loyal than boy scouts, more noble than Templars. We'll fight to the death to protect your honor and your lives."

Luke threw in, "When we're not busy fighting each other."

Tav dropped his pretentiousness. "Which happens more than we like to admit."

Grace chuckled. She pointed to Micah. "And what of your silent man?"

Micah shrugged his good shoulder. "The group was going before me. I was just hanging around when Tav—"

Three pebbles flew across the clearing and hit Micah with the force of beestings. "Ow! Okay, okay!" Micah started again. "Tav saved my life and let me join the Knights so he could keep me alive. I've been with them since Junior High." Micah stared at the ground. "I tried to hang myself when I was twelve."

He shoved the dirt at his feet around in small circles. Remembered pain burned his cheeks. "Had the rope too long to break my neck but not long enough to get out of it. I started praying to anyone who could help me. Promised I'd give them my life if they got me out of the tree. Tav passed me, stopped, and cut me down. Made me promise I'd never do something so stupid again."

Jere harumphed. "There's still been stupid. Just not *that* stupid."

Micah raised his head. "Thanks, Jere. Love you too, brother." He faced Grace. "Tav introduced me to the One I'd pledged my life to. Told me what it meant to follow—really follow—Him. How it would be a lifetime commitment, not a passing fancy. Not a 'get out of hell' free card. Jesus died so I could have life. But it cost Him everything. I pledged everything in return."

Chay cleared her throat. "One condition for me to join you: you do not talk to me about your god. Ever."

Four hands went in the air. "We promise."

Tav added, "We don't promise we won't talk to each other

about Him." Micah watched Grace hide a grin.

Jere muttered. "All day. Every day. Outloud."

Chay dropped her head and let out a growl.

A wildcat screamed from the woods close to the clearing. The angry, bitter, ear-piercing screech made Ben huddled into Micah's arms.

Chay jumped to her feet and picked a substantial tree branch. Tav, Jere, and Luke also stood. To Micah, they looked more at ease than they should. He called, "Guys… Ben is terrified."

If Ben's scared, it's not his brother.

Luke checked around for another branch. Jere drew his knife. Tav picked up his backpack. The big cat shrieked again, closer. It growled as it paced the perimeter of the clearing. Micah couldn't see it, and no one pointed to where it might be. Instead, they watched from all angles. Ben quivered and quaked, lying on Micah's chest. Micah yelled as loud as he could, "Go on! Get away from here!"

The others raised the call, and everyone barked, "Get out!" "Hi-yah!" "Leave, cat!" Chay added a few more colorful phrases, but again, Micah refused to let them penetrate his brain. *Holy Spirit, my ears hear, but my soul doesn't have to. Please.*

Moments later, there came the sound of something moving away in the brush. The cat called from below the hill, then from further off, and further still.

A group exhale let off steam and nerves. Micah hugged Ben and comforted him. "It's gone, Ben. The bad cat is gone. He won't bother us again."

Ben raised his head to meet Micah's eyes. He whispered, "Maow."

Micah hugged him again. "Right, buddy. The maow is gone." He lifted Ben to his feet. "And we should move on, too. We should cover more ground before we lose the light."

Everyone packed. Ben carrying Micah's backpack won Micah a sideways glance from Chay. He explained, "Hurt my shoulder the first day. It got infected. Jere cleaned it out, and I'm trying to let it heal."

Grace nodded. "Makes sense." She glanced at Jeremiah. "Are you a doctor?"

"Nope. I got boys. I know how to repair about anything."

Grace laughed. "So I've been told by parents of boys. Are you married?"

As the group walked, they made small "get to know you" talk. And kept their eyes open for the anvil. Or the letter G. Or a sign of civilization.

* * *

Three hours later, they stopped at another grassy clearing. Tav looked around and jutted out his lower lip. "Seems like a good place to spend the night."

Luke cocked his head. "Listen." Micah caught the sound of gentle waves lapping. Luke grinned. "Water!" He hustled to drop his pack and went in search of the noise. After a minute, he yelled, "Yes! A pond. With fish."

He stepped back into the clearing. "Looks like it's deep enough we could even bathe in it." He grinned. "Some of us could use a bath."

Ben raised his hand to his nose and pinched his fingers together. Micah laughed. "Are you insulting us?"

Ben closed his eyes and continued to hold his nose.

Jere humphed. "Let's catch the fish before we pollute their habitat."

Grace offered, "If there's fish, there might be frogs. We could gig a couple of those for a nice meal." She pulled a knife from her pack and walked towards the pond.

Chay groaned. "I'd rather starve."

Tav offered, "We have MREs." He dropped his pack and dug out the camp shovel to prepare a pit for the fire.

Chay gagged. "I'll eat frogs." She followed her mother.

Chay, Grace, and Ben wandered over the hill. They hadn't been gone but a few minutes when Ben came running back to Micah's side. He grabbed Micah around the middle, then dragged at him, demanding Micah come.

Micah laughed. "Okay, bud. I'm coming. I'm with you."

The sparkle in the boy's eyes read joy, not terror. Nothing untoward had happened to the women.

In his excitement, Ben yanked on Micah's bad shoulder. Micah pulled back. "Ben! That's the bad shoulder, bud. Ease up."

Ben froze. Micah knelt to catch Ben's eyes. "It's okay, Ben. It is. It's a little sore, still. So slow down, and I'll follow you."

Ben slowed to a tiptoe. Micah shoved him lightly. "Not that slow. Walk normal."

Ben smiled and resumed his pace. Running over the hill, running back to see if Micah still followed, running back over the hill. A frenetic puppy.

Finally, Micah reached where Chay and Grace stood. A burned-out and dilapidated fireplace stood in the remains of what might have been a cabin. No walls, no floor, no ceiling. Only a broken and disused fireplace.

Chay poked around the ruins. She lifted a crumbling brick. "I'd say this is over a hundred years old. The way the grass is all grown over it, I'd also say its heydey may have been seventy-five years ago."

Micah's eyebrows rose. "Are you an archeologist?"

"Not yet. Mom is."

Grace assented. "And you called it very well, Chay. Good observations."

Micah circled the area with his wrist. "You think we could set our fire in here? Maybe use the flat stones for cooking?"

Grace snorted. "We'd need a botanist to say whether this is poison ivy, oak, sumac, or any other skin irritant."

Micah held up a finger. "I have just the person. Be right back." He trudged back over the crest, calling, "Tav. We need you."

Tav asked, "What's up?" He followed Micah back to where the women stood.

Micah pointed. "Take a look. Anything allergy-producing in this vegetation?"

Chay considered Micah's leader. "Are you a botanist?"

"Nope. Just allergic to most everything." He examined the foliage. "I don't see anything threatening. We'll clear it out, then swim in the pond."

The group shifted their supplies close to the remains of the cabin. Micah and Ben gathered dead wood to start their fire for the night. Luke, Grace, and Jeremiah went to capture dinner. Dry leaves and kindling caught quickly in the prepared space. And by the time the hunter-gatherers returned with fish and game (mostly fish) to eat, the coals burned red. With enough fish to go around, Micah didn't have to ask whether Luke or Jeremiah caught the most. And the frogs proved a nice addition, though they did not taste like chicken. Ben tried to catch a snake to add to the meal, but Micah discouraged him. "When I can do better snake identification, we'll try it, okay, buddy?" The boy seemed disappointed. Micah wasn't.

Everyone bathed and hung non-essential clothes on the rocks to dry. The essential clothing remained on its wearer to dry *in situ*.

As Micah cleaned the area so as not to entice predators, he noticed a lump in the weeds. He poked it.

It clanged. Metal.

Micah scraped off the overgrowth.

Tav walked over. "What's going on?"

Micah pointed to the object he cleared. "What does that look like to you?"

Tav knelt. He dug with his hands to reveal more of the chunk of metal. Finally exposed, Tav whistled low.

Chay demanded, "What is it? What did you find?" She pushed her way in front of Micah.

Tav sat back on his haunches. "I believe we've found an old anvil." He gazed at Grace. "Do you concur?"

She eyed the mound from side to side. Finally, she nodded. "I do believe you're correct. Why is it important?"

"Because it's the next marker we need." Tav dug into his pack and pulled out the game pieces and the compass. He showed it to Grace and Chay. "See? This is the heading we followed. We line it up and look for the G next."

Chay and Grace exchanged glances. "No wonder we're not getting anywhere. We thought there was only one direction per card. Like we needed to figure out which one to follow." Luke and Jeremiah joined the crowd at the side of the brick pile.

Tav explained, "We've been using all three. Once we found a marker, we looked for the others." He shrugged. "Everyone is trying to figure out the rules as we go along." He laid the compass on the anvil, checked the direction. "Card says Five North. The next marker should be a G. And we should find it along the path."

Micah suggested, "There's enough light. Can we search the area for the G? In case we can see it from here?"

Tav chewed on it a while. "Yeah, let's try it. But we don't need everyone to go. No one should be wandering in the dark."

Luke raised his hand. "I'll go. I'll take Ben with me. He's got the sharp eye."

Chay stepped up. "You're not leaving me behind. I'm coming with you."

Tav tipped his head. "Grace?"

"No." The woman declined. "I'll stay here and get warm by the fire."

Luke extended his hand to Ben. The boy grabbed Luke's hand and held it tight. He smiled and pranced and pulled Luke along. Jeremiah accompanied them.

Grace watched the four leave. She sat with her knees curled to her chest. "He's a special child." She smiled at Micah. "He must bring a lot of joy to your life."

Keep lying? Or admit the truth? Micah swallowed hard. "He does." He bowed his head. "He's not my brother. We found him here in the woods when we washed ashore. He saved our lives."

Grace's eyes narrowed. "So, you're playing this game and not looking for his parents? Don't you care—"

"It's not what you think. He has a brother, or someone like a brother, in the hills. Hiding like Ben is. Except the brother is older. He told us they were both in the foster program, and their guardian died. He and Ben have been living off the land, trying to avoid the authorities."

"So, they're runaways."

Tav corrected her. His voice carried some bitterness. "Throwaways, according to the brother. The guardian seemed like a convenience for the foster program."

"You believe the older boy?"

Tav raised his chin slightly. "I do. I've been where they are. Not wanted. It eats at your soul. If we can fill Ben's life we will. And make no apologies."

Grace held up her hand. "Did not mean to hit a nerve, Tav. Honest."

Tav gathered and threw a handful of dirt on the ground. "I'm sorry. I think I'm stressing about this whole thing. I don't want the little guy abandoned."

She smiled a sad smile. "Was Luke abandoned?"

Tav shrugged. "In a sense. We still have our parents. They're living, anyhow. But they've disowned us both. So I look out for Luke, yeah."

Actual thunder sounded in the distance. Storms threatened. Micah caught Tav's eyes. Both men nodded. Tav stood and hollered, "Knights, assemble!"

Grace appeared confused. "What's wrong?"

Tav explained, "If those storms make it to us, it'll be a miserable night for everyone. I'd like to use what's left of the cabin to form some sort of shelter. Make a lean-to with the blankets and anchor them with the bricks. We might still get wet, but it wouldn't be as bad as being in the rain."

"Clever thinking. I'll see what we have to help."

Luke, Jeremiah, Chay, and Ben all reappeared. Tav explained the need, and the teams set to work. Within an hour, they constructed a functional shelter. Ben delighted in running in and out.

Micah chuckled to Tav. "We get home, I'm going to build him the biggest tree fort he's ever seen. And Jere can bring the boys over, and we'll all spend the night. We'll pretend we're back in the forest."

Tav huffed. "I'd better be invited to the party."

"Of course. And Luke, if he's not fallen in love with someone."

"We're still about chastity, you know."

Micah grinned. "Didn't say a word, Tav. Didn't say a word."

The group rested back and watched the fire and the stars. They would slip into the shelter before full nightfall. Chay asked, "None of you have a harmonica, do you?"

Tav took back his role as spokesman. "No."

Chay's voice carried relief. "Oh, good. I'd have to kill someone." She pointed to her mom. "And don't you dare. You swore the last time you'd leave it at home."

Jeremiah rotated to a semi-sitting position. "Come to think of it…."

Chay groaned. "No!"

Jere lay back down. "I was going to say I never did learn to play one. Always hated the sound."

Chay shook her head. "You're evil. The strong, evil type."

Jere chuckled. "I have my moments."

A coyote howled in the distance. Ben snuggled under Micah's arm. Micah kissed him on top of his head. "Night, Ben."

Cold chills swept through Micah. *God, help me. Help me know Your will from my fear. Show me what's right in Your eyes. Protect us all, Lord.*

* * *

SATURDAY

Coffee? Someone was brewing coffee? Who would dare usurp his privilege? Micah sat, rubbed his eyes, and noted Quinn seated at the fire outside the makeshift tent. The older man poked the burning wood with a stick. As all good campers do.

Micah turned out of his cover. He checked to see if Ben still slept and panicked. No Ben. Micah combed the shelter for his little brother. A smallish lump lay between Chay and Grace. Figured. Abandoned for a better offer. Micah sighed, then joined Quinn at the fire.

Quinn chuckled. He kept his voice low. "Deserted for a woman. The boy has no loyalty."

"But plenty of common sense. When did you get in?"

"About an hour ago. Your pot and I have been having a good conversation."

"Oh? It tells you all our secrets?"

"You have any to tell?"

Micah held up a finger. "Hold that thought." He made a trip to the woods, then came back. "No. No secrets. Grace and Chay joined us."

"So, I see. You could do worse for teammates."

"About how we saw it." Micah grinned. "Grace is death on gigging frogs. Join us tonight, and we'll fix you some."

"I might." Quinn poured a cup of coffee for Micah and

one for himself. Good, strong coffee. The two men sipped and drank and enjoyed the peace.

Micah saluted Quinn. "You brew a wicked coffee, sir."

"Coming from you, that's quite a compliment."

Jere rolled over and muttered something about a "river bottom" but did not rise. Grace snuck out from her sleeping bag. She caressed the small head cocooning with Chay, smiled, rose, and joined Quinn and Micah.

"Good morning, gentlemen."

Micah pulled out another mug. "Coffee?"

"Is the sun shining?"

Micah directed a gaze skyward. "Yes, yes, it is."

"There's your answer. Please."

Micah poured and handed her the shimmering liquid. She took a sip, sighed, and sat beside Micah. "I think I'll adopt you."

Quinn shook his head. "No, he's mine."

I'd trade in a heartbeat. But that's not what You want, is it, Lord? Mother is my assignment. I understand. But it's nice to be appreciated by someone. Even strangers who are becoming friends. Thank You for giving me the encouragement.

Grace asked, "Since we're off the clock, how many teams are still out here?"

"Of the six teams that started from the river, only three still search." Quinn swallowed a mouthful of coffee, then added, "I count the six—seven with Ben—of you as one team. The WVU team is still going, as is the all-female team from Duluth."

Micah debated asking. Grace beat him to it. "We all have the same cards. Why aren't we tripping over each other? Or at least crossing paths?"

"The challenge is everyone assumes they know which starting point is which. And in what order they go in. If it were easy, the gold would have been found years ago."

Micah poured more coffee for Quinn. "Did Magary want the money found?"

"Certainly. Mr. Magary never anticipated it would be

hidden this long. But there's the beauty of it. The money is still there. Still waiting."

Ben tiptoed out of the shelter. He spotted Quinn and ran to him. He hugged the monitor, sat for a second in his lap, then bounced to hug Grace. He sat in her lap long enough for her to hug him, and he raced to Micah and sat. Ben wrapped Micah's free arm around him and sighed. He leaned back against Micah's chest and smiled.

Grace's voice trembled. "I wish we could all be as content as this little fellow." She asked, "Have you seen his drawings?"

Quinn nodded. "Kid's got an amazing talent. I hope his next parents recognize and promote it."

Micah tapped his leg. "Ben's brother said Uncle Petey tried to pay for drugs with gold coins. The woman said they weren't real." Micah's eyes narrowed. "You think someone could have found the treasure already?" He kept his suspicions about Sissy to himself.

Quinn raised his eyebrows. "Interesting question. Someone will have to locate the box to find out, won't they?"

"I suppose." Quinn wasn't going to give away any secrets. The monitor finished his coffee. Micah went to refill it, and Quinn waved him off. "I'm good. I've got to check in on the others." He smiled at Grace. "I understand you cook a mean frog. I'll be back tonight to try them."

"If I catch any more." She laughed. "There's quite a few down in the pond. I'm not big on carrying them with us while we search for symbols."

Micah chuckled. "I'm sure Ben would love to help, wouldn't you, Ben?"

Ben leapfrogged out of Micah's lap. He sprang around in front of Grace and Quinn. A soft whispered, "Ribbit, ribbit," accompanied the jumps.

Grace's hand flew to cover her mouth. "He does speak!"

Micah waited until the frog hopped back to his lap, then hugged Ben. "Yes, he does. But only when he wants to."

Ben smiled at the three adults. Quinn stood and put his hand on Ben's head. "You take care of all these people, you got that, Ben? They need you to look out for them."

Ben gave his one solemn nod. Quinn hugged him, moved off, and disappeared into the forest.

Grace shook her head. "And he's off."

Micah quipped, "Truer words were never spoken."

Grace turned to him. "What?"

"Never mind. Let's get this bunch up and head out of here. We've got treasure to find." Micah rose to his feet. He pulled the coffee pot off the fire to let it cool and stop percolating. He checked the color, added some water, and shrugged. "I can be kind."

Grace smiled. "Yes, you can. You are amazing young men."

He shrugged. "We're men, anyhow." Grace shook her head.

* * *

It took nearly an hour to get everyone up, fed, packed, and finally chasing the newest heading: Five North. All eyes looked for a G symbol. High, low, everywhere in between. Micah drew the letter for Ben so he would know what to look for. They walked for two hours, then took a break. Ben alternated between walking with Grace, Tav and Micah, or Luke and Chay. Or Jeremiah bringing the rear guard. After the break, the positions switched, with Tav taking the rear, Micah and Jeremiah in the middle, and Luke, Grace, and Chay in front. Ben scampered between them.

Another hour in, Ben came from being with Tav to Micah's side. He picked Micah's hand and tugged. Micah studied the boy. "What do you need, Ben?"

Ben pulled Micah back to walk with Tav. Tav hugged him and said, "Thanks, Ben. Saved me from having to yell. Or run."

Micah eyed Tav. "What's up?"

"Keep walking. No problems. We're just shooting the breeze."

Micah faced forward and matched Tav's stride. "Okay, now what?"

"I'm hearing something or someone following us."

Micah resisted the urge to look over his shoulder. "You think it's another team?"

"If it was, why don't they declare themselves? We're not out here in secret."

"No, but if someone wanted to verify they were on the right track, following someone else would help."

"How can anyone know if they're on the right track? The only way to be sure is to find the coins. Or not find any more markers."

Micah shrugged. "I'll give you that. You think it's an animal?"

"I don't know. We haven't heard any animals except the cat the other night. And it wasn't following us. It found us."

"True. And Ben's brother never makes any sound when he comes and goes."

They walked a few yards. Micah suggested, "You drift up front and alert the others. I'll hang back here and watch the rear. I'll listen for anything, and we can compare notes later."

Tav nodded. "Just don't fall too far back. If it is an animal, I don't want to have to pluck you out of its jaws."

"You and me both."

Tav picked up his pace and joined Jeremiah. Ben stayed with Micah. Micah slowed slightly to put more distance between the groups.

Nothing sounded out of place. The breeze through the trees rustled the saplings and brush. Nothing different there. Micah walked with Ben at his side for nearly an hour, then stopped.

There it was. The muffled sound of a footfall on the springy forest floor. It stopped one light thud after Micah did. Micah's stomach twisted. Could Tav be right?

Ben cocked his head and stared at Micah. Micah pursed his lips. "Nothing's wrong, buddy. Just taking a quick break." Ben bounced up and down until Micah started again. He couldn't risk the "start-stop" trick again, or whoever might be behind them would be suspicious. Nor could he send Ben running ahead. Best to keep walking and listening. Listening hard.

Aware someone snuck behind them, he picked up the sound more often. Whether from fear or cognizance didn't matter. What would he do about it?

An indeterminate time later, Luke called a halt with his fist in the air. The group huddled. Chay sneered at the Knights. "Do you actually practice this stuff?"

Grace laughed. "No, they're making it up as they go along." She nailed Tav with a sharp eye. "Am I right?"

"A knight never tells." Tav grinned. "Let's take an early lunch break." Only after everyone became comfortable did he reveal his reason for stopping. "I thought I heard someone trailing us earlier."

He looked to Micah for confirmation. Micah nodded. "Heard it, too. Not far off, but trying not to be caught."

Grace's eyes grew concerned. "Why? There're no rules against groups walking in the same direction."

Tav pulled some innocent weeds. "You're right. Which makes the deal so strange. I don't like being followed, but there's not much we can do. Except stay vigilant. Until whoever wants to declare their business."

Chay's voice became dark. "And what business do you imagine they have with us?"

Tav repeated his thought, "I don't know. I can't even suggest anything."

Jeremiah pumped a fist into the ground. Carefully. "I suggest we don't hang around on this heading. Let's give 'em a show of finding the marker, head a different direction, and come back later."

He pulled his knife and began doodling on the ground. "We can memorize landmarks, use the compass to get back on track, and start over."

Luke suggested, "We could go back and confront them. See what they want."

Micah brought out his knife as well and began digging in the sod. Aimlessly. At least so it would appear to someone watching. He kept his voice low. "I'd be for challenging them if we didn't have Ben to worry about."

Grace leaned forward. "I say we keep walking until they approach us. Keep doing what we're doing. Looking for the marker. But we can bypass it when we find it. And like Jeremiah said, head out, then double back later."

Tav eyed the group. He directed, "Any other discussion?"

No one spoke. "Fists in."

Grace and Chay watched the Knights insert their fists into the circle. Tav motioned with his hand they should follow suit. Tav instructed, "Silent count of four, make your vote. Thumbs up, we follow Grace's advice. Thumbs down, we don't. Tie vote means we discuss it some more."

Grace lifted her head. "You're going to include us in the inner workings of the Knights of the Octagon?"

Luke shrugged. "Why not? You're here. You've got as much stake in this decision as we do."

Chay asked, "So, are we honorary knights?"

Tav said, "No. There are no honorary knights. There are knights, and there are—"

"Peasants."

Micah punched Jeremiah in the arm. "No peasants. Knights and not knights. We vote all at once so no one is swayed by someone else. Honest opinions."

Tav questioned the women. "Ready?"

Chay and Grace each put a fist in the circle. Ben did as well. Micah put his arm around the boy. "Yes, you get to vote, too."

Tav nodded. Micah counted to four, raised his thumb.

Eight thumbs went up. Micah laughed. "No, Ben, you only get to vote one time." Ben withdrew one hand and put it behind his back.

Grace chuckled. "I'm flattered."

Jeremiah snorted. "Don't be. We're all going to blame you if this goes south."

"I see how you are." Grace rose to her feet. "Let's get the show back on the road."

And they were off again.

Another hour of walking. Micah and Tav headed the column. Micah spotted a flat stone half-buried in the dirt. He slowed but didn't stop or point. He signed *Survey stone. Tie your shoe.*

Jeremiah, Grace, and Ben had the middle. Jeremiah slowed. "Hey, Ben, your shoestring's loose. Let me tie it."

Ben stared down at his foot. He looked up and grinned at Jeremiah, then held his foot up. The string was indeed loose. Jeremiah knelt. "How long has this been untied, buddy? It's not safe."

Jeremiah came back to his feet and kept walking. Micah did not look back. Luke and Chay strolled at the rear of the column. Luke called out, "We need to verify the direction. We're still following Five North, correct? We haven't veered, have we?"

The group bunched to check the compass. Tav pointed along the direction. "Five North. Still headed true."

Within the huddle, Micah turned to Jeremiah. "You see it?"

"Yep. G right in the center."

Luke added, "Looked like there was a year on it. Looked like a seventy to me. Or something in that range."

"So now we keep moving along Five North. We'll come back here when we've shaken the tail."

"Let's do it."

Jeremiah picked a tree branch and leaned on it to walk. "I think everyone should get one of these. Sure makes it easier to walk."

Micah saw the indentation Jeremiah made with his walking stick. He found a suitably sized pole and gave it to Ben. "Here, buddy. See if you can walk like Jeremiah. He says the stick makes the walking easier."

Ben followed Jeremiah with gusto. The only way he could have left a better path was if he'd been on a pogo stick. There would be no missing the trail back to the marker.

Chay grinned. "You guys really are making this up as you

go along, aren't you?"

Luke shrugged. "It keeps us from getting bored. And mostly out of trouble in school."

Jeremiah humphed. "Mostly."

They walked nearly an hour past the G marker and stopped. Tav threw down his pack. "We're on the wrong heading. I know we are. We missed it back there."

Jeremiah grumbled. "I told you we should have gone back. I told you twenty minutes ago. But you wouldn't listen. You'll listen to your brother, but me? Never."

"Because you're never right. Just like Mick."

Micah picked up the argument. He couldn't drop his pack because Ben carried it, but he could protest. Vociferously. "Leave me out of your fights! I'm tired of being the fall guy around here. I never wanted to come anyhow!"

"Fine!" Tav threw his hands in the air. "We'll go back. Turn around and see where it gets us. We'll be walking in circles by nightfall."

Luke didn't bother to join in. Micah figured they gave enough justification for reversing fields.

Chay decided to play, too. "I don't know why we're following any of you. Once we get on the right path again, I'm headed out on my own. This is stupid."

Grace wouldn't be left out. "Who are you calling stupid?"

"This whole trip is stupid! You and your treasure hunts."

The group reversed field and quick-stepped back the way they came. If anyone followed them, they were about to be run over.

Sounds of brush being swept aside greeted them. Whoever shadowed them scattered to avoid detection. Micah and the group slipped through the path they'd already made, leaving no noise. Would the ruse work?

The group bypassed the marker several yards before calling a halt. Another huddle. They argued. They moved closer to the G. Argued some more. Veered off the path. Pulled out the compass. Yelled at each other. Finally agreed they would follow a new heading. 275 West. And look for the G symbol.

The column reassembled. Tav, Luke, and Chay headed the front. Jeremiah and Ben took the middle. Micah and Grace brought up the rear and listened intently for any sound of being followed.

Nothing. They heard nothing but birdsong and wind in the pines. Micah and Grace walked in silence for about twenty minutes before Grace asked, "You think we lost them?"

Micah huffed. "I think I lost me. That was the most bizarre ruse we've ever tried to pull."

Grace's eyebrows rose. "You mean you've done this before?"

Micah chuckled. "We used to have to lose girls who followed Tav. Starstruck with his amazing good looks, you know."

Grace grinned. "Yeah, I know how girls are. Why didn't any of you take a girl up on her offer?"

Micah lost his levity. "Home life. Tav and Luke fought their father. I took care of my mother. No time for female companionship." *Not allowed, either.*

Micah continued. "Jeremiah did, as he told you, and now has the two boys. And no wife."

Grace nodded. "I understand how things go. I have a daughter and no husband." She smiled a sad smile. "Life."

"Yeah."

The group walked until the sun slipped below the treetops. Time to find a place to camp. Hopefully, near water. With fish. MRE supplies ran low. If they couldn't supplement their rations, they'd have to throw in the towel on the search. And have nothing to show for the week but sore feet, a sore shoulder, and Ben. Which made up for everything else.

If Micah could keep him. *He's not a puppy. I can't bring him home and say, "Look what I found." I want to. Why can't I? He could live with me. He could.*

Except I'd need a birth certificate for him. Not to mention Mother's reaction. It's not going to work, is it, Lord? You're not going to let me adopt him.

Micah walked on.

Tav and Jeremiah scouted and found a place near the water to camp. Nice clearing for a fire, the chance to catch fish and maybe a frog or two, and even springy ground for sleeping. Perfection. If you camped outside under the stars, anyhow.

Grace taught Luke how to gig frogs. Chay hung out with her mom and Luke, though she declined to kill the frogs. Jeremiah taught Ben how to fish. Micah and Tav cleared the ground for the fire and lit the blaze for cooking. As they prepped the site, Micah noted, "Luke and Chay have hit it off. I don't hear her complaining about being out here anymore."

Tav grumbled. "He needs to keep his head in the game."

Micah smiled. "I think he has."

Tav sneered, "The wrong game."

"What's eating you? He's found someone he likes talking to. It's not a problem."

"I don't want him to lose sight of going to college. We worked hard to give him this chance. I don't want him to mess it up."

Micah threw three logs on the ground. "Did we ever ask him what he wanted?"

Tav's jaw fell open. "What's that got to do with anything?"

Micah shook his head. Tav shrugged. "Yeah, I did ask him. And he wants to go. He even wants to try to walk on with the football team."

Micah's head snapped up. "What? With your dad out there shadowing Addison? This will be his freshman year, right?" Addison, the youngest Vaughn boy, would attend college on a football scholarship. The scholarship Tav lost, and Luke refused. But their dad would have one son in the game.

Tav rested his hands on the shovel. "Yeah. Luke swears it's the only way Dad will breathe the same air we do. It's been four years. Luke will have a beard. He somehow thinks Dad won't recognize him."

"He's not wrong. Your dad only saw whoever was first man up."

"Tell me about it." Tav double-checked the firepit to

ensure no errant sparks would fly out to start a forest fire. "Bring on the amphibians."

The group gathered for dinner. Plenty of fish, several more frogs than the last time, and even a snake. Micah shivered. Ben spotted the creature, and Jeremiah dispatched it. Rather than waste the resource, he brought it back.

Grace knew how to cook reptiles, and passed around the tender meat, insisting they all try eating some. She shamed anyone turning the delicacy down until they ate it. Ben seemed the most enthralled with the meat.

Micah smiled at the picture of Ben eating heartily. The boy needed to put on weight. When they got home, Micah would be sure Ben got the "good goods" in life. *When.*

Quinn appeared before dinner finished. Micah waved the man in. "We saved you some."

Quinn's face seemed drawn. Micah eyed him sideways. "What's wrong?"

Quinn took a plate of food, ate half of it, then admitted, "We lost a team today."

"Lost a team? What do you mean?" Tav sounded stunned.

"Their GPS stopped moving. We waited a day to see if they were simply resting, hunting, swimming, or whatever. But the tracker never moved. By the time we got to the location to check out what happened, we found two…"

He hesitated and motioned to Ben. Micah moved to take the boy off, but Grace stopped him. "Ben should hear this as well. Whether he comprehends it will be another matter. But he should know."

Quinn's face grew darker. "Two bodies. Wild animals covered the cause of death. A coroner will be able to tell, however."

Tav asked, "Four-person team?" He got to his feet.
"Yeah."

Tav assumed the lead. "Any sign of the other two?"

"No. No drag marks, no signs of anything."

"Who died?"

"Win and Nance. And they held all four cards. So, there's

no way to tell where Sissy and Doug may have gone."

Silence. Chay studied her hands. "Are you suspending the game?"

Quinn shook his head. "I don't have the authority to tell individuals you can't camp in the wilderness. I can only tell you this hunt just became a whole lot more serious."

Tav took his seat again. "What are you going to do?"

"The authorities are here combing the scene." He scowled. "Right now, we can't even call it a crime scene. Not until we know the cause of death. They could have been killed by a bear."

"But doubtful."

No need for Micah to speak. Tav hit all the angles Micah would have brought up.

Tav motioned to the camp. "You're welcome to spend the night here. Safety in numbers." He sniffed. "Not that you can't take care of yourself, I'm certain."

Quinn shrugged. "Still nice to get most of a night's sleep."

Micah didn't have to guess what the "most" signified. They would be setting a watch. With seven people, the guard cycle would be short. But someone would mind the camp.

They split the watch into hour-and-a-half intervals. Micah and Ben took the first watch. They patrolled around the perimeter of the group as the others slept. Ben thought this great fun. He assumed the role of the sentry, marching stiff-legged, his arms at his side. Micah wondered if he should put the boy back in his tree camo? They carried it with them. Of course, anyone watching the camp wouldn't be fooled by a four-foot bush marching around and around. No. No sense in hiding him.

Were Sissy and Doug killers? Ben identified Win as a woman who scared him. But she wasn't the woman at the cabin the night Uncle Petey died. Ben drew a different woman there. One who looked amazingly like Sissy. But he'd been too traumatized to say if it was Sissy or not. Could there be two killers?

The thoughts kept him busy for the duration of his shift.

Micah needed to ask Grace about her faith story. What brought about the change from the hard-bitten, rough-talking woman to the Grace of today? He'd promised Chay he wouldn't talk about Jesus in front of her. There was a story there as well. So many stories. So little time. Hopefully.

What symbols did the fourth card hold? A fish. A boot. The letter Y. And then what? If they found the Y and started along its heading, how would they know what to look for? Quinn said they would be given direction. No one reached the end yet. No one finished the third leg, either. Except the Knights.

Smoke tickled his nose. Micah checked the fire pit. The blaze remained contained, still sparkling and shimmering. Nothing amiss there.

But smoke still filled his nostrils. Micah peered hard into the trees. Down the hill. Beyond the shrubs.

There. A glow that shouldn't be there. A small glow. But small glows get big in a hurry. Micah grabbed Ben by the shoulders. "Watch me, Ben. You need to wake Tav. Then you need to do this." Micah held his hands in the ASL sign for fire. He wiggled all ten fingers, moving them up from his waist. "Like this, Ben. Wake Tav. Show him."

Ben nodded once. He wiggled his fingers in response. Micah placed Ben's hands down around his waist and pulled them up. "You have to move them up, Ben. Wiggle your fingers and move them up. Now go!"

Ben raced up the hill. As Micah raced down the hill to the fire, a gust of wind spread the flames. The small glow became a major threat. Micah beat the fire with his shirt. He spun in the dirt to smother what he could. Knelt to scoop handfuls of soil and rock and toss them on the glowing embers. "Come on, Ben. Do it, buddy. Make him understand."

Shouting would win him a lungful of smoke and ash. Instead, he continued to suffocate the flames. "God help me. Please!"

Help arrived. Everyone but Grace and Ben pounded down the hill to help extinguish the blaze. The six made quicker work of stamping out the forest fire than Micah could do alone. Micah appreciated their silhouettes in the glow, throwing dirt, stomping embers, and stripping shrubs and tree branches that embers set ablaze. Half an hour of hard, heart-stopping work brought the fire to an end. And left the group in darkness again.

But Grace and Ben stood at the crest of the hill, waving flashlights to give the firefighters a homing beacon. Grace's light swept back and forth in even arcs. Ben's circled and pointed at the sky, the trees, the ground, anywhere he could direct the illumination.

Micah's group coughed and choked and cleared their lungs as they climbed the hill. Micah gave Ben a long, warm hug as soon as he reached the boy. "Good job, Ben. You sent Tav. Thank you. We got the fire out. You're a hero." Ben hugged Micah back and continued playing with the flashlight.

The weary group grabbed water and drained it. They cleaned and covered any and all minor burns. Micah's shirt proved a total loss, but his undershirt could be salvaged. He pulled a spare shirt from his pack and covered the burns.

Tav cleared the smoke from his throat. "Did you teach him to sign 'fire?'"

"Yeah." Micah melted to the ground. "I figured it would be the easiest for him to repeat. I'm glad you figured it out."

Quinn coughed hard. "Quick thinking on your part. I take it you were over the hill when you spotted the fire?"

"Smelled the smoke first. I went to look for the source. I didn't expect a fire."

"Still good thinking. I'll call the authorities in the morning to determine how the blaze started."

Tav defended the group. "It wasn't our fire. We keep it contained."

Quinn waved him off. "I know. I see the way you boys"— he stopped and added—"and girls, handle yourselves. The flames spread out too far to have been started by a floating ember. I'd bet the Rangers find someone deliberately set the fire."

Micah turned to Grace. "Thanks for keeping Ben out of danger. I know you would have been a help down there, but staying with Ben mattered more."

Grace agreed. "He seemed upset, so I kept him with me. I told him I needed him to protect me here." She hugged him. "And he did a fine job of it, too."

Micah's throat constricted. Ben was becoming a real boy.

His brain snapped back to attention. Stupid thoughts. He addressed Quinn. "What now?"

"Nothing now. We'll make decisions after we get facts." He stood. "I'll take the next watch. I'm awake anyhow. I need time to think." The game monitor found a spot outside the camping circle, leaned against a tree, and seemed prepared to ward off intruders. Micah and the rest of the camp settled into their respective sleeping positions around the fire. Micah closed his eyes and let the darkness close in. And offered a prayer they would wake again in the morning. All of them.

* * *

SUNDAY

Quinn left them in the morning. He called in the coordinates of the fire to the Rangers. He congratulated the team on making it to the fourth leg and encouraged them to keep going. Then he left to rejoin the investigators at the scene where Win and Nance died. The team returned to the G marker. They lined the new course, 195 W. Fish, boot, Y. All the symbols standing between them and the treasure.

Intensity marked their steps. Micah didn't feel gold fever, but his nerves told him to, "Hurry. Hurry." His brain argued, "Someone else will get there first. You know they will. You'll never win this. Never. You don't deserve to win."

Micah fought back the only way he knew how. He covered the march with prayer. *Lord, You hold all of us. You hold this treasure. Yes, I'd love to have part of it. Love to be able to provide for Ben. Love to buy out my mother, too. You could make the dreams possible without me finding a million in gold coins. You could think it, and all the wishes would come true. But Your will might be something different. I want to want Your will. I'm not there yet. Help me get there.*

Ben's delight in simply being with people, walking in the sun, playing with sticks and rocks made the anxiousness less intense. Micah closed his eyes. *Lord, let me be a child again. The one before Dad left. Before Mom got to be…Mother. Help me be the child who lives for the joy of living. Please.*

They stopped at noon for a rest. The trees thinned out,

and they approached a natural gorge. The shade of the rocks provided a break from the constant dizzying switch from sun to shade to sun to shade. Tav pulled out the cards to reverify what they already knew. "We're looking for a boot. Or a fish."

"Or the letter Y. We know, Tav. We know." Jeremiah griped. "You've told us a dozen times."

Chay motioned to the cards. "Which one will be first?"

"Therein lies the trick. It could be any one of them."

Grace nodded. "Which's what threw us off the first time. We saw all three in the same area. I didn't know which way to go."

"How'd you choose?" Micah wondered if women knew a secret manner of deciding between options. Other than voting or Ro Sham Bo.

Chay scowled. "Race wanted to be the leader and insisted we follow him because 'he knew his way around the forest.' I wouldn't follow him anywhere until he put away the rifle. Stupid git."

Grace chuckled. "I wouldn't—"

"I know you wouldn't, Mom. So, I did."

Tav went back to the start. "We decided the formations needed to be something which would have existed at least fifty years ago and would not change significantly over time."

"Rocks."

"Or signs or carvings. Or trees, but ones which had been there and would stay there. The X we saw in the tree existed when the treasure was hidden and will exist another hundred years or more."

Jere added, "Unless someone cut it down and burned it."

"Or a rockslide took out the stones Magary used. Intangibles that might prevent anyone from ever finding the gold. But it's still worth trying."

"Are you convincing yourself?" Grace smiled at Tav.

"Maybe." He dropped his eyes to the ground. "Eventually, we have to throw in the towel. But not yet. Not until we run out of MREs."

"What do you think the fish will look like?" Chay studied

the card. She gazed at the four knights. "Given what you've seen, take a guess."

The Knights fell silent. Micah took a stab at it. "We've seen trees used twice. More often, it's a rock formation."

"Except the anvil was real," Chay objected.

"Yeah, but there's not going to be a fifty-year-old fish swimming around these parts."

"It has to be stationary." Luke pointed out the less obvious.

"So, we can line a direction. Right." Micah's eyes narrowed and lost focus. "Fish, fish, fish. A fish farm?"

"Fish and game sticker?"

Tav nodded. "Might work. I could see it being a sticker."

"What about the boot? What would it look like?" Grace joined the round-robin discussion.

Jeremiah suggested, "A rock formation? Like the snowman."

Micah threw in his guess. "What about an opening in a hillside? A mine entrance or two rocks which have a gap? It could be almost anything."

Grace stood. "We should get moving. We're not finding anything sitting here."

Micah climbed to his feet. "Come on, Ben. Let's move 'em out." Ben stood and began pulling people up. Tav and Luke let the boy strain against their weight before moving. Jeremiah stood, picked Ben up, and put him over his shoulder. "I'll carry this pack."

Ben flailed in the air, smiling and laughing without sound. But his eyes widened and sparkled. He caught Jere around the neck and hugged the man. Jeremiah returned the hug, set the boy down, and said, "Okay, you can walk. I think Mick can carry his own pack, though. I'll give you something else to carry." He handed Ben the fishing pole. "You carry this, and if we see water, you get to catch dinner. Okay?" Ben nodded with his bow at the waist, then skipped to walk beside Jere.

Micah called, "You stole my brother!"

Ben rushed back to Micah's side, hugged him, and ran

back to Jeremiah. Jere laughed. "Ha! Now I'm the favorite."

They walked along the ridge. A natural path formed between two wide courses of rocks. The trail began an incline. Not steep, but determined. Jeremiah and Ben procured the lead. Tav, Chay, and Grace took the middle. Micah and Luke brought up the rear guard.

An hour into the march, an explosion rocked the hills. The ground rumbled, and rocks slid past them. Micah and Luke stopped and did an about-face. Both men scanned the mountain behind them. A cloud of dust rose in the air and fanned out toward them. Luke yelled, "Rock- slide! Run!"

Micah put it in high gear and sprinted alongside Luke. The three in the middle stayed just ahead. Jeremiah picked up Ben and ran with the youngster over his shoulder.

No one looked back. *Run. Run. Don't think. Run.* Jeremiah yelled, "We have to get out of this gorge!"

Micah searched frantically for an exit, a space, a way to escape the funnel. He and Luke caught up to the middle. Tav's limp intensified. He began to hobble. He shoved Chay and Grace ahead of him. "Go! Go!"

Micah and Luke caught him. Micah grabbed Tav's arm on one side. Luke grabbed his brother's other side. Together they carried Tav along faster than he could manage alone.

And still no exit.

Run.

Run.

The rumble growled, reverberated, resounded down the ridge. Pebbles bounced past them, followed by stones and rocks. Boulders would be next. Would there be…

An opening. Jeremiah swung around the pillars of rock and headed clear of the gorge. Chay and Grace slingshotted around, followed by Micah, Tav, and Luke. They scrambled close to the protection of the hill, curling into balls to protect their heads and bodies. Errant shards of stone and rock crashed over them, bouncing down the mountain, splintering trees and shrubs in their path.

The body of the avalanche poured like lava down the

slope. The dirt and rock spread as it reached the turn. The mass widened to flow down and around the pillars behind where the group cowered. Had they climbed high enough?

Micah kept his eyes open. He watched the team. *Please, God. Protect them. Save them. Help them through this. Please.*

Panic gave way to peace. All would be well. *"I am with you in the fire. I am with you in the flood. I am with you always."*

The thunder passed. The dust settled. Pebbles stopped jumping on and beyond them. The slide continued to rumble down the hill.

Only when the ground stopped shaking did heads lift from the dirt. Tav's voice shook as he ordered, "Sound off."

"Jeremiah. Ben. Shaken but uninjured."

"Luke. Present. Uninjured."

Grace answered, "Grace. Uninjured."

"Chay. I…I think I'm uninjured. Except maybe my pride." Her voice trembled.

"Micah. Not permanently injured. Grateful to be alive."

Tav finished the roll call. "Tav. Jury's still out on the injuries. I think I'm fine. When my knees stop shaking, I'll let you know."

No one moved from their spot. Breathing. Breathing felt good. Being alive felt good. Micah turned to a sitting position. He closed his eyes, picked a note, and began singing the Doxology. His voice shook, but he held the line.

"Praise God from whom all blessings flow."

Tav and Luke joined the second phrase. Their voices sounded no steadier than Micah's.

"Praise Him all creatures here below."

Jeremiah and Grace merged on the third section. And wavered.

"Praise Him above ye heavenly host."

"Praise Father, Son, and Holy Ghost. Amen."

Micah couldn't swear it, but he would bet he heard Chay on the "amen."

Tav climbed gingerly to his feet. Luke caught his arm and supported his brother. Micah rose, dusted himself off. He moved to where Ben and Jeremiah snuggled together. Micah ripped the sleeve off his undershirt and held the rag against the back of Jeremiah's head. "You're bleeding, bro."

"Can't hurt this head."

"You're not invincible." Micah applied pressure to stem the blood flow. The wound wasn't deep. Micah pulled the rag away and said, "I think that will hold it."

"Thanks." Jere pointed at Micah's shirt. "We can't take you anywhere nice, can we?"

"Nope."

The others gathered around. Tav suggested, "How about we find a camp early and call it a day? I don't think I'd recognize a boot if it kicked me right now."

Grace let out a deep sigh. "You got my vote. Or do we have to do this with a thumbs-in-and-up vote?"

Luke jumped in quickly. "No vote. Just yea or nay. I'm all for an early break."

Jeremiah looked down at Ben. "What do you say, buddy? Should we find a camp and go fishing?" Ben nodded once. Jeremiah raised his glance to meet Tav's. "We're in."

Chay pointed to Tav. "What he said. I'm in."

Micah raised a thumbs up. "Unanimous. Let's do it."

They rose and started downhill, picking up kindling and dead limbs fallen in the slide. At least they would have wood for the fire.

They came across animals who had not fared as well as the team. A rabbit. Squirrel. Two quail. Grace pointed them out. "Listen, I know it's awful to think of. But there's meat here, and we should gather it while we can." She pulled a bag from her pack. "We can put the carcasses in here until we reach a camping spot. Then I'll teach you how to clean and cook them."

Micah consented to carry the load since Luke supported Tav and Jere carried Ben. And since Grace offered to clean and cook them, he should at least haul them.

The slide's damage disappeared into the valley. The team maintained their 275 West heading. Tav and Grace took the lead. Jeremiah, Chay, and Luke filled the middle. Ben walked with Micah again. At times the boy held Micah's hand and swung it repeatedly. Other times, Ben padded along, his eyes down. What did the youngster think about? Perhaps remembering his brother? Wondering why he joined this crew? Or how to get away from them?

Could Ben be capable of such introspection? Could any maybe-seven-year-old? What became of Ben's brother? They hadn't heard him in several nights. Was he still out there? Did he kill Win and Nance? What about Sissy and Doug?

Too many questions. No answers.

Grace held up a fist. Everyone stopped. Movement in the brush caught Micah's attention. Race and another man stepped out. Race of the rifle which lived on his shoulder.

Ben huddled into Micah, hiding behind him. The boy trembled. He'd seen Race before and not reacted like this. What made the difference now?

Micah wanted to close the distance so he could hear but didn't want to bring Ben closer to danger. He'd have to wait for someone to fill him in. He noticed Jeremiah left Chay and Luke unsupervised and moved to stand beside Tav. Even unarmed, Jere could be intimidating.

Hand and facial gestures served as good indicators of the tenor of the discussion. Not good. But eventually, a consensus must have been reached. Race and his partner fell in with Grace and Tav. Jeremiah dropped back with Chay and Luke, and the march continued.

So, an eight-way split now? Maybe not. Jeremiah dropped his hand to his side and signed, *Enemies closer.*

Micah breathed out a small sigh. Jeremiah's sentence fragment was part of an old maxim: "Keep your friends close and your enemies closer." How convoluted could this hunt be? Should they cut their losses and leave?

Except Grace and Chay were now part of the Knights. Leave no person behind. The team would stick it out.

The group walked another hour. Micah spotted a clearing a degree off the trail, but sufficient for their purposes. He whistled shrilly. Tav threw the "stop" fist. Everyone turned to look at Micah. He pointed to the opening in the trees. Race and his companion hesitated to join the others. Maybe the two thought they could go on alone? Good luck.

Of course, they had found their way to catch up with Micah's group. Either Race knew something the Knights didn't, or the man's companion was sharper than the rifleman. Micah would find out soon enough.

The group huddled together to examine the clearing, declared it suitable, and made camp for the night. They gathered more firewood. A larger pit needed to be cleared, with a stone firewall around it. Ben and Jeremiah went to look for a source of water. And fish. And frogs.

Grace taught a class on how to skin and feather game. Micah buried the offal deep. Deep, deep. "No bear smelling this" deep. The work pulled at his bad shoulder. Neither Race nor Fly, Race's companion, moved to help with preparations or clean-up. Micah wanted to quote Apostle Paul, "He who won't work shouldn't eat," but the Lord's, "Love your enemies," ended the thought argument. Kind. Micah would be kind. And nurse his shoulder tomorrow.

Ben stayed close to Jeremiah. He could hide behind the big man better than he could Micah. And hiding mattered. Micah would have to find a way and a time to ask the boy about Race. Or could it be the gun?

Quinn didn't join the group for dinner. Micah felt sorry for the man, considering the wildlife feast they enjoyed. It filled every stomach and then some between the supply of game and fish. Grace insisted they dry the leftovers to serve as jerky for the next day's journey. Race disparaged the need for food after tomorrow. "We'll have the treasure by noon."

Tav raised his eyebrow. "What makes you think so?"

"Because we've got two teams here. That's more than Magary ever imagined would look for his money. He never thought eight people would work together."

Grace stated, "He was right. Eight people haven't worked together. You left the first day. You're only here now because you cheated the system and followed the GPS on our cards."

Race sneered. "I don't call it cheating. I call it using my head."

Chay growled. "We'll see what the monitor calls it when he checks in."

Fly shook his head. "He's too busy with those two who died. He'll be with them for a couple of days."

Micah resented Fly and Race being clean-shaven. And clean. Almost fresh-pressed. Like they'd dropped onto the field directly in front of Micah's team.

Race didn't lose the sneer. "Shame about them. Real shame. Too bad the authorities will keep Quinn occupied while we locate the treasure."

Micah started to object but stopped at the sideways motion of Tav's hand. Right. Better to not speak. No arguing with a fool. Or a fool's partner.

"I'm going on guard. Come on, Fly." Fly climbed to his feet and joined Race.

The two men walked into the forest. But not so far they couldn't hear what was said in camp.

Tav picked up a stick and wrote in the dirt. *Race kill W & N?*

Grace scribbled with her fingers. *No.*

Sure?

Life on it.

All lives on it.

Trust me.

Fly?

Unknown.

Ben scribbled in the dirt. He drew lines and shapes. Houses. Mansions.

Tav asked, *How find us?*

Grace ventured, *Cards?*

Chay traced her fingers through the dirt. *Give cards. Tell take hike.*

Would it help? Would having all four cards make a difference to the man? And encourage him to leave? Micah waited on Tav.

Tav doodled. Then wrote, *Worth shot. Do it.*

Speaking of, Race and Fly walked back to the circle. Race complained, "You done playing in the dirt? I want someone to spell me."

Micah stood and took a step toward Race. "I'll do it. My hands are sore anyhow."

A big cat purr-yowled in the woods. Race fired off several shots in the direction. The cat screamed. Micah shoved the muzzle of the gun in the air. Race reversed ends of the rifle and brought the butt slamming into Micah's head. Micah staggered and crumpled to the ground.

Five bodies came to their feet and surged forward. Race dropped the barrel and pointed it at the middle of the group. "Nobody moves."

Chay streamed ahead to stand in front of the muzzle. "Go ahead. Do it. You're too much a coward to shoot someone looking you in the face."

Stand-off. Micah saw it even from the ground. Race tried to stare the young woman down, but it was he who blinked and raised the barrel. Chay seethed, "Get the gun out of here. Now."

Race turned away. The group descended on Micah, pulled him to a sitting position, and checked his head. Micah tried to joke, "Can't hurt—"

Jere cut him off savagely. "Don't say it. Sit there and bleed."

Tav retrieved the first aid kit. Chay wet a cloth and held it against Micah's head. He winced and closed his eyes. He heard Luke call, "Jere. Get Ben."

Micah opened his eyes. There were two of everything. He closed them again. Maybe he'd wait. He heard someone moving, heard Jere murmuring to Ben. "It's okay, buddy. It's okay. Mick's not hurt much. Just banged his head. He'll be fine. Wait!"

Micah opened his eyes to see Ben flying full force at Race, catching the man, then pummeling him for all his slender frame could. Race raised his hands in defense. Luke stepped in and threatened, "Don't touch him."

"Get him off me!"

Ben whaled away. His face twisted into a mask of concentrated malice. Luke tried to intercept the boy's throws, caught his fists, and knelt in front of him. "Ben. Stop."

He didn't. Maybe he couldn't. He continued to try to punch and strike and hit and attack. Luke wrapped his arms around the boy and held him. Tears flooded Luke's face. Micah's face. He could only whisper, "Ben, Ben. It's okay, buddy. It's okay. It's okay."

Five minutes passed before Ben ran out of energy. His punches slowed. His face relaxed. His eyes closed. He dropped his head into Luke's chest and collapsed. Luke picked him up and carried him to Micah's side. He set the boy down so Micah could hug and hold him.

Micah looked into Luke's face. Not all Ben's punches had missed or been blocked. Luke's cheek bled, and one eye swoll closed. Jeremiah stepped over and stared him up and down. "You two. What would you do if I weren't here?"

Luke grunted, "You are, and look at us."

"My point exactly."

Chay carried the water to Luke's side. She pressed the cloth against Luke's cheek. Her voice shook. "What you did…holding him…how did you know to do that? How could you?"

Luke motioned to his brother. "He used to hold me the same way when I wanted to punch out Dad." Luke smiled sideways, favoring the left. "From the time I wasn't much older than Ben."

Chay leaned into Luke's chest. "You. You men. Why am I here with you?"

Luke put an arm around her shoulders. "Because you're lost like we are."

Moisture trickled down Chay's face. Micah noted the same moisture fell on Grace's cheeks. The older woman turned away and hid her face. She walked to the packs, pulled out two game cards, shuffled them, and handed them to Race. She glared him down. "Here are our cards. I give you our share if you find the treasure first. Get out. Take your buddy and leave. I don't care if it's dark. I'm sure you have your super night vision equipment. Go find your own campground. Go find the treasure. But don't you come anywhere near us again, you hear me?"

"Or what?" Race took a step toward Grace.

Grace continued to give him the death stare. "Or I'll kill you like I did the game we ate. I'm a dead shot with a rock. Do not try me."

Race's eyes flared. Fly reached out and touched the rifleman's arm. "Come on, Race. We don't need these people to find the treasure. Now we have all the cards again. We can find our own way."

Race backed up but kept his eyes on Grace. She didn't move. He picked up his rifle and pack and walked away with Fly.

The group listened until they could hear no more movement in the brush. Then they listened another five minutes.

Tav grinned and clapped his hands silently. He bowed low and saluted Grace. He kept his tone quiet. "Well played, Grace. Well played. Absolute mastery."

Jeremiah added, "Magnificence."

Luke threw in, "Outstanding."

"A pinnacle performance." Micah finished it off alliteratively.

Grace curtseyed and bowed. "Scared myself. I didn't know I had that kind of *chutzpah* in me."

Chay walked over and hugged her mom. "I am so proud of you. You never stood up to Howard."

"Yeah, well, Howard was then. This is now. And Howard is long gone."

Micah continued to hold Ben but asked the group, "If Fly is new, how did he know about Win and Nance?"

"Race told him." Grace tilted her head. "What are you

thinking?"

"I don't know. It seems strange he simply shows up, all clean and pressed and neat, and knows about the murders."

Luke added, "And Quinn being held up by the authorities. If they haven't checked in with the monitor, how do they know anything?"

Jeremiah harumphed. "I'm more interested in who is trying to kill us. Setting the fire? Causing the rockslide? Someone wants to not only beat the competition, they want to eliminate all of us."

"You think someone deliberately set the rockslide?"

"I heard an explosion. After that came the avalanche. There wouldn't be any mining in this area. And no one should be blasting with civilians in the hills."

Jere's point made sense. Uncomfortable sense. Sissy and Doug remained missing. Could they be the ones behind the attempted murders? Could someone else…

A cat growled. A pack of coyotes answered. Micah looked into the woods but saw nothing. Cats and coyotes didn't hunt together, did they? Or were the coyotes chasing Ben's brother?

Micah called out, "Come in and get warm. We have leftovers."

It took nearly five minutes but a tall, gangly youth in a ghillie suit stepped into the light of the campfire. He sat. Wearily. Tav put together a plate of food and handed it to the youth. The young man took it and devoured the contents. *Not eating much, huh? Leaving the river, you're not scavaging like you did. Food's harder to come by.*

Micah kept his thoughts to himself. Maybe they could keep the youngster with them and out of trouble. Micah waited until the youth finished and handed his plate back to Tav.

"Thanks. That's good eating."

Tav took the lead. "When's the last time you ate?"

The boy shrugged. "When we left the river, I suspect."

"Good thing you left Ben with us. At least he got regular meals." Tav shifted in his seat. "What's your name? What can we call you?"

The boy fell silent. "BB. For Ben's brother. At least for now. Until I kill the ones who—"

"—killed Uncle Petey. Right, we know. Any idea who or where she is? We certainly haven't seen any strangers around here."

BB hung his head. "No. I been shadowing anyone I come across, and I can't find her. I'm starting to think she's gone. I went back to the cabin, but someone burned it down."

Tav shook his head. "I'm sorry, BB. I need to know one thing. Did you have anything to do with the deaths of two treasure hunters?"

"Two people got killed? Is it why all the Feds and Rangers is all over the hills? No, I didn't kill anyone. I wanted to. But I can't find her."

Tav nodded. "Okay, you're welcome to stay with us. You'll have food, anyhow."

Jere cleared his throat. Tav looked at Jere, then turned back to BB. "Someone may be trying to kill one or all of us. But you're welcome to stay. If you want."

"I'll think about it."

"How old are you, BB?"

"Old enough." Tav glared at the boy. BB sighed. "Fourteen. And a half."

"Fourteen. And you want to spend your life in prison?"

"No. I…I want to make it right for Petey."

"Killing someone won't bring him back. It won't do anything but put you behind bars."

"She can't walk free."

"She won't. Ben gave the authorities a description of what she looked like. They'll find her."

"How did he give anyone a description? He doesn't talk."

"No, but he draws. And his drawings may as well be a photograph. The authorities know exactly what she looks like. And they'll bring her in."

"So what? She walks free."

"No, she goes to trial. You and Ben testify against her."

BB snarled. "Right. Ben still doesn't talk. How's he gonna

testify?"

Tav smiled. "Ben talks plenty. You just have to know how to listen."

Micah looked down at Ben. The boy fell asleep. It was the best thing for him now. Micah lay him down and covered him.

Tav noted the movement. He addressed BB. "You're welcome to come in, sleep near the fire, take your suit off and be comfortable for one night. In the morning, you can decide what you're going to do."

BB fell quiet. After a few moments, he gave in. "Yeah, I guess. It'll be good to sleep somewhere safe." He eyed Tav. "Unless whoever is trying to kill you comes after you."

Tav waved the boy to the fire. "Might be they've come and gone. Get comfortable. Sleep. We'll take care of any threats tonight."

BB lay down, and within minutes, Micah heard a contented sigh and a light snoring. Or heavy breathing, depending on who you asked. Either way, BB slept.

The group gathered for a goodnight discussion. Grace smiled. "Got him with food. Good work."

Tav shrugged. "He's a kid. Just needs some help."

Chay asked, "What do we do now?"

Tav gazed at Jeremiah, Luke, and Micah. "We get some sleep. Rotate the watch. And stay on guard. In the morning, we'll figure out our next steps." He stood. "I'll take first watch."

Jere offered, "I'll spell you."

Grace threw in, "I'm after you."

Chay lifted her head. "Me next."

Luke raised a hand. "Me after you."

Micah started to speak but stopped as three immediate "No!" votes yelled back. Tav put a hand on Micah's shoulder. "You're in no shape to be on guard. Rest. We'll check on you each shift to make sure you're still breathing."

Micah sighed. "I feel useless."

Jere quipped, "You are useless. But you're fun to have around. Sometimes we need you."

Micah exhaled. "Thanks, Jere. Love you too." Micah settled down to sleep near Ben. His head pounded. Sleep would be a good idea. Yeah, right. Micah closed his eyes and began counting. "One hundred. Ninety-nine. Ninety-eight. Ninety-seven." He never reached ninety.

* * *

MONDAY—WEEK TWO

BB was still there when Micah woke in the morning. His lanky silhouette shadowed the firepit on the west side. Micah made room to stir the coals and make coffee without disturbing the youth.

Luke wandered over from his guard position and sat next to Micah. "How's the head this morning?"

"Better. Sleep helped." Micah poured water from the camel pack into the pot.

"What do you think? Who's after us?"

"No idea. Someone who doesn't want us to find the treasure would be my guess."

"But if they know where it is, why bother? Just grab it and claim it."

"Exactly." Micah added the ground coffee. "Makes no sense to me."

"Do you think…" Luke trailed off. He looked at the sleeping boys and continued, "…it has to do with them and the drug deal?"

Micah stopped, then put the coffee pot in the fire. "It could. Doesn't change what we're doing. We're still going after the coins."

Luke remained silent. Micah stared at him. "Are you thinking we should give Ben to whoever it is?" He kept the heat from his voice. Luke knew better. The Knights would never…

Luke shook his head. "No. Of course not. One for all and all for one. I thought it might change how we march, that's all. We need to have a better awareness of what's going on around us."

"Agreed."

"Agreed what?"

Quinn came out of the forest. Luke dropped his head and swore softly. Micah nudged him. "Obscenity jar."

Quinn repeated, "Agreed what?"

Micah chuckled. "We need to be more aware of our surroundings."

"I see." Quinn glanced from Micah to Luke. "Who's on guard duty?"

Micah motioned. Luke raised his hand. "Me."

"Nice challenge when I came in."

Luke growled. "Don't rub it in."

Quinn laughed. "No problem." He jerked his head to BB's form. "Who'd you adopt now?" The monitor sat.

"He said to call him BB. Ben's Brother."

"He the vengeful one?"

"Yep. I think we've talked him off the ledge."

"Good job. Proud of you boys. And girls."

Micah poked the fire. "We thought you'd be tied up with the killings."

"No. Authorities have those. I'm just the monitor. I've got people to take care of on my own."

Luke raised an eyebrow. "Speaking of, do you know Race and another guy are on the hunt?"

Quinn stared from Luke to Micah and back again. "No, I did not know. Tell me about it."

Luke detailed Race's appearance and the altercation with Micah, then Grace. He finished with, "Race backed down, and the two of them left. We figure we won't see them again."

Quinn rubbed his chin. "Interesting." He eyed Micah. "Why is it always you who gets damaged?"

Micah shrugged. "Just lucky, I guess. I'd say I'm the

biggest target, but that would be Jeremiah. So I don't know."

"Anything else you want to tell me about?"

Micah moved the pot so it would boil faster. "We almost bought it in a rockslide."

Quinn's jaw dropped. "What?"

"Yeah. I heard an explosion, then a rockslide behind us. We managed to dodge it, but much of the valley is now covered in scree."

"An explosion? When did this happen?"

"Yesterday." Micah looked to Luke for confirmation. "Noon?"

"Earlier. We hadn't been walking for more than an hour or two."

Micah nodded. "Right. Earlier."

Quinn scowled. "You get shot at. Twice. A fire starts near you. Now a rockslide." He stared off into the distance. "Be nice if you could stay out of trouble for a day or two."

Micah laughed. "Yeah, we'd like it, as well."

"Maybe I ought to stay with you a while. See if it's the game or something else." He motioned to BB. "Or someone else."

Luke's voice became soft. "Which was my question."

"We'll find out. Coffee ready yet?"

Micah watched the brew percolate. "Another couple minutes." He grinned. "You should have been here last night. Talk about a feast. We found game. Casualties of the slide. Grace skinned 'em and cooked 'em like she's been doing it all her life. She is one amazing woman."

Quinn raised his brows. "Oh?"

"Yes, oh."

"I'll have to get to know her better."

Micah laughed. "You should."

He rose and retrieved the coffee mugs. Micah poured some for himself, Luke, and Quinn. They silently saluted each other and drank from the life-giving fluid.

The others roused in short order. They made breakfast of the jerky from the night before. Quinn pronounced it delicious.

BB decided to follow the group. "Until I figure some things out." He removed his ghillie suit and stuffed it in his pack.

Ecstatic to have BB with them, Ben danced and skipped in circles and hugged BB. Repeatedly. Ben did go over to Luke while Luke sat on the ground. The boy stared at Luke's wounds. He reached out slowly and gently touched Luke's swollen eye. Luke kept his tone light. "Yeah, buddy. It's fine. No worries."

Ben lowered his eyes, then reached in and hugged Luke hard. He stood that way for a moment. Finally, he backed up. The boy smiled, leaned in, and kissed Luke on the forehead. Ben skipped over to sit beside BB.

The adventurers cleaned up, packed up, headed up, and moved 'em out. The monitor watched them set their heading without indicating whether they followed the correct path. Micah shook his head to himself. There could be no reading the man. Must be a deadly poker player.

Tav reminded the group, "Fish, Boot, or Y. Keep your eyes sharp."

Micah snuck a look at Quinn to see if the monitor would react. Nothing. He got nothing. *God, if You want us to have the treasure, we will. You know how I would love to have it, to have the money to support Ben and BB.*

He stopped. Ben *and* BB? When did BB come into the equation? Of course, if BB was Ben's brother…or Ben thought he could be…then Micah would adopt both. He would have to. No question.

One question. Mother. She'll never allow it. She'll pitch a fit and end up in the hospital. And I'll be the ungrateful son. The less-than-worthy son. The "worse than an unbeliever" son. Mother first, right? Right?

Or is it?

Ben held BB with one hand and Micah with the other. BB scowled but consented to being led by his younger brother. He grumbled, "Holding hands with a kid. Don't tell anyone I did this."

Micah chuckled. "Get over it. Ben is happy you're here."

They walked in twos and threes. Threes to accommodate Chay and Luke, and Ben and BB. One needed a chaperone. The other needed assurance. Jeremiah led. Chay, Luke, and Grace took the middle. Micah, BB, and Ben made the second half of the center. Tav brought up the rear with Quinn. They would switch off at intervals.

Suddenly, Jeremiah threw his fist in the air. He circled it. Everyone joined into a circle. Micah asked, "What is it? What do you see?"

Jere pointed to a boulder. "Look at the way it's cracked."

A single fissure split the rock. Two breaks extended from the base of the slit. One went east, the other west. Jere traced the cracks with his hand. "I see a Y."

Micah stared at it. "You think it's been that way for fifty years? Nothing is growing in it."

Grace nodded. "The split looks recent. Within the past year or two. With all the pine seeds, you would expect something to have started growing."

Jeremiah nodded. "You're probably right." He didn't give a hand signal. He merely started walking again. The group came over the crest of the hill. Chay pointed to the gully at the bottom. "A river. Oh, goody."

Micah eyed the water. "Doesn't look too wide."

"Not if you can swim. If you can't, it may as well be a mile."

Luke cocked his head. "You can't swim?"

"Sink like a rock. Never learned to float or stay above water. I swim along the bottom of the pool. Bottom of a body of water? Not so much."

Micah studied the water feature they would have to cross. It didn't move fast, but it did move. Rocks bordered both sides. The way the water swirled, rocks hid in the middle, too. Now what?

The team gathered and slid down to reach the border of the river. Ten yards across. No telling how deep. But it wouldn't matter if they couldn't all get across.

Micah stepped back and let Jeremiah and the Vaughn

brothers begin plotting. Grace moved beside him. "Don't you get in on the planning?"

Micah shook his head. "No. Jere and Tav visualize what needs to be done. Luke collects the supplies, and I swing the hammer."

Chay objected. "That doesn't sound fair."

"Fair doesn't enter into it. We pull to our strengths. I don't see in three dimensions." He shrugged. "Never have been able to. Describe a building, and I'm like, 'Okay, fine.' But I can't see it. Better to leave the job to someone who can figure things out."

Quinn nodded. "I knew I liked the way you boys think."

Tav and Jeremiah pointed to two solid boulders on either side. "The tricky part will be getting across with the first rope. We don't know what the stream holds. There could be whirlpools."

Jere suggested, "Giant catfish."

Grace laughed. "We could noodle it for dinner."

Chay grimaced. "Mother."

Quinn tipped his head. "Have you noodled before?"

"Yes, and I have the jaw marks to prove it." She bared her arm to show white scars encircling her elbow. "Seventy-five-pound cat. Arkansas."

Quinn pulled up his sleeve. He bore several scars as well. "Sixty pounds. Mekong Delta. You got me beat."

Grace laughed. "Maybe the only thing I'm better at than you."

Tav's eyes carried confusion. "What's noodling?"

Grace smiled. "It's catching large catfish with your fist as bait. You insert your arm into the fish's nest. When it chaws down on you, you pull it out of the water."

"And it doesn't mind?"

Quinn laughed. "Oh, it minds plenty. You go fighting with a fifty-pound cat, and it'll try to pull you in and under. Takes a real man—or woman—to handle something so strong."

Tav shook his head. "Why would you want to do

something like that?"

Quinn appeared shocked. "Why? Sport, man, sport! Man against nature. The thrill of victory. The agony of defeat."

Tav pulled back. Grace laughed. "Good eating on a catfish. You can feed a family of four for days on one of those."

"Did you eat it?"

She smiled. "No, we did catch and release on the biggest ones. Preserve the gene pool of the monsters."

She focused on Quinn. "You?"

"Survival of the fittest. We ate what we caught. Or gave the fish to the locals."

Tav tapped his foot. "Can we get back to the obstacle at hand? Getting across this stream?"

Quinn waved to him. "Be my guest."

Tav and Jere knelt to draw in the dirt. "What we're going to do is run two lines across. We'll secure them to the rocks on either side, then ferry the packs across. People can walk across the bottom rope and hang on to the top."

Chay looked skeptical. "Will the ropes hold?"

Tav nodded. "We'll make sure of it. We won't take chances."

Luke added, "We can belt you to the top line so if you do fall, you won't get washed away."

Chay grumbled. "Thanks. I needed that image in my brain."

He touched her arm. "We won't let anything happen to you. You're a Knight of the Octagon. Part of the team. We protect each other."

"When we're not killing each other." Jere threw in the reminder of their humanity.

Tav nodded. "Truth." He looked at Luke. "Draw for short straw?"

Grace asked, "Loser gets short straw?"

"Winner. He gets the honor of taking the rope across."

"The honor of dying, maybe." Grace sounded less than convinced.

Tav passed his fist in front of his chest. "But with glory." He smiled. "We're not crazy. But yeah, winner gets to swim across."

Quinn slipped his shirt off. "Count me in."

Four knights all echoed, "No." The man leaned back.

"You're too important to the team." Tav circled his hand to indicate himself and Luke. "We're expendables. Mick's too banged up to go, Jere has kids, so it's us two." Tav looked at Grace. "Sorry, but we can't let you take the chance."

Grace glared. "Why not?"

"Because you're the only one who can gig and cook a frog. The team needs you."

"And it doesn't need either of you?"

"We're interchangeable." He ducked his head. "No death wishes. No delusions of glory. We know what we need to do."

Quinn shook his head. "You boys are something else. Okay, I'll hold the straws. So neither of you cheat and try to deliberately draw the short one." The monitor picked up two sticks, broke one shorter than the other, and put them both in his hand. He edged the markers up evenly and held his hand out.

Luke drew first. Tav pulled his and, without looking, raised it in the air. Luke threw his stick down and turned away.

Tav stripped off his shirt and undershirt. Ben watched and decided he would, too. He tossed the shirt down with emphasis. Chay shook her head. "Too much testosterone here."

Quinn began cussing. Micah jerked his head, then understood. Ben's back was covered in scars. The boy had been beaten multiple times.

Chay covered her mouth. Grace groaned. Ben tipped his head, unsure. Micah hugged him. "It's okay, buddy." *No one will ever hurt you again. Ever. Lord, make it true, please.*

Luke laughed. "Hey, let's all take our shirts off." He stripped down to his chest. The younger man tied a rope to the boulder and began pacing off the distance Tav would need to get across, plus have the extra to tie. He looped the rope around his waist and started marching up the stream.

Grace asked, "What is he doing?"

Micah nodded. "Geometry. If you take off far enough above the far shore, you end up at the spot you want without being carried beyond it, missing the bank, and having to start over."

She shook her head. "And you were all dropouts?"

"Life. It happens."

Micah watched Luke add more rope. He tied himself off to the anchored rope. He measured the distance again.

Tav eyed his brother closely. "Don't get any ideas, Knight. Integrity, remember?"

Luke lowered his head. "What about protecting each other?"

Tav walked alongside his brother. "I can handle it. You'll be able to pull me back out if I get in trouble."

Luke hesitated, hesitated, finally took the rope off his waist and gave it to Tav. Tav chest bumped him quickly. "I got this, Luke. I'll see you on the other side."

Tav tied the cord around his waist and waded into the water. His eyes widened. "Cold!" He slipped into the stream.

Micah held his breath. Reflex. He didn't breathe until Tav's head came above the water. He strained against the current with Tav. Twisted. Ducked. All in mimicry of what Tav did. Over. Under. Over. Under.

Under. Under. Under....

Quinn muttered, "He's been down too long." He stepped up to grab the rope, but Luke waved him off. "He's good. He's good. He'll be up in a second."

Luke muttered, "Come on, Tav. Come on."

Tav's head broke water. He paddled and stroked and worked and let the current carry him until, finally, he crawled up on the far side. He sat up and raised one fist in the air. And held it. And held it. And held it.

Luke returned the gesture. He saluted his brother, jerked his arm down, and fist back. "Yes!" He grinned. "That's my brother."

Quinn chuckled. "Yes, he is. Now let's finish this bridge, or he might die of hypothermia."

They sent the second line across and fastened it to the top of the rock. Two lines traversed the water. They trollied the packs over easily. Then came the time for the people. Chay looked doubtful of the rig. Quinn volunteered, "Let's put some real weight on this to test it." He strapped himself to the top line, wrapped the safety lead around his waist, strode out, and deftly walked the line to the middle of the crossing. He grinned and shouted, "Hey, look…no hands." He stepped off the rope and splashed into the stream. The top line held, and he jerked upright. With only a little effort, he regained the bottom rope and finished his way across.

Grace went next. She eschewed Quinn's theatrics and went straight across. Chay stepped into position. Luke reassured her, "Take it easy. It's not a race. Not a competition. We've got you going and coming. Everything will be fine."

Chay glanced from the stream to the ropes to the far side to the ropes to the stream. She reached up and kissed Luke. "For luck." She stepped out and made her way across the bridge to the other side.

Micah murmured in Luke's ear, "There are advantages to being on this side."

Luke murmured back, "Tell me about it."

Micah grinned, "Well, you know…"

Luke waved him off. He turned to BB. "Your turn, BB. Show Ben how it's done."

BB's face lost all color. His eyes grew wide, and he shook his head. "I don't know…"

Ben hugged him and turned to Micah. Micah roped the youngest boy in. "You be careful."

Ben zipped across until he almost reached the far side…then zipped back to the near side. Again, he zipped back over.

BB grumbled. "Show off." He allowed Micah to strap him into the upper handhold and wrap the rope around his waist. Micah could feel the boy shaking. The Knight put his hand on

BB's shoulder. "You can do this. Go for it."

BB inched out and over the water. He made it halfway before he froze. Luke yelled, "Go on, BB. Keep going."

But the boy couldn't move. Micah tugged on the rope. BB jerked back, too terrified to go any further. Micah eyed Luke. "Go on. Help him."

Luke tied off and walked out to take BB by the arm. He not-so-delicately shoved the boy forward and kept pushing him until they both stepped off the bridge. Micah sighed. *Thank You, Lord.*

Finally, his turn. Micah stared at the ropes. He hated the thought of losing them. What if he…no, that wouldn't work. But what if… No, maybe…

Tav yelled, "Quit reinventing the wheel, Mick! Get over here."

Micah wrapped the tow rope around his middle, untied the top and bottom ropes. In chorus, Tav, Jere, Luke, and all the others screamed, "Mick!"

Micah stepped into the current. He flailed his way as the team pulled him across. He would land fifteen yards further downstream, but hey…he saved the ropes.

Then came the wrath of his teammates. Tav started the attack. When he ran out of words, Luke continued. Jeremiah glared and shook his head. Even Ben bopped him very gently. Micah waited until they ran out of steam, then said, "I know. Stupid. All derivatives of the term. I won't do it again, I promise. I didn't want to lose the ropes. We might need them."

He smiled. "Besides, I knew who had me. Quinn isn't going to lose his barista."

Quinn growled, "Boy…one of these days."

Micah climbed to his feet. "Okay. We're across. Which way do we go from here?"

The compass directed them back on track, and the team set out again.

After another hour of walking, Tav, now in the front, called a halt. "Break. Everyone take a seat."

He passed out the last of the protein bars. "Eat. Drink.

Then we need to look for food for tonight."

Micah grumbled, "And keep watching for signs." He called to Grace. "Were you talking to talk with Race? Or can you really dispatch an animal by throwing a rock?"

Grace smiled. "Oh, a little of both. Helps if you can see some game. I haven't seen an animal worth taking down since we started this morning."

Chay snorted. "I haven't seen an animal, period."

Micah started to say something snide but decided against it. Something about having eyes for Luke. But best left unsaid.

Tav held up his snackbar. "Which is why I'm saving some to use for bait. When we get to a more stationary spot, I'll scatter some of this around. Maybe we can draw in some critters worth cooking."

Micah stopped eating his. "You want some of this back?"

"No. I kept part of one to feed the dinner hopefuls. We'll see if it works."

Micah finished his bar. His head pounded. He called, "Who has the first-aid kit?"

Luke pulled it out of his pack. "What do you need, Mick?"

"Something for the headache. Strong."

"Which, the headache or the pills you need?"

"Both. I'll take ibuprofen." Luke passed him the bottle of medicine. Micah pulled out six tablets and washed them down with water. He closed his eyes and let the pounding have its way for a few minutes longer.

Jere asked, "How many did you take?"

"Six."

"You want to have a liver? Don't do it again. Four max. Got it, Andres?"

Micah sighed. "I got it. I got it." He muttered, "Mother hen."

"I heard you."

"No, you didn't. You just think you did." Micah laid his head back and stretched his neck.

"I did, and you take the lead. If you're going to fall out, I want you where I can see you."

Micah stood and took his place at the front of the pack. Everyone else assembled behind him. Ben scrambled to be with Jeremiah, holding the big man's hand as he had Micah's. Then he grabbed BB's hand and pulled him forward. BB pulled back. "I can walk, Ben. I'll choose where."

Ben's smile disappeared. He stepped in front of BB and delivered a sharp kick to his brother's shin. BB yelped, "That hurt!" He rubbed his ankle. "You've never kicked me before." BB glanced around at the group. "Who taught him?"

Micah laughed. "No one. I told you Ben could talk. He just doesn't do it with words." Most of the time. "Mew" and "Ribbit" might not count as words. Not yet. BB fell in line beside his brother and Jeremiah.

Another hour of walking. Micah squinted. A glint of light appeared in the trees on the side of the hill. Micah stopped but didn't throw up his hand. He wanted to see if the glint repeated itself.

It did. Micah's brain processed the image. *Like sun off a mirror. Or a glass…*

Micah shouted, "Down! Everyone down!"

The group hit the dirt in unison. A shot rang out from the hills. Quinn ordered, "Cover!" Everyone scrambled in the ground for a tree or bushes to hide behind. Three more shots rang out in quick succession. Micah leaned against a tree and breathed hard. He snapped a glance at his team, trying to make sure they all had shelter. He couldn't see anyone. Good thing. If he couldn't, the shooter certainly couldn't.

Which didn't stop whoever it was from firing round after round in their direction. Puffs of dirt and dust exploded in the ground around him. Chips plummeted from trees as the bullets struck again and again.

Quinn called, "Can anyone see the shooter?"

Micah yelled, "No." "No," echoed several other voices. Micah risked a look at Quinn and saw the man withdraw a long gun from his pack and assemble it. He sighted it at the trees. Trying to find the target.

Micah's eyes narrowed. *Give him something to shoot at.* Stupid thought, but Micah spun into view, hesitated, then spun back under cover.

The ruse worked. The shooter fired again. Quinn crouched and let out a spray of bullets toward the flashes.

Quinn's shots reverberated in the forest. Nothing else did. No one fired back. Either Quinn hit his target, or the target skipped out. *How does it feel to be shot at?*

Knowing Quinn had a gun made Micah braver. And safer. Or at least it felt like it. Unless someone started firing again.

Quinn popped off another three rounds for effect. Still nothing from the hills. Micah looked to Quinn for orders. Quinn stood with extreme caution.

Nothing.

He stepped into the light.

Still nothing.

He motioned to the others to stand. Slowly.

Nothing.

Everyone breathed a sigh of relief.

Quinn glared at Micah. "What kind of fool stunt was that?"

Fool wasn't the word Quinn used, but it would translate. Micah shook as he stood. "I don't know. I don't. But don't expect me to do it again. Ever."

Quinn growled at him. "Boy, if you ever…"

Micah asked, "Everyone okay? Anyone hit?"

Reassuring calls of "I'm okay" came back.

Tav. Chay. Grace. BB. Luke. "Ben's with me. He's good."

Micah called "Jeremiah."

No answer.

"Jeremiah!"

Nothing. Micah raced to where the man lay.

A bullet pierced his chest. Micah leaned onto the man to listen for a heartbeat.

Nothing.

Micah began chest compressions. "No. No. You do not get to die on us. You don't."

Hot, angry tears flowed down Micah's cheeks. He

pumped harder. "No, Jere! No!"

Quinn stepped beside Micah, followed by the others. Quinn moved Micah aside. He listened, then shook his head. "He's gone, Mick."

Micah screamed to the sky. "NOOOOOOOOOOO!" He tried to push Quinn away. "We can—"

Quinn repeated, "He's gone, Micah."

Tav grabbed Micah around the shoulders. "Leave him, Mick."

Tears rained down Luke's face.

Micah looked at his hands. Blood. Blood on his shirt. Blood on his chest. He stared at his friend, his brother. He stared at Tav. "No. No."

Heartbreak replaced anger. Micah dropped his head to Jeremiah's chest and sobbed. "Jere. Jere. Not you. Not you."

Grace moved to pull Micah away. She surrounded him with her arms. Held him close to her heart. Soothed him with words she whispered.

Tav and Luke knelt beside Micah and Jeremiah. Tav lifted Jere up to hug him. Luke followed. They sat back on their haunches. No one spoke.

Ben crawled between them. He lay his head on Jeremiah's chest. After a moment, he lifted it, reached up, and kissed Jere on the forehead. Ben poked at the blood on the man's chest. It covered his finger. Ben raised his hand and looked at his finger. He drew the finger under his eye and down. Tears. Tears for Jeremiah? Maybe the only tears the boy had.

Quinn stepped away from the group. He punched in numbers on his phone. Held it to his face. "Yes. I want to report a murder. You heard me. At these coordinates. Right. Get someone in right away." He listened. Micah heard anger burn in Quinn's tone. "I said right away. Airdrop someone. I don't care. Get someone out here now!"

He lay his phone down. Knelt again with the others. He began. "Our Father, Who is in Heaven. Holy is Your Name."

Micah and the others sobbed, "Your kingdom come. Your will be done on earth, as it is in Heaven. Give us today the food we need. Forgive us when we fail, as we forgive those who fail us. Do not lead us into temptations to evil." Quinn broke from the traditional recitation and added, "Temptations to avenge ourselves. Temptations to blame ourselves. Temptations to hate and malice and anger and bitterness. Deliver us from these evils, Lord." He looked up, then finished with the group, "For Yours is the Kingdom and the power, and the glory forever. Amen."

Six adults and one teen settled cross-legged to wait. Ben moved around the circle, hugging and kissing each person. He lingered where the hugs needed to be held longer. Micah held him the longest. He buried his head in Ben's shoulder and wept. Openly. Unashamed. "Lord, why? Why Jeremiah? He has babies. His sons. Why not me?"

There would be no answer. Not now. Micah lowered his head and prayed again, "Your Kingdom come. Your will be done. Not mine. Yours. Even now."

Micah slipped his shirt off and covered Jeremiah's face. He expected the man to sit up and say, "Fooled you." Prayed he would. Even now.

But he didn't. Micah sat back.

Quinn waited fifteen minutes and made another call. He stepped away from the circle. "Yeah. How long? Make it less. Yeah."

Luke gazed over at Micah. "You're bleeding, Mick."

Micah shook his head. "No. It's Jeremiah's blood. I'm fine."

Tav glanced over. "No. You're bleeding. Your back is bleeding."

"Forget it. It's his, not mine. Leave it alone."

Tav lurched to his feet. "I'm not going to leave it alone. You're bleeding."

Micah yelled, "It doesn't matter. Jeremiah's dead. Oh, Lord in Heaven. He's dead."

Tav yelled in return, "And I'm not going to lose another brother!" Tav grabbed the first-aid kit and began dabbing at Micah's back.

Micah could feel the burn. A bullet must have grazed him. On top of everything else. But he hadn't felt it. It hadn't mattered. It still didn't.

Tav pulled off his shirt and gave Micah his undershirt. "This will stretch. It'll keep the wound clean." His eyes burned fierce. "Keep it clean. You hear me, Knight?"

Micah nodded. He would comply. Not because he wanted to. But he knew how to follow orders. For now.

It was half an hour longer before a helicopter hovered over their spot. Ben looked into the sky. He peeked from Micah to the chopper to Micah to the chopper. Micah explained. "It's a helicopter, Ben. They're going to…" He caught himself. "They're going to take Jeremiah…away. To, uh…keep him safe. For now. For a while."

Three persons rappelled from the chopper. They untied and approached Quinn, who stepped out to meet them. Micah's group lost all control of anything, including themselves. They were extras in a play. Set dressing to be moved around. Sit and be quiet. Speak when spoken to. Micah preferred it that way. Quiet. Alone with his thoughts. And prayers.

And since the attention shifted away from him, he could pray. Properly. *Lord. Take care of Jeremiah. I know he's with you. I know he's having the time of his life. Assure him we will take care of his boys. They will never want for anything. Except maybe a father. And we'll try to be there for them as much as possible.*

Two more people rappelled down. They brought a stretcher. One of them examined Jeremiah's wound. He turned to Quinn. Micah didn't hear the conversation. Didn't want to.

The men loaded Jere's body onto the stretcher and hoisted it to the chopper, which hovered overhead. Still, no one moved.

Three officials spread out in the area, taking pictures, and picking up bullets. The fourth man walked with Quinn over to the circle of mourners. No one stood. He nodded to the group. "People. I'm Deputy Whitehouse. I'm sorry—"

"Don't. Don't say it." Tav jumped to his feet. "You're not,

and we know it. Do your job. Ask your questions."

Grace laid a hand on Tav's arm. She squeezed it, and Tav returned to sitting. Grace gave the man a straight-lipped smile. "We're hurting. It's fresh. What do you need to know?"

"What you saw. Who you saw."

Grace glanced around. Heads nodded in unison. Grace said, "We saw nothing. A glint in the sunlight. The shooter opened fire. We saw nothing but our own fear."

"How many times did the shooter fire?"

Grace stared at the ground. "I don't know. Ten. Fifteen. I didn't count. I wanted it to stop. That's all I thought about."

Quinn and the fifth newcomer, a forest ranger, walked up the hill toward the shooter's position. Micah pulled himself together. "I think he fired seven rounds before Quinn could get his rifle out."

"Was the shooter still firing?"

"They stopped. I rolled out to draw their fire."

Tav's head came up sharply. "You did what?"

Micah waved him off. "Never mind. It's not important. The guy saw me and started firing again. Quinn returned fire, and the shooting stopped."

"Did anyone hear the shooter leave?"

All voices answered in the negative. Micah added, "I don't think they did leave. I think Quinn hit them."

"You know for a fact Quinn hit them?"

Tav seethed, "The only fact we know is our friend is dead. For no reason we know of. He's got kids. Two little boys. What will they do for a father? That's the only fact we're concerned with."

Deputy Whitehouse nodded. "I understand." He walked over to join Quinn and the ranger. They disappeared into the brush. Were gone a minute. The three deputies joined them. Micah could hear them moving through the bush. If they found anything, they didn't say.

Quinn walked back and sat on the ground with the group. He did not speak. The deputy, the ranger, and the remaining three men rose on their rappel lines back to the helicopter. Five minutes and they were gone. Then the chopper disappeared.

Tav swallowed around his tears. "Where will they take him?"

"Into Erskine. It'll be a few days before Jere's people are notified and brought out. The coroner will take good care of him."

Grace spoke for the group. "What's this all about, Quinn? Who shot at us? What do they want?"

Quinn stared at the ground. "I wish I knew. I wish even more I could tell you. I don't, and I can't." He held Micah's gaze. "The first time someone shot at you, who could the shooter see? You? And who else?"

Micah thought back. Way back. Jeremiah's lifetime back. "Maybe all of us? They were above us on the hill. They could see everyone. We weren't hiding."

"Where was Ben?"

Micah's head snapped up. "What? Why?"

"Just tell me where he was."

"Behind me. I slipped, or the shot would have taken him out."

"The second time?"

"I don't know. We scattered."

Tav interrupted. "No. Ben went with Jeremiah to go fishing." His voice cracked.

"And he stayed with Jeremiah this time, too." Quinn finished the timeline.

Tav's voice trembled. "Are you saying the shooter is after Ben?"

"No. I'm saying it can *look* like the shooter wanted to hit Ben." Quinn spoke sharply and firmly. "Whoever they are, they're a terrible shot if they've tried three times and can't hit him."

Could it be Ben's fault Jeremiah had died?

How far back did blame go? If Tav hadn't suggested they go rafting…if Micah hadn't rented the watercraft…if Luke hadn't picked this canyon…if BB hadn't pulled them out of the water? Who should ultimately pay for Jeremiah's death?

God.

The answer always came back to the One Who allowed it. Always. Blame God.

Or accept He had a plan—has a plan—and it is good and right and loving and perfect. Even when it doesn't look like it from this side.

Blame God?

Or praise Him for the time with Jeremiah. Be thankful they got to know him at all. And knew they would see him again.

Which would it be? Bitterness? Or grief with thankfulness?

Micah closed his eyes. Bowed his head. Made his choice.

"Father God, Lord Jesus Christ in Heaven, thank You. Thank You for giving us time with Jere. Thank You we can pour out our grief to You, and You understand what it feels like. You lost a friend. Lazarus died, and You wept. Even more, God, You lost Your Son. Someone killed Him, too. But it was us. We killed Him. He stepped into our place and took our death.

"But You didn't stay dead. You came back. You live. Jeremiah lives. We will live. We hurt, we're angry, we're devastated. But You are Good. You are Love, and You are God. Heal us, Father. In Jesus's Name."

He held the amen. Maybe someone else wanted to make their choice known.

Maybe not. After several seconds, Micah added, "Amen."

Voices murmured, "Amen."

Micah swallowed hard. "What do we do now?"

Quinn's voice stayed quiet. "The authorities want you all to stay here. To wait for them to come back and investigate this thoroughly."

Micah's head snapped around. "Are you saying we have to stay put? Just sit and wait and do nothing until they get around to coming back? In what, a day? Two days? And in the meantime, we mourn and cry in this spot? I don't think so."

He looked at his people. "What do you want to do?"

Long silence. Tav couldn't keep the bitterness from his voice. "Go home. I don't want anything to do with this quest anymore."

Luke stared at the ground. "But the money would help the boys. Jere didn't have life insurance. This could make a difference for them."

Micah looked at Grace. She waved him off. "Not my call. This is for you three to decide."

Chay backed her mother. "I agree. You three have to do what's right for you."

Micah turned to Tav. "Do you want to split up? You go home. Luke stays here?"

Tav shook his head. "No. We're in this together. If I get outvoted, I'll stay with you."

Luke faced Micah. "Your call, Mick."

Micah lowered his head. *Lord? Help me.*

Peace like Elijah's mantle poured over him. Micah nodded. "We keep going." He didn't look to Quinn for confirmation.

Tav exhaled through clenched teeth. "Then we go together."

Micah promised, "Two more days, Tav. Only two more days. If we don't find anything, we're done." He looked at Chay and Grace. "You two can continue searching." He shrugged. "Nice of me to tell you what you can and can't do, right?"

Grace smiled. "It's okay, Mick. Everything is awkward now. We'll sort it out."

Micah turned to Quinn. "What are you going to do?"

The monitor shrugged. "I'll hang around with you and the team if you don't mind."

"What about the authorities?"

"They can hunt me up later."

Micah looked around at the team. He did a silent four count. Raised his thumb.

Six adults all raised theirs in unison with him. BB cocked his head and narrowed his eyes. After a moment, he raised his thumb as well.

Ben raised both hands and held them in the air. He jumped up and down and ran around to kiss Quinn and everyone else.

BB shook his head. "You think he really knows what's going on?"

Tav snorted. "You want him to kick your shins again? Of course, he knows what's going on."

BB took Jeremiah's pack. He searched the faces and asked, "If no one minds. I'll carry his."

No one raised an objection. The compass was pulled out, the direction relocated, and they were off again. Fish. Boot. Y.

* * *

Once again, they searched for a camping place before nightfall. Tav's plan of leaving a trail of MRE crumbs proved fruitful. Or animal-full, anyhow. Grace brought down two pheasants and stunned three squirrels. Quinn dispatched all five critters. They set up camp near a rock pile. Maybe it had been a rock wall. No one could tell for sure. But it had been in place for many years.

Grace guessed sixty to seventy. Micah's eyes narrowed. "Long enough to have been here when Magary came this way."

Luke reminded, "If he came this way."

Micah frowned but dipped his head. He walked over and examined the stones closer. He ran his hand along the top of the wall. Stones were expertly placed to ensure the wall would not fall at the first high wind. Micah let his gaze drift down the face of the barricade. He brushed against the wall, disturbing a layer of dirt, dust, and ivy. He noticed a horizontal rock missing. To the right of it, two vertical "bricks" shifted apart, leaving a gap.

Micah's eyes widened. His heart seized. He yelled, "People! Come look."

The group gathered. Micah traced the opening with his hand. "What do you see?"

No one spoke. Finally, Tav sniffed. "Well, it's not a fish."

"It's a boot. I swear it is. Who's got the compass? Where

are the markers?"

Tav pulled out the game cards. The compass aligned. A heading projected. For the morning. Not tonight. Tonight needed to be rest and recovery. And tears and prayers. And a requiem for the fallen.

Dinner proved a quiet affair. The preparation of the game couldn't have been better. But for all Grace's skill at cooking, no one had the heart to eat. They dried the meat and would have it the next day. And the next.

The group reclined around the pit as the fire popped, sparked, and sizzled. Micah asked, "How would he want to be remembered?"

Tav grunted. "He wouldn't. He'd say, 'Eh, move on. Don't mention it.'"

Luke's eyes twinkled, but his face remained somber. "Yeah. He'd want to be thought of as a good father."

Tav snapped, "He was a good father. He tried to be a good husband. But Shelly…" He trailed off, unable or unwilling to continue his thought.

Micah tilted his head. "What did she want when we left? It surprised me she came to the house to see him off."

"Probably begging him to reconsider. Again."

"She spent more time poking around the gear than she did talking to Jere. It made no sense."

Quinn sat up. "Who are you talking about?"

"Jeremiah's ex. She showed up the day we left."

"They on good terms?"

"Those two?" Tac scoffed. "Oil and water have a better chance of staying together. She hated him for winning custody of the boys. No one expected her to show up when we left."

Quinn's eyes narrowed. "What is her full name?"

"She's Shelly, no e, Acosta. Lives in Wade." Luke supplied the name.

"1517 Montrose." Tav filled in the rest of the information. "Why?"

Quinn pursed his mouth. "Just collecting information. The more you know, the easier it is to put pieces together."

Micah didn't feel up to badgering the monitor about what puzzle he wanted to assemble. Sadness washed over him. He raised his head to the stars. "Lord, I am going to miss him."

Tears splashed down his cheeks. Micah didn't bother to wipe them away.

Ben did. Ben moved over to sit beside Micah. He patted Micah's cheeks, collecting the moisture on his hands. Then Ben stepped over to Tav and repeated his actions. Ben rubbed his hands on his cheek, scrubbing away some of the blood streaks. Ben walked over to Grace. He cocked his head to the side. Grace choked, "Sure, buddy. You can have my tears, too." Ben cupped his hands below her cheeks and gathered more water. He slipped next to Chay. She filled his hands with her sorrow.

Finally came Quinn's turn. The man closed his eyes. A slow, wet trickle of pain trailed down his face. Ben patted the man's cheeks, kissed them, again rinsed his face. He sat beside BB and looked up at his brother.

BB's voice tightened. "I didn't know him, Ben. I didn't. I'm sorry he's gone. I'm sorry everyone is hurting."

Ben lowered his eyes. Micah watched the boy. After a moment, he realized Ben was crying. Micah got up and moved to where Ben sat. He pulled the boy to his chest. "That's right, Ben. We're sad. We can show each other we're hurting. It's okay. You can be sad, too. No one will hurt you for being sad. Or for crying." He hugged him. "Real men cry, Ben."

Ben laid his head on Micah's chest and wept. Silently. But he wept.

* * *

TUESDAY—WEEK TWO

Morning brought new determination. Find the fish. Find the Y. Find the treasure and go home. Stay out of trouble. Avoid getting killed.

If the shooting stopped, they would know… What would they know? Jeremiah was the target? Or the shooter gave up? Maybe he'd been wounded and would come back later? Micah still knew nothing. Except he needed to find a fifty-year-old fish and a letter Y.

Tav leaned on Luke and Grace for support of his bad knee. It slowed them down but didn't stop them. The woods cleared out, giving way to rolling meadows. The trees gave way to open sky, sun, and clouds. Micah drew a deep breath in and let it out with a rush. Air. Sunshine. Life. Finally.

There were still rocks. Boulders dotted the countryside. The group searched each one diligently to see if they could find a fish. But nothing came close. At least not anything they saw.

Micah walked with Quinn. He could ask his questions, and maybe the monitor would answer. At least he could try. He started with something neutral. "Who owns all this land, Quinn?"

"The Feds. It's all federal parkland."

"Is that why we never crossed any fences?"

"Right. It's parceled out, but not so as you'd notice."

"How many acres?"

"I don't know exactly. Someone willed the land to the government a long time ago. I think they took possession about twenty years ago."

"Did Mr. Magary know the land would change hands?"

"He knew."

Micah turned sharply to face Quinn. The monitor's tone carried a sense of…pride? Satisfaction? Micah asked, "You know more of this story, don't you?"

Quinn laughed. "I'm just a monitor out here to keep people out of trouble." He lost his levity. "Didn't do a very good job of it, did I?"

Micah recognized the feelings of guilt. He said softly, "Not your fault, Quinn. Whatever happened, it wasn't your fault. No one blames you. Don't blame yourself."

Quinn nodded once. They walked on in silence.

Tav and Luke led. Tav threw his hand in the air. Quinn chuckled. "You boys do love your regiment, don't you?"

"Since we couldn't be pirates, we became knights." They joined Tav and the others. "What is it?"

"There are markers here. Poles. Maybe they indicate a border?"

Angle iron posts, the kind that support stop signs, dotted the landscape. They had holes up and down their length but weren't connected to or by anything. Weathered and rusted, they stood unheeded for many years.

How many? Enough to be original to the search? Micah inspected the first few that matched their heading. Nothing. Two more stretched out ahead, still on the 110 East heading. Nothing on them, either.

Off to the left, barely away from the trail, a pole stuck in the ground. It leaned severely, and the dirt around the base appeared as semi-dried mud. The rod looked like it would fall at any minute. Tav went to investigate. His voice jumped an octave. "It's here! The fish. Come on."

Micah noted Quinn's eyes flare. Did he see something wrong?

An ichthus, the Christian fish symbol, was formed from

wire and attached to the pole. Micah watched Quinn. This wasn't what he expected. Micah stared at the mark. What could be wrong with it? Why couldn't it be the right one?

Grace spoke. "Awfully shiny for being out here fifty years."

Chay agreed. "There should be rust or wear or dirt. It looks too clean."

Tav glanced from mother to daughter. "You think someone did this on purpose? Someone trying to confuse anyone who follows them?"

Chay's eyes narrowed. "It's the sort of thing Race would do."

"Could he have moved the correct symbol?" BB got into the game.

Micah side-eyed Quinn. The man remained silent. But his eyes…his eyes. Micah stated the obvious. "If he moved the symbol, it's game over. There's no way we can find the coins if we can't trust the signs."

Quinn pulled out his phone. "Let me make a call. Give me a minute." He stepped away from the group to get some privacy. Then began tapping and texting.

Tav whispered, "I'd give my share of the loot to know what he's doing."

Luke asked, "Give it to who? Me? Because I'd take you up on that. I bet he's talking to someone, telling them to move the treasure. If someone's going to cheat, the monitors will make sure no one finds the coins."

Tav shook his head. "No bet. Because I'm thinking he's doing the same thing. I just wanted confirmation."

Chay grimaced. "Race. It has to be Race. He's been a slime bucket this whole game."

Micah reinterpreted the words Chay actually used to describe Race to something less worthy of the obscenity jar.

Quinn came back and put his phone away. "Consider this a false flag. Ignore it."

Micah gave a straight-lipped smile. "Sure glad you're with us. It could have been bad."

Tav asked, "But who would do it?"

Luke snorted, "Does it matter?"

Tav touched the fish. "Yeah, I think it does. Why would someone go to the trouble of setting up false markers? If they're ahead, keep going. We're not going to pass them, right?"

He looked at Quinn. "Don't you think it's strange?"

"Are you thinking it's a trap of some sort?" The monitor's eyes narrowed.

"I'm thinking I don't know. But maybe we should find out?"

Quinn's eyes took on a faraway focus. He shook his head, finally. "Too dangerous." He motioned to Ben and BB. "You've got kids to look after." He stared at the ground. "I'll follow the trail and see where it goes. Or to who it leads."

Micah shook his head. "Not by yourself. Call in help, at least."

Quinn smiled. "I think I can handle…"

Tav drawled, "Yeah, and you'd smack any of us if we gave you attitude. Come on, Quinn. Admit it. If this is Sissy and Doug, they've already killed two people."

Micah's voice tightened. "I don't want to lose another friend."

"What are you proposing?"

"Splitting up. Send the boys and two guardians ahead, following the real trail. The rest go with you."

Quinn's smile looked evil. "And how do you choose who goes where?"

Chay and Grace stepped forward. "Yes, boys, how do you propose to choose?"

Tav cleared his throat. "The way we usually do. Ro Sham Bo."

Micah held up a hand. "Too many of us, and it'll take too long. I propose something simpler."

"Draw straws? That's not easier."

"We all pick numbers between one and one hundred. Quinn calls out a number. The three closest go with Quinn.

The other two go with the boys."

Quinn raised an eyebrow. "How far?"

Micah tipped his head. "What?"

"How far do we chase down this false trail? An hour? Two hours? Overnight? Have you thought it all the way through?"

Tav cleared his throat. "Um, we'd leave it up to your judgment."

Micah read the man's eyes. "No cheating, Quinn. No saying 'far enough' just to get rid of us. We want to help."

Luke kicked the dirt. "We want to keep you alive." He looked into Quinn's eyes. "We owe you."

Quinn shook his head slowly. "You don't owe me anything, boys." His voice tightened. "If I agree to this, I'll play it straight. I'm not certain I can go along with you putting yourselves in danger."

"We've been in danger. We're still in danger. If Sissy and Doug are behind this, maybe we can keep Ben and BB out of danger."

BB stepped up. "I want a chance to go, too."

"No." Six voices in unison voted him down. Micah added, "You have to stay with Ben and keep him safe. He trusts you. He needs you."

BB dropped his eyes. He wasn't happy. Ben walked over and hugged his brother. He stared up into BB's face. BB glanced down and smiled. "Okay, little guy. I'll stay with you."

Quinn stepped away from the group and walked around the false fish. He studied it a moment, glanced at the group, glanced at the fish, nodded. He dipped his head side to side. "Fine. Three go with the boys. Two come with me." He held up his hand before anyone could object. "I only have two eyes. I can't keep track of three of you."

Chay asked, "How do we know you won't cheat?"

Tav stood up and pronounced, "We are Knights of the Octagon. Honesty and integrity are our primary values." He dropped the formality. "We don't cheat. Even when we don't like the arrangement, we don't cheat."

Chay sniffed. "I might."

"That's between you and your maker." Tav looked around. "Okay, so maybe just this once, we all write the numbers down in the dirt. Quinn calls his number. The two closest go with him."

The group picked up sticks or held out fingers. They all faced away from each other. Tav instructed, "Silent count of four. Write your number."

Everyone wrote.

Quinn called, "Done?"

"Done." Tav announced it for the group.

"Fifty."

Chay groaned. "You did not call fifty. I knew you weren't going to call the exact middle. You couldn't."

Quinn smiled a straight-line smile. "But I did."

Micah wrote forty-five. Tav, forty-eight. Grace and Chay wrote thirty and twenty-five. Luke wrote forty. He held Tav's eyes. "No, I didn't throw the game."

Tav jerked his head to the side. "Never thought you would." He placed a hand on the younger man's shoulder. "Take care of Ben and watch out for yourself."

Luke hugged Tav and Micah. "Come back. Alive."

Micah nodded. "Always."

Tav and Micah huddled with Quinn. "We follow the direction they wanted us to go, right?" Tav pointed toward a stand of trees. "Over this way."

Quinn nodded. "It would seem to be the way. But we'll see what happens when we get closer."

The three walked side by side, Quinn in the middle. Tav asked, "Honest opinion. Sissy and Doug pull this trick?"

Quinn didn't answer for a moment. "If I have to guess, I'd say yes. But I don't like making guesses."

"We'll see what happens."

The ground remained soft from the recent storms. Not squishy enough to leave boot marks but sufficiently supple to show a trail. As the men followed the compass north, the path veered ever so slightly to the west. A degree or two over ten yards. Not enough to be "in your face" wrong, but still, off course. Micah pointed out the discrepancy. Quinn nodded. "They want us to follow the trail, not the compass."

Micah guessed, "And they don't want us to notice?"

Quinn raised his eyebrows. "That would be my take."

The trio halted before the tree line. Micah could see how the trail moved alongside the line. Not going far into the forest but hugging the outer reaches. Why not lead them in? Micah gazed at Quinn.

Quinn answered as if reading Micah's mind. "Gives them a cleaner line of sight. Better aim."

"If they were the ones shooting at us, they need all the advantage they can get." Tav snorted.

Quinn reminded him, "They hit Jeremiah."

Tav's face fell. Micah guessed his confidence did as well.

A voice yelled out, "Stop where you are. Hands in the air."

The trio complied. Doug and Sissy stepped clear of the trees. Neither appeared armed. Doug smiled. "Boy, are we glad to see you! We've been wandering out here in these woods for days."

Sissy added, "Ever since we split up with Win and Nance. They insisted they knew the way. I knew they were going wrong. But they wouldn't listen."

Quinn asked, "So you split up? Did you keep any of the cards?"

Doug nodded. "Yeah, but we lost them a day or so ago. We got caught in the storm, tumbled down a hill, and lost all our gear."

Sissy glanced at Micah and Tav. "Say, aren't you the men with the young boy? The one who didn't talk?"

Tav stole a glimpse at Quinn, then nodded. "Yes, ma'am. We are."

"Where is the boy? I want to apologize for seeming rude to him. He seemed like a nice kid."

Quinn motioned over his head. "We left them back a ways. They're going on ahead."

Doug smiled. "Oh, fantastic. You'll let us come with you? And we can get out of this cursed wilderness? We would really appreciate it."

Quinn pursed his lips but shook his head. "No, I'm afraid not. I'll give you directions to get back on track, but I can't take you to another team. That would be unfair."

Sissy's voice whined. "Why? We're part of the hunt like everyone else."

"True, but it's against the rules to take a team further ahead than they've gone on their own. Each team must find their way without assistance from the monitor."

Sissy turned to Tav. "You wouldn't mind letting us follow you, now, would you? We can join your team. Since Win and Nance dropped out…"

Quinn interrupted. "They didn't drop out. Someone murdered them."

Sissy half-screamed. "Murdered! Oh, no!"

Doug appeared shocked. "Murdered? How?"

"The coroner is still determining cause of death. Law enforcement suspects they were knifed to death."

"How can they tell?"

"The condition of the bodies. Coroners can decipher between knife wounds and animal wounds. Forensic science has come a long way."

Doug stuttered. "We liked them. Who would want to kill them? Why?"

"We're still working on a reason. But one suspicion is a drug deal gone bad."

Sissy's eyes widened. "Drugs? They never seemed the type to be involved with drugs."

"They weren't. Whoever killed them was."

Doug cleared his throat. "How can you possibly know?"

Quinn smiled. "I can't share that information at this time."

Sissy fiddled with her pack. "Are you sure you can't take us to join your people?"

Quinn shook his head. "We can take you back to where you got lost. You'll have to find your way forward from there. Or we can arrange to take you to the river, and you can pick up your boat and sail home. Those are your choices."

Sissy pulled a gun from her pack. "No, those aren't our only choices. I hoped we could do this the easy way. But you insist on making it difficult. You will take us to your team. Now."

Quinn raised an eyebrow. "Guns? Since when? I thought you were the up-close, stick-a-knife-in-them kind of villain."

"When it works. Guns are so noisy. Draw a crowd."

Micah snarled, "Why were you shooting at us?"

Doug cocked his head. "Shooting at you? Why would we?"

"Exactly what I'm asking you. Three times you shot at us. The last time you murdered Jeremiah."

Sissy shook her head. "I'm sorry to disappoint you, but we never fired at you. We certainly didn't kill your Jeremiah, whoever he might have been. We have no interest in you at all."

"Why do you want to join us?"

Doug pulled out a gun as well. "Walk. Talk later. Move."

Quinn turned. He caught and held Micah's eyes. Micah caught Tav's. The three men began to head back the way they came.

Mostly. They followed the path, veering off a degree or two in the opposite direction. Meaning they trailed deeper and deeper away from the correct way. They would pull Sissy and Doug away from Luke and the others at any cost.

But if I die, who will take care of Mother? Don't I have an obligation to her to live? She certainly says so. All the time. It's my life's purpose. Care for her. Nothing else. I can't die.

Lord, tell me there's more. I'll lay down my life for Ben and the others. Mother will have to fend for herself. You can take care of her. I know You can.

So why do I feel so trapped? Is this really what You expect of me? All You expect?

Micah walked with his hands at his side. He saw Quinn stretching his hands, working out the kinks in his fingers. Then he dropped his hands to his side. He held out three fingers.

Then two. Then one.

Countdown. Micah signed to Tav, *Ready.*

Tav signed *Ready.*

The men walked on. Quinn strolled to the top of a hill. Small trees dotted the ridge and the side of the knoll. Quinn tripped and fell, hitting the ground hard. Doug stepped back two feet and ordered, "Up. Get up."

Micah and Tav reached out to help the monitor halfway to his feet. Quinn nodded his head less than a quarter of an inch. Tav and Micah reacted. Quinn threw himself backward into Doug. Micah and Tav turned on Sissy and lashed at the gun in her hand. The pistol went off. Micah grabbed her arm and thrust it into the air. Another bullet fired. Tav grabbed her wrist, forced the gun arm down to the ground, and kicked it. Sissy screamed but let go of the weapon. Micah grabbed it and tossed it to Tav. Tav aimed the gun at Sissy and ordered, "Don't move."

Quinn forced Doug to the ground and wrestled the weapon from him. He pointed at the man's middle and threatened, "On your feet, and don't move."

The monitor reached over and took the pistol from Tav. "Thank you, sir. I appreciate the help." He looked at the two Knights. "Either of you hurt?"

Micah actually checked. "I don't feel anything unusual."

Tav breathed out. "Me, neither."

Quinn ordered, "Check Mick. I don't trust him."

Tav inspected Micah's torso. "Don't see anything new."

Micah frowned. "I'm good, I tell you."

Quinn grimaced. "Just making sure." He motioned for Doug and Sissy to sit. "We're going to be here awhile. You may as well get comfortable."

Sissy sank to the ground. Doug did as well. Quinn ordered, "Packs off and throw them aside. Slowly."

Again, they complied. Slowly, as Quinn commanded. Micah moved over, picked up the backpacks, and brought them to Quinn. Quinn motioned for Micah to open them.

Sissy snarled, "You can't hold us. You're not a cop. You

have no right to look in our bags."

Quinn smiled his tight-lipped smile. "Ma'am, you have no idea who I am or what I have a right to do. I suggest you sit and be quiet."

Sissy didn't take the hint. She yelled, "Get your hands off my stuff, or you'll be facing time in jail! I'll sue your…" She continued with words and descriptions Micah ran through his "Jesus filter." Garbage stays out.

Micah opened the pack and pulled out two plastic-wrapped blocks, tied with strings, of some white substance. He carefully laid them on the ground, touching them as little as possible.

Quinn glanced sideways at them. "My, my. I wonder what those will turn out to be?"

Doug sneered, "Powder sugar for my mother."

Micah dug out two more packages. "Mother must do a lot of baking."

"She's very into cookies." Doug hissed the words.

Micah dug into the second bag and produced an equal amount of what looked to be the same substance. The last thing he pulled out was a handful of gold coins. All of them fakes.

Quinn shook his head. "You haven't been carrying this all along. Too much chance of losing it. This must be a recent acquisition. Friends along the way?"

"This is your fiction. You tell me."

Quinn smirked. "Transporting illegal drugs on a federal reserve? Sounds like prison time. Federal prison time. Add the murder charges, and we're looking at some serious detention. Maybe even life without parole."

Sissy exhaled. "Fine. What do you want? How do we make this go away?"

Quinn seemed surprised. "Go away? What are you talking about? Make what go away?"

"The drugs. The murders. Which I'm not admitting to. But you want to pin them on us, so what do you want to make it all not have happened?"

Micah started to object, but Quinn waved him off. "I have the lead."

Micah nodded and stepped back. He sat down some distance away from any danger. This would be Quinn's show. And he would handle it his way.

Quinn raised an eyebrow. "Someone committed two murders. Win and Nance were your partners. You disappeared without a trace. No drag marks. No unknown footprints. What happened? Did they find your stash?"

Doug sneered. "This is your fantasy. You go ahead with it." He picked up handfuls of dirt and let it sift down through his fingers.

Quinn put a hand to his jaw and rubbed it. "Well, let's see. If they didn't find your drugs, maybe they had information you wanted. And when you mentioned it, they got upset? But what information, hmm?"

Quinn looked over at Micah and Tav. "Think, boys. What knowledge could someone hold that drug runners would be afraid of?"

Tav suggested, "Their identities as drug runners?"

"Maybe. But if Nance and Win knew that about Sissy and Doug, they'd never partner with them. Think again."

Micah pictured Win in his head. Then Sissy. His insides turned cold. He'd seen them both in the drawings in the dirt. Women Ben had been afraid of. Two women. One Ben had known. One knew Ben. The other...

Micah sat up straight. "Win knew Ben and BB. She served as their county worker."

Quinn nodded. "Okay, good. Now, how does…"

He trailed off, smiled without mirth. "I see. I get it now. Win mentioned she'd seen Ben before, didn't she? Figured out she'd seen him in the cabin." He turned to face Sissy. "The cabin where you killed Pete Winston." He stared hard at Sissy. "Did someone put a hit out on him? Or did he get inconvenient?"

Doug lifted his head. "There was no hit. Winston tried to pull a double-cross. Tried to pay us with fake gold. I don't know where he got it, but there was no way I would take it as payment for good horse." Doug laughed. "Idiot thought the stuff was real."

"But you knew real gold existed around there, right? Somewhere out this way. So you killed him?"

"He pulled the gun on me. I had no choice."

"You think the witnesses will say the same? Oh, wait, you were going to eliminate the witnesses. As soon as you found both of them, am I right?"

Sissy shrugged. "Again, I'm not admitting to anything. You began talking about making this go away."

"No, you talked about it. I talked about you giving up your supplier."

Doug growled. "For what? A murder charge you can't prove? What witness do you have? A dumb kid who can't talk? That'll go over well in court."

Micah's gut burned. Quinn smiled wide. "I'll put my 'dumb kid' against any lawyer you can find who will represent you. And your supplier. The kid ID'd you at the cabin. Both of you. You know how juries love kids, don't you?"

Sissy and Doug exchanged glances. Micah came to his feet. He didn't know why, but something told him to move. He stretched.

Doug spoke to Sissy under his breath. She shook her head. He spoke some more. Again, the shake of her head. The third time, she nodded. Doug looked at Quinn. "I'll give you his name and number."

Doug reached in his pocket. Quinn trained the gun on him. Doug pulled his hand out very slowly. He flipped something in his hand at the last moment, and Quinn doubled over. Micah jumped forward to tackle Doug. He recognized the throwing blade in the drug dealer's hand too late to stop his bull rush. Doug turned on Micah. Micah grabbed the man around the middle and drove his shoulder into the man's chest.

Bad move. He'd hit him with his sore shoulder. Micah writhed in agony but would not let go. He spun onto his back and flipped the drug runner over his head, landing sitting on top of him. Doug exhaled with a loud "Whooof." Micah pinned his hands and held him.

At the same time, Tav wrestled with Sissy and her knife. She sliced across the front of him. He danced back. She twirled the knife to throw it, but Quinn rose up and knocked it from her hand. Tav and Sissy pounced on the blade. Both grabbed it at the same time. Tav slammed their hands onto the dirt. Sissy refused to let go. Tav smashed her hand again and again. She rolled to the side and kicked Tav in the thigh. He yelled but didn't let go. Quinn staggered over and kicked the blade away. Tav spun and pinned Sissy's arm behind her back. He grabbed her free hand and forced it behind her as well, holding her on the ground.

Micah yelled, "Quinn! Are you okay?"

"Yeah. Scratched. Takes more than one blade to get me down." He yanked the small blade from his belly and held his hand to his middle. "I'm fine."

The monitor stood, shaking as he pulled out his phone. "I need a team in here, and I needed them yesterday. Thirty minutes. No longer. Right."

Quinn sat down, still holding his side. He shook his head. "College boys. I could use you on my team."

Micah started to ask, "What team?" but decided he didn't want to know. Not now. Maybe later. After Sissy and Doug were removed.

It took the full thirty minutes before a helicopter dropped in. There was enough clear space for it to land, and five commandos jumped out.

Micah couldn't hear above the sound of the blades whirring. He saw Quinn talking to one of the commandos. Two grabbed Sissy from Tav. Two grabbed Doug. They loaded the drug dealers into the chopper. A medic came over and patched Quinn's side. One of the commandos spoke to Quinn. Long conversation between the two of them.

Finally, the commando came over and ducked his head at Micah and Tav. "Nice work, boys. Thanks for backing up our man. Quinn told us you wouldn't let him come alone. Good job." His eyes grew stern. "You neither saw nor heard any of this. Unless we call you to testify in court, of course. Beyond that, this never happened."

He saluted Tav and Micah, then jumped in the helicopter. The bird took off, banked to the west, and disappeared.

Micah and Tav exchanged glances of disbelief. Tav circled his index finger and looked at Quinn. "What just happened?"

Quinn smiled. "What are you talking about? I didn't see anything." His voice hardened, but only slightly. "And you didn't either." He turned to Micah. "You hurt your shoulder again, didn't you?"

Micah shook his head. "No. Since nothing happened here, how could I hurt my shoulder?"

Quinn chuckled. "Okay, smart guy." He looked around at the area and shook his head. "Guess we should get back with our real team."

He started walking. Micah and Tav fell in beside him. Micah whispered, "What is your real team? I can guess those people, but—"

Quinn gave Micah an innocent look. "What people? I didn't see any people?"

Micah sagged. "And I didn't either. Right. Forgive me. I'm still learning."

Quinn chuckled. "Don't worry about it, Mick. It's not something you'll ever need to remember."

Tav snorted. "How will we forget this figment of our imaginations?"

"By remembering exactly what it was. A figment of your imagination. No, you can't tell the team. I'll tell them anything they need to know." He stopped at the pained look on Tav's face. Quinn walked a few paces, recanted. "Okay, you can tell Junior, but only after you get home. Not here, and not while anyone else is around. I'll tell BB and Ben their Uncle Petey has been avenged, the killers will face justice, and they can go back to being kids again."

Micah walked in silence for several yards. He had to ask. He had to. "The coins. The fake coins. How did Petey come by them? Are they part of Magary's quest? Are we looking for fool's gold?"

Quinn shook his head. "I don't know how he came by the coins in his possession. I know the treasure exists. I know the money is real. Beyond that, you'll have to trust me. And never mention it again."

"Right. I got it. I got it."

They caught up with the remainder of the team before nightfall. Quinn handled the questions of who, what, where, and how. No one in the group looked satisfied with the answers, but no one questioned the monitor outright. Grace retained other questions for Quinn.

"What do you get out of this? Who pays you to supervise…excuse me…monitor these searches?"

"Money comes from the Magary estate. It's what he wanted."

Chay side-eyed him. "Why don't you find the money for yourself?"

"Because we work for the estate. We're fiduciaries. Sworn to protect the interests of the game. We're paid well enough."

Micah shook his head. "People of honor. You want to join the Knights?"

Quinn smiled. "I'll think about it. Maybe you boys want to join us."

"Does it require travel?"

"Not as much as you think."

Tav stuck out his bottom lip. "I'll think about it." He began scattering crumbs to draw in food for the evening.

And the evening ended the ninth day.

* * *

WEDNESDAY—WEEK TWO

The next day's hike brought them off the hills and into pastureland. An occasional cow could be seen grazing in the distance. Quinn warned, "Keep them in the distance. The more distance, the better."

Luke cocked his head. "They're moo cows. What kind of trouble can they cause?"

Grace chuckled. "You don't want to find out. There's a half-ton of muscle and bone. Add they can average seventeen miles per hour at a full run. Top speed is twenty-five miles per hour. You do not want to mess with a cow. No cow tipping. Not while I'm around."

"Cow tipping?" Micah was incredulous. "Is that really a thing?"

"Depends on who you ask. Sort of like snipe hunting."

Luke shook his head. "Snipe hunting? What's snipe hunting?"

Micah swallowed his laughter and his smile. It might be too soon for the levity and practical jokes. Jere would have pulled the prank.

He didn't have to choose when Quinn described the trick. "You stand in the dark with a flashlight and a pillowcase. You yell, 'Here, snipe,' and wait for the snipe to run into the bag."

Luke nodded. "I see. I take it the one calling gets left holding an empty bag?"

"You got it."

Chay offered, "Snipe actually are a marsh bird. But they don't come when called."

Luke dropped his head. "Sounds like a Jeremiah gag. He picked on me for being the little brother." He sighed but said no more.

They reached a stone marker in the center of the field. Micah and Tav examined it closely. They tipped it up to look at the end in the ground. Nothing. Tav called, "Luke. Chay. You two double-check this pillar. I don't see anything. I want to make sure you don't, either."

Chay, Grace, BB, and Quinn all investigated the column. There was a place on the face that looked as if it had been ground away, but no fish or Y could be seen. Rock chips and sand littered the area. Micah asked, "Ben, do you see anything on here?"

Ben rubbed his hand across the face of the post. He rubbed the scratched area several times but finally shook his head.

Tav made one last appeal. "Quinn, since you're with us, can you verify this column has no markings on it?"

Quinn stepped in and checked out the pillar. He rubbed it top to bottom. His eyes narrowed, and the monitor frowned. He stepped away. "I can verify there are no markings on this pillar. I also suggest a course correction." His eyes sparkled. "Y, you ask? A guess."

Tav and Micah exchanged knowing looks. Micah smirked. "Y, of course. We definitely will play the hunch."

BB looked lost, but he finally nodded. "Right. Why would we keep going the way we are? Y not?"

Tav pulled out the laminated card markers and dug out the directions. "235 South. Right. All we need is the fish. Then we get more information about the location of the treasure."

Quinn raised his eyebrows. "So, I said."

The group went fishing.

* * *

Tav and Micah led the column. Quinn, BB, and Ben took the center. Luke, Chay, and Grace brought up the rearguard.

Micah reminded the group, "Eyes open. Looking for a fish."

BB kicked a weed. "Why? Quinn will tell us where it is."

Tav corrected the young man's misconception. "No. Quinn will tell us if it's been moved, or faked, or if someone has otherwise cheated. We could miss it on our own, and he won't say a word."

Quinn smirked. "True."

Micah added, "His job is to ensure a level playing field. Not root for one team or another. Much as we want him to pull for us."

Quinn laughed. "I would if I could. But I would be cheating."

BB suggested, "But if you like us…"

"No."

Ben gave an exaggerated sigh, shifted his backpack, and marched forward. Quinn pointed. "Take a lesson from your brother."

BB repeated Ben's shifting of his pack. "He's not really my brother. We been together since he was a baby, so he may as well be. But he isn't kin."

Micah drifted back to be closer to the discussion. "Where are your parents, BB?"

"Don't know. No one would tell me. I had to be four, five maybe, when I got taken to live with Petey. There were a few others, but they came and went. I think they got adopted. Girls, mostly. But no one wanted me. And no one wanted Ben. Two different times people adopted him, but they brought him back. Said he was stupid. Dumb. Wouldn't talk. Wouldn't make no noises at all. They didn't want a defective baby. So, he lived with Petey and me."

Micah bit his tongue. So much he wanted to blurt out. Like "I'll take you. Both of you." "You can come live with me." "I'll be your brother." He would not make promises he could not keep. *Lord, You know. If You want me to adopt them both, You'll have to work it all out. All of You and none of me. Because it's how it has to be.* Micah resumed his place with Tav at the head of the column.

An hour later, the sky began to cloud. It went from bright blue to threatening gray. Storm clouds built on the western horizon. The team crossed a clearing where another crumbling ruin lay ahead. A home? A house, anyhow. There were the remains of a garden. Overgrown yard ornaments dotted the area. What might once have been fountains now looked like mounds. The stone underneath peeked through in patches.

Tav stopped and waited until the rearguard caught up. "We'll set up camp here. If the weather gets bad, we've got some shelter."

Luke muttered, "If the place doesn't fall in on us."

Micah shrugged. "You can always sleep in the rain."

Luke ducked his head. "Eh. We'll see which is worse if the storm unloads."

As the group unloaded their packs, Ben began digging around the shrubs covering the concrete structures. He pulled at the trailing vines and exposed a Venus figure pouring water from a bucket. Or poured water when water ran. Ben immediately covered her up again.

Micah chuckled. "Not into art, huh, bud? Me neither."

Ben moved to uncover a second creation with a generous basin. The water feature looked like an idealized fish spouting water from its mouth. Ben's eyes grew wide. He grabbed Micah's hand and pulled him. Micah nodded. "Yeah, I see it. It's a…" Micah stopped. He yelled, "Fish! Ben found the fish!"

Everyone gathered to look. Tav patted Ben's shoulder. "Good job, Ben. Thank you. That's great." Tav retrieved the card. "Last course. 280 West."

Chay objected. "But the fish is headed in the opposite direction. It's looking east."

"But its body lines up with the point on the compass. We head west."

Chay and Grace exchanged glances. Chay shook her head in disgust. "No wonder we weren't getting anywhere."

Grace buried her head in her hand. "I'm surprised we found you boys." She stopped. "You men."

Luke grinned. "Well, I'm glad we could help out. You've made this trip enjoyable."

Tav added, "And kept us fed. That's worth half the gold as it is."

Grace chuckled. "Let's find the treasure first. Then we can worry about divvying it up."

BB glanced west. "Shouldn't we go find it now? Before someone else gets there?"

Tav pointed to the darkening skies. "We'd be heading into the storm. I know. We all want to find the loot and head home." Tav's head jerked. "Wait. How do we find our way back to the river? I'm not big on the idea of simply reversing the paths." He eyed Quinn. "Or is it part of the 'directions to follow'?"

Quinn smirked. "Wondered when you would ask." The monitor sat leaning against a semi-standing brick wall. "I have the coordinates to the beach. We're less than a day away from the starting point."

Tav pulled his fist back. "Yes!" He stopped. "Not exactly much to go back to. But if we find the money, maybe I can quit two of my jobs."

The group took seats around the shell of a house. Micah noted the expression on BB's face fall. He guessed what the boy might be thinking. "BB."

The boy turned to him. "What?"

"If the counties can work out their differences, I'd like to apply to be your guardian. You and Ben."

BB gave Micah the side-eye. "Why?"

"Because you saved our lives. You and Ben both. I care about Ben. I'd like to care for both of you." Micah lowered his head. "But the logistics need to be taken care of. Unless anyone objects, I'll keep you with me until then." *Objects? Like Mother? Lord, You'll have to deal with her. Show me what you want me to do.*

Quinn quoted, "'What pleases God is to look after widows and orphans in their need.'" He cocked his head. "Is your mother a widow?"

Micah's eyes flared. "No. She's not a widow. She says my father abandoned her." Micah shrugged. "I guess she's a type of widow."

Quinn pulled up a weed and began stripping it into pieces. "Not necessarily. If she could work to support you, she isn't."

Tav threw in his opinion. "Your mother could work. She chooses not to. She put you to work to support her."

Micah picked up a rock and threw it. "She's sick."

"In the head, maybe."

Micah's head jerked up. "Wait a minute."

Tav held up both hands. "It's the truth, Mick. We all know it. Your mother is as capable of working as I am. I've seen her around town while you're working. She's not disabled, and she's not sick. Other than being mentally ill for putting you through what she has. You know it, too. Except she's got you tied up in guilt with the 'worse than a non-believer' misquote."

Grace added, "Listen to him, Mick. He's telling the truth. Being a widow doesn't entitle someone to enslave their children. Not in this day and age. We're not helpless."

Chay grinned. "Absolute truth. Pity the man who thinks he has to 'take care' of me." She glared at Luke with a smile underneath.

Confirmation? I'm taking it as such. Lord, help me know what to do.

Micah chewed the inside of his cheek. He eyed Tav. "I'll work on it. Right now, we should make a shelter for the evening. And find someplace to light a fire. It will be a wet, cold night if we don't."

The team set about hanging covers to create a wind and water break. BB and Ben scrounged dry wood for a fire. Micah pulled out the coffee pot to serve as a cooking vessel. They turned the dried meats into a passable stew with water and some spices from Grace's kit. No one complained, anyhow.

Just after dinner, the rain came in. With it, wind and cold. The group huddled near the fire. Ben shivered whenever lightning flashed. BB tried to assure him, "The lightning won't reach you, bud. We're safe in here."

Micah watched Ben and thought he knew what the problem might be. "It's not the flash that scares him. The flash means the thunder will follow. I think he's afraid of the noise."

Ben buried his head in Micah's shoulder. Tav touched the boy's arm. "When Luke was little, I used to tell him the angels were bowling." The man looked at BB. "Does he know what bowling is?" Tav stopped. "Do you?"

BB snorted. "We may live back in the woods, but we're not totally ignorant. Yeah, we know what bowling is."

Tav exhaled. "Sorry. Sometimes I use a reference people haven't heard before. Makes it tough to get the joke if you don't know the allusion."

Micah snickered. Seemed to happen a lot with Tav.

Bowling angels didn't help Ben's courage. But the thunderstorm passed quickly. The sun came out again. Long enough to cast a golden light on the countryside.

Micah decided it would be best to take a trip to the trees before nightfall. He walked a ways from the remains of the house. Two small hills or humps faced away from the forest. They looked like blast berms, built to direct explosions away from targets. Easily ten feet tall, they were covered in earth and grass. So much so they looked like small hills dropped in the middle of the house area. But why would there be such things in the middle of a homestead? It didn't make sense. As Micah passed the first one, he noted a door. A door in the side of a hill? How did that work? And why?

Micah tried to pull the door open. It stuck, refusing to move. Too much dirt around the opening. He looked at the house, then at the hump. Maybe the house didn't have refrigeration when it was built. Perhaps the door led to a cool area where they could keep food fresh. Or fresher, anyhow.

Satisfied he'd discovered the reason for the hump's existence, he started back to join the group. He passed the second door, stopped.

In the half-light, Micah made out carvings in the sideposts. Ichthus. Pointing down.

His being quieted. Did he see the prize? Could it be so close? Should he tell the others? He looked over and saw Quinn staring at him.

The monitor wore an enigmatic smile. His eyes twinkled. He raised his eyebrows. Tipped his head toward the others. Shook it. Very slightly.

Micah acknowledged Quinn's instructions. He would keep the secret until the morning. There would be plenty of light. Who knew how deep they would have to dig, how much dirt they would have to move? Better to wait. Let everyone get a good night's sleep.

Except Micah. The thought of finishing the quest excited him. But he laid down near the fire, stretched out, and called, "Night, people. See you all in the morning."

Quinn suggested, "How about a word, Mick?"

Micah choked, began again. "'Lord, You knew us before we were born. You know every hair on our head. You know all our days. You know the plans you have for us. You ask we trust You as a good Father. Keep us always in step with You. In Jesus's Name, amen."

"Amens" echoed around the fire. Micah didn't try to sort out who spoke and who didn't. Wasn't his job to determine it. Just his job to be faithful. *Keep me walking with You. Always.*

* * *

THURSDAY—WEEK TWO

Micah got up with the dawn. He stirred the fire. Gathered water. Went to fill the pot with coffee. But a clunk in the can stopped him. A lump, the size of a quarter, rattled against the sides of the rapidly emptying can. He poured the grounds into a mug and looked. A white object slid out. Micah picked it up. Plastic on one side, metal on the other. He held it at eye level, turning it over and over. What was this thing?

Recognition dawned. His being went cold. Froze. His eyes narrowed focus. He'd never held one before, but he knew. He knew.

Quinn turned over. "Coffee ready yet?"

Micah could barely speak. "Look at this."

Quinn rose and strolled over to join him. "What?"

Micah handed the piece to him. "Is this…?"

Quinn took the item, rolled it around in his hand. "Where'd you find it?"

"In the coffee. Buried at the bottom."

An AirTag. Someone put a tracker on them. Spied on them. Knew where they were all the time.

Micah shook his head. Not possible. The device only worked when someone with a phone and Bluetooth came near the tag. The Knights lost their phones when the raft flipped.

But…other people hadn't. Quinn had his phone.

Micah watched Quinn. Watched the monitor hold the tag

in his hand. Hold it to his phone. Type information. Wait for the response. Swear. Proficiently.

Quinn held Micah's eyes. "I'm sorry, Mick. I am so sorry. My phone must have activated it when I visited you. The frequency pinged the owner. They knew your coordinates."

Micah nodded. Still numb. "And used it for what?"

"To send the shooter after you. Every time I showed up, they knew where you were."

Micah swallowed hard. "Not the first day."

"You had your phones until you went overboard. He could have tracked you downstream, then waited for the signal to reappear. Then it was a matter of following you. After that, it was all me."

"But Grace and Chay have phones, too. It wasn't only you. Race and Fly came in." He stopped. "Is that how Race knew where Grace was? Did he tag her, too?"

Quinn's eyes flared. He expressed a few more opinions, then nodded. "I would bet money on it. He tagged them the first day. Left the field to let them do all the dirty work. He showed up to throw them off the trail by thinking the cards alerted him. But all the time, there's a tag."

Micah closed his eyes. "Who tagged us?"

Quinn's voice grew soft. "I have the registry of who sold it and where. We'll back-trace it to its owner."

He knew. Micah knew. But he wanted the confirmation. "Where?"

"Wade."

Jeremiah's suburb. The shooter hadn't been after Ben. He'd been after Jeremiah.

Micah wanted to sink into the ground. Disappear. It wasn't enough someone killed Jeremiah. But it was a deliberate act. Cold-blooded murder. Someone hired a hitman. And they did their job. Sloppy. Not a high-powered affair. But adequate.

Quinn put his hand on Micah's shoulder. "We'll nail her, Mick. She won't ever see those boys again." He stopped. "Unless you can think of anyone else..."

Micah shook his head. "No. His folks loved him. He owed

them money, but he worked to pay them back. They wouldn't. Never."

Quinn nodded. "I needed to ask, son."

"I know." Micah's throat choked. "Can we not tell the others? Yet? Let them have this last day?"

Quinn squeezed Micah's shoulder. "Sure. We need Grace and Chay to look for a tag on their gear. But we don't have to say anything about this one."

"Thanks. I don't know why it makes it worse, knowing someone planned his death. But it does."

"I understand."

Micah's hands shook as he prepared the coffee. Would he ever not associate Jere's murder with the drink?

Maybe in a hundred years.

The team woke. Ben ran to Micah and hugged him as he did every morning. The boy stepped back and studied Micah. Micah smiled. "Hey, bud. You sleep well last night?" The usual routine.

The second long, hard hug wasn't. Micah laid his head on Ben's. "Thanks, Ben."

Ben bowed his head once. Walked over to hug Tav. And Luke. And Grace. And Chay. Finally, he skipped over to Quinn. He stood still and tall in front of the monitor, a soldier ready for inspection. Quinn smiled at him, laid his hand on Ben's head, and laughed. "Good man, Ben. Ready for action. How 'bout we eat first?"

Ben nodded over and over. And over. Micah smiled. "I guess breakfast gets the Ben seal of approval."

"I guess it does."

Quinn called Grace and Chay over. "I'm concerned about how Race knew where to find you."

Chay grumbled, "So am I."

Grace shrugged. "It was the cards. But I gave them to him, so we shouldn't have any more trouble with him."

Quinn shook his head. "The trackers in the cards are registered and encoded. He shouldn't have been able to follow you with them. No one should be able to follow anyone in the game."

Grace tipped her head. "How then?"

Quinn probed. "What broke you up your first day?"

"We couldn't work together. Race insisted he knew the way but wouldn't even try to follow the symbols. We didn't get three hours out before you rescued us."

Quinn nodded. "Right. You think the fight might have been a little flimsy?"

Chay offered, "I thought so from the beginning. Like Race didn't want to go once he got to the landing point. It seemed weird since he was so gung-ho at the start."

Quinn continued his questioning. "Do you think Race would be the kind of person who wanted others to do the dirty work? Would he, say, put an AirTag in your gear so he could follow you from a safe, comfortable spot, and swoop in at the end?"

Chay and Grace's eyes both widened. Chay swore. "Why…" She stopped. "Sorry, Ben. That foul, corrupt, unscrupulous, shameless excuse for a human being." She grabbed her backpack. "He insisted we all have these keychain fobs on our packs." Chay ripped the offending tag from her bag and handed it to Quinn.

Quinn waited as Grace ripped hers off as well. The monitor turned the fobs over and exposed the AirTags. "He's been tracking you. I imagine when you joined with the Knights, he needed to check on you and see which way you went."

Grace growled through clenched teeth. "And picked a fight so I'd throw him out. Which I did." She sighed. "And I thought I had been the hero."

Tav put his arm around her. "You were. I don't care if he left voluntarily. Your threat was real. It scared me, and I'm on your side."

Grace chuckled. "Thank you, Tav." She cocked her head. "Are you going to tell us what Tav stands for? Is it really your name? Your birth name?"

Tav hemmed. "When this is over, I'll tell you. For now, leave it the way it is."

Grace kissed him on the cheek. "And I love you for it."

Chay turned away and pretended to gag. "Mom! You're old enough to be his mother. Stop!"

Grace chuckled. Tav shook his head. Grace got busy and divided the remaining MREs. "They're all gone." She eyed Quinn. "Unless you can arrange a food drop, we're done."

Quinn chuckled. "I'm not responsible for feeding the masses."

Micah pointed, "Unless I'm wrong, the mound there is a root cellar." He pronounced the oo as in "foot."

Chay cocked her head. "Excuse me? A what?"

"A root cellar. You know. A place they kept roots."

"You mean a root cellar." She pronounced the double oo as "boot."

"No, it's root. You don't say 'boot ball.' You say 'football.'"

"And you don't say the point was 'moot.' You say the point was 'moot.'"

Tav whistled. "Hey, can you two gammarians quit? I don't care how you pronounce it. All I care about is, are there veggies in there?"

Micah bowed to Chay, spreading his arms wide. She curtsied in return. Micah addressed Tav's question. "Not sure they'll be fit to eat, but there might be something worth looking for."

The group walked to the door. Tav pointed to the ichthus on the doorposts. He stared at the fish fountain, then the doorposts. His eyes widened. "Mick…"

Micah nodded. "Yeah, I think so."

Tav turned to Quinn. "Is it? Is it really?"

"One way to find out." Grace and Chay pulled out their flashlights and the lantern. Tav, Luke, Grace, and Chay all combined to ram the door open.

Steps led down into the hillside. The temperature dropped twenty degrees. Spider webs lined the ceiling of the cellar. Tav started forward, stopped. He turned to Grace. "Would the archeologist prefer to see the artifacts *in situ* before they are disturbed by grave robbers?"

He caught himself, hung his head. "No graves."

Grace smiled sadly. "No graves. Come on. We'll go together."

Tav turned to Micah. "Get the shovel. We might need it."

Micah retrieved the shovel. The group started down. All except BB. Micah eyed the young man. "Is there a problem?"

"Yeah. I don't like dark underground places. They get too close, you know?"

"I understand. You can keep watch up here. Call out if something or someone gets near the place."

BB looked relieved. "Thanks, Mick. Uh…you won't tell the others, will you?"

"Our secret." Micah joined the others and entered the dank cellar.

Spacious enough to hold eight people easily, timber joists and supports made the room at the bottom safe from collapse. Micah addressed Grace. "Tornado shelter?"

"Probably. Also, a place for vegetables in the winter. Which there don't seem to be any of."

Tav shrugged. "Too dark to grow much down here."

Micah set the shovel into the ground closest to the back wall. "Any likely spots we want to try?"

Luke complained, "You mean we have to dig up the whole basement?"

"If it's worth doing…" Tav corrected his brother.

Micah addressed Quinn. "How deep do we have to dig? Wouldn't a metal detector be handy?"

"What did I tell you at the beginning?"

"All we needed was the camp shovel."

"That's all you need."

Tav took the spade and drove it into the ground at the center of the space. He pulled it out and repeated the action. Over and over in a straight line from the middle to the wall. He duplicated the pattern to the opposite wall. He quartered the room to no avail.

Luke took the shovel and mirrored Tav's action on the

diagonal. A star began forming. Chay followed Luke. Grace followed Chay. Ben begged for the shovel from Grace. She hesitated. "I don't know, Ben. The ground is kind of hard."

He hung his head and stuck out his lower lip. Grace laughed. "Fine. You dig where you want."

Ben studied the patterns on the floor, then went behind the stairs. He disappeared in the dark. Grace grabbed her light and followed him. Ben jumped on the spade but couldn't penetrate the dirt more than an inch. He jumped again and again but made no headway. Luke stepped up. "Here, little guy. Let a heavyweight do it. You pick the area, and I'll dig it for you."

Ben paced back and forth, pounded his foot on the ground. He dug his heel in, mashed the dirt around, then stepped back.

Luke grinned. "I got it. I'll try right there."

But "right there" produced nothing. Micah sat on the next-to-the-bottom step. It shifted slightly. Micah looked down. The riser wasn't fastened in like the others. It slid forward. Micah's eyes widened. He yelled, "Luke, give me the shovel."

Luke came around to see what Micah wanted. Micah jumped to his feet. He took the shovel and forced the stair forward. It jerked, protested, and finally creaked along, leaving a gap. Micah pried at the bottom riser. It copied the second step. Once they were removed, there became room to probe the space below the treads. Micah handed the shovel to Tav. "You do it."

Tav shook his head. "You've kept us going. You should have the pleasure."

Chay stomped forward. "Give me that thing. You two will argue all day." She grabbed the shovel and jumped on the blade.

A loud "chunk" rewarded her efforts. Chay crowed. "We hit something!"

She handed the shovel to Luke. He gave it to Tav. Tav stepped into the work and shoveled the object. In ten minutes, an oversized banker's box sat on the floor of the shelter. Micah yelled up, "BB! We've got a box! Come to the top of the stairs."

BB peeked through the opening but remained in the sunlight. "What kind of box?"

"A treasure box! I don't know."

Tav laid his hand on the top. "We're about to find out."

Pulling the top off required another five minutes of concerted effort. But in the end, it slid up and off. And the team gazed at their prize.

The box held gold coins. Hundreds of them. Thousands, maybe? A million? A paper with a handwritten note lay on top of the coins.

Tav moved the paper aside. He clutched the coins. Pulled them up. Looked at them. His face fell. He stared at Quinn and gasped, "They're fake! They're not even metal!"

Micah's stomach dropped. Luke's face turned beet red. Grace and Chay both looked devastated.

Quinn nodded. "Exactly right." He sat on the steps and faced the team. "Do you have any idea how much gold weighs? If each coin weighed one gram, you'd have one million grams. Or a thousand kilograms. Roughly one ton of gold. Are you prepared to carry that much gold anywhere?"

The team grew quiet. Very quiet. Quinn wasn't finished. "Now, suppose you could move a ton of gold. How are you going to protect yourselves from every bandit in the world who gets wind of what you have?"

Quinn settled on the step. "The paper you shoved aside? Try reading it."

Tav picked it up. Grace held her flashlight over the words. Tav read aloud, "You have found my treasure. Your reward is being kept safe at the Woodman's Bank in Centralia. Your monitor has the information you need to redeem your prize. My requirement for a four-person team still stands. All four members of the team must present themselves at the bank to be awarded your monies. I appreciate the teamwork and cooperation necessary to complete this quest. Congratulations. Signed, Warren Q. Magary."

Tav added, "There's a date and a seal." He extended his hand to Quinn. "Thank you. We would not be here without you."

Quinn shrugged. "Eh. That's what the monitor does."

BB called from the doorway, "I see two guys walking this way. One of them has a rifle on his shoulder."

Quinn pointed to the papers. "I would suggest you find a place to secure those."

Tav looked around, yelled, "BB. Throw down Ben's pack."

BB complied. "Why?"

"Because no one will believe we'd trust a kid with something this important."

BB added, "Especially a 'dumb kid.' Which is what they all think he is." He threw the pack down. Micah inserted the papers into the backpack and handed it to Ben to put on. Micah put a hand on Ben's shoulder. "Which we know he's not. Not in the least."

BB chuckled. "And I got the bruised shin to prove it."

The group climbed the steps to meet Race and Fly. Quinn was the last man to come up the stairs, a shade behind the others. Micah thought he saw Quinn arrange something on top the coins. Maybe. Maybe not.

The two intruders came up to the house and smirked. "So, found the treasure, did you?"

Tav nodded. "Oh, we found something. Not what we expected, but we found something."

"We'll take it from here."

Tav waved his hand. "Go right ahead."

Race's eyes narrowed. He lowered his rifle and pointed it at the team. "Fly, go check what's in the cellar. Bring it here."

The team fanned out around Race but moved slowly. No one gave him a reason to start shooting. Grace and Chay might think the rifleman incapable of killing anyone, but Micah wasn't sure. And wasn't going to take chances.

Fly came back up the steps as fast as he went down. He held a fistful of the pretend coins and a packet with writing on it. "It's fake. It's all fake."

Race grabbed the packet and tore it open. He read it to himself, hurled it to the ground. He stomped the paper. Race pointed his weapon at Quinn and snarled, "You. You were in charge. Where is the money?"

Quinn shrugged. "What did the paper say?"

"I asked you where the money is." Race extended the rifle toward Quinn. "Tell me. Now."

Fly picked up the paper and read it aloud. "Teams of four only. Verified to have fulfilled all requirements. Sorry for your luck."

Race reversed the end of his gun and swung the butt at Quinn. The monitor caught the weapon and forced it to the ground. Quinn swung a fast right cross and decked Race, pulling the rifle from Race's hands. Race sprawled on the ground, grabbing at his jaw. Quinn beat the gun against the doorpost. There came a satisfying "chunk," and the weapon flew into two pieces.

Quinn threw the barrel after the stock. "Pick it up, take it, and leave. You've got twenty-four hours to be off this property before you're arrested and thrown in jail. Now move." Quinn eyed Fly. "That goes for you as well. Go."

Fly helped Race to his feet and headed away from the farmhouse. They disappeared behind the treeline, headed west.

Micah led the team in a deep and repeated bow to Quinn's superiority. "Bravo! Bravo! Even if you can't really order him off. At least he believed you."

Quinn snickered. "Who says I can't?"

Grace cleared her throat. "It's government land. You said so yourself."

"Yes, but the previous owners maintained the right to use it when they wanted for special purposes. Like this treasure hunt. Mr. Magary secured those rights to himself and his posterity in perpetuity." Quinn smiled. "As his designated and duly appointed representative, I have the authority to toss him out."

Micah grinned. "And you did so very clearly."

Quinn cautioned, "I have the authority. The power is another matter. If he refuses to go, I'd have to tie him up and physically remove him. Which makes him a danger to us yet."

Tav pointed to the cellar. "Do we take the box with us or leave it here?"

"You can leave it for now. We'll send a team to clean up the remains."

Micah stared at the monitor for several minutes. He called, "Ben…let me see those papers in your pack for a moment."

Ben stripped off his pack. Micah dug out the letter and reread the signature. "Warren Q. Magary." He eyed Quinn. "The Q wouldn't stand for Quinn, would it?"

"Why would you think so?"

"'We.' You've talked about being part of this game and its organization. It's a logical question."

Quinn jerked his head to the side. "Logical, maybe. The Q stood for Quincy."

"But was Warren your grandfather?"

Quinn's eyes sparked. "Let's say not."

"Because he wasn't, or you just don't want to say?"

"Yes."

Micah shook his head. "Fine. Keep your secrets. All except one. How do we get out of here?"

Quinn pulled up his phone. "Here's our route back to the rocks where we started. Take us about a day. You'll be home by tomorrow evening." He smiled at Grace. "And yes, we'll do a meal drop. We don't have a safe place to land a chopper, or we'd ferry you all out of here."

Tav grew solemn. "Can you take us to Erskine first?"

Quinn nodded. "Yes. Of course. We'll make sure you're there before Jeremiah's folks arrive. The estate is providing transportation for them to come to Erskine. It will transport all of you home."

Grace touched Tav's arm. "We'd like to come, too." Chay nodded. Grace continued, "We didn't know him long, but we were part of the team." She stopped. "If that's okay."

Tav closed his eyes. His voice tightened. "Once a Knight, always a Knight. We'll make sure you're there."

Quinn picked up his backpack. "Let's head out. I'll phone in a 'to-go' order, and they can drop it where we'll be."

BB quipped, "Can we order pizza?"

Quinn shoved the boy. "You'll be lucky if they don't drop us more MREs."

"I'd take Grace's snake over those."

Grace smiled as she picked up her pack. "Maybe we can oblige. I saw a few slithering past on the way here."

The team gathered their gear and began the walk back.

* * *

ERSKINE—THREE DAYS LATER.

Micah paced around the family waiting room. Neatly upholstered wingback chairs lined the walls. Two matching couches. Tav paced the opposite direction. Luke sat against the wall, staying out of the way. Micah checked the clock for the tenth time. Still no word to say Mr. and Mrs. Acosta had arrived to see their son.

Tav groaned. "This is killing me. Why is it taking so long for them to get here?"

Micah guessed, "Maybe they couldn't find anyone to watch the boys?"

Luke harumphed. "In their family? There's always someone available. Jere's got three brothers and two sisters. Those boys will never lack for a sitter."

Tav flopped down in a chair. "Must be traffic. Has to be."

Footsteps and voices sounded in the hall. Micah looked through the window in the door. Mr. and Mrs. Acosta, sober and stern, walked up the passageway. Behind them, Shelly Acosta marched. Mascara ran down her cheeks, her eyes puffy and red.

Micah's fists clenched along with his jaw. He seethed, "Shelly came."

Tav swung on the door and stared out the window. He stepped back. "Of all the—"

Luke grabbed him. "Stop. Right there. I bet they haven't

charged her yet. Maybe they're waiting on evidence. Or the shooter to confess. Be cool, Tav. You can't blow this. I'd be right there with you if I knew she'd already been convicted. But she hasn't. We have to be cool."

Micah lifted the only prayer he could. *Lord, forgive me. I can't forgive her yet. Forgive me. Hold on to Tav, and Luke, and me. Give us Your peace. And strength. Hold the Acostas in Your arms.*

The door opened. A sheriff's deputy escorted Jeremiah's parents into the room. Tav hugged them. Micah followed, then Luke. Shelly moved to Tav, but he stepped away. His voice cracked as he faced her. "It's too soon. Too close. I'm sorry."

Shelly protested. "Too close? What about me? You don't think this is hard for me? I tried to make up with him before the four of you left, but he wouldn't say anything. He—"

Micah took Shelly's arm. "Not the time, Shelly. Give Mama and Papa space."

She turned a sweet smile on Micah. "Of course, Micah. You always have been so caring."

Quinn walked in behind the entourage. He caught Micah's eye. Motioned to Shelly. Micah nodded a half inch. Quinn nodded back.

Chay and Grace stepped in as well, followed by BB and Ben. Shelly's eyes widened, then narrowed. She fumed under her breath, "Who is that?"

Micah kept his tone even. "Friends we made on the trip."

"Why do they get to be here? I thought this was 'family only.'" She sneered the words. "I fought to be allowed to come, even though I'm family. I'm his wife. They shouldn't be here."

Micah bit back all the words he wanted to say. He swallowed hard, prayed harder, and said, "Jeremiah wanted them to be here." *I'm sorry, Lord. But it would be true if he could have a say in it. He wouldn't want any of us to be here, including himself. But since he is, they are.*

Shelly's head whipped around. "He said he wanted them here for *this?*" Her voice rose, preparatory to a full-blown scene.

Quinn stepped up and took Shelly's elbow. "Ms. Acosta?

May I have a word with you?"

She stared him up and down. After a second glance, she raised her nose and sniffed. "Of course."

Quinn led her out of the room.

There was an audible exhale from several corners of the room. The deputy motioned to a chair. "Please. Sit. We'll bring your son in so you can see him."

Autopsy. They did an autopsy. How will he look? Will they have cleaned him up? Left him…

The door at the far end of the room opened, and a gurney trollied in. Jeremiah lay stretched out as if peacefully sleeping. No blood. No wounds. No bruises. Just Jere. Fully dressed, sleeping. Forever.

Mrs. Acosta fell across Jeremiah's chest. Her husband leaned beside her. They held one another. Both reached up to touch Jeremiah's face, his arms, his chest. Both wept aloud.

Micah, Tav, and the rest of the team stood in the rear and waited. Who hugged who didn't matter. Whose tears fell most, or not at all, didn't matter either. Micah grieved. And prayed. *God, please. Hold the Acostas. Hold all of us. We know You know grief. Send Your love to fill the emptiness. Send Your hope to still the hurt. Come as our Father, Who makes all things right. Not now, but one day. It's the only healing there is. Thank You, Lord.*

Eventually, the Acostas rose. The funeral director introduced them to the team members they didn't know. Mr. and Mrs. Acosta hugged one and all and left. Grace, Chay, BB, and Ben paid their respects. Quinn came in after the women and children left. Tav, Micah, and Luke gave the man time with Jere. They would wait to the end.

And then it was the end. Tav lay his hand on Jeremiah's chest. His voice cracked, and he whispered, "We created a ceremony, a protocol, a ritual for everything. But not this. Never this."

Tav leaned forward and kissed Jeremiah on the cheek. "I love you, brother. Hold a place for us at the table."

He stepped away. Luke grasped Jere's hand, held it, kissed his forehead. He moved aside.

Micah laid his hand on Jeremiah's head. He whispered, "Into Your hands, we commend our brother. Love you, Jere."

The three Knights huddled up and cried.

* * *

Quinn waited outside the door. The Acostas would ride back to Weld with Jeremiah. Quinn pulled Micah aside after the goodbyes were said. "Need a word with you, Mick." He motioned to Tav and Luke. "They can listen, too. Remember I told you the name Andres sounded familiar?"

"Yeah?"

"I looked it up. Seems there was a missing family by the name of Andres. About eighteen years ago. A man who worked with us went out on assignment. When he came home, his family had disappeared. No trace. He spent a year looking for them and finally found them. Because of the nature of his work, he couldn't force a reconciliation." Quinn raised his eyebrows. "You'll need to trust me on why not."

Micah's soul stilled. Something inside knew. He knew. Micah dropped his hands to his side and stood stone-still. And waited. And listened.

Quinn continued, "So he did what he could do. He wrote letters. Every week, he wrote to his estranged wife and his two sons. One letter to each of them. He sent them money. He bought the boys savings bonds. Birthday cards. Graduation cards. He never missed a week of writing. He loved his boys. Loved his wife. But she threatened to…" Quinn trailed off. He studied the floor, studied the wall, met Micah's eyes. "She threatened to blow his cover and put his and a great many coworkers' lives in danger if he ever came to the house where they lived. He thought the letters he sent would let the boys know how much he loved them and wanted to be part of their lives."

Micah whispered, "But she never gave them to the boys, did she?"

Quinn shook his head. "No. They were all returned to sender. Of course, someone kept the money he sent his wife.

But anything addressed to the boys came back to him as 'undeliverable as addressed.' He kept every letter."

Micah sank down in a chair. He thought he'd cried all his tears for Jeremiah. He was wrong. A well still existed. He couldn't muster any volume to his words. "Is he alive?"

"Oh, of course. Of course, he is. I wouldn't have told you otherwise. He wants to meet with his son." Quinn put an arm on Micah's shoulder. "If his son wants to meet with him."

Micah stood. He looked at Tav and Luke. Tav warned, "You better meet with him. I'll run you out of the Knights if you don't. You understand, soldier?"

Micah smiled through the pain in his gut. "Yes, sir. I understand." He turned back to Quinn. "Is he here?"

"In the chapel. You want an escort?"

"No." Micah breathed out. "I'll do this alone."

Quinn clapped him on the shoulder. "Good man."

Tav and Luke both slapped him on the back. Micah settled himself, walked to the chapel. He opened the door.

An older man sat in the front pew. A lighted cross rested on a wooden altar below a stained-glass painting of the moon and stars. Creation had been put on display for those who needed a different perspective than death.

The man turned as Micah walked in. Micah's breath caught as he looked at the face he saw in the mirror every morning. Older, more drawn, grayer, but still the same face.

The man stood. He held several ten-by-fifteen manila envelopes. He stepped out of the pew and approached Micah.

Micah went numb. One thought. One word. "Dad?"

The man laid the envelopes down on a side table. He opened his arms wide. "Mick."

Micah buried himself in his father's arms. "Dad. Thank You, Lord. Dad." Micah's knees wobbled. Too much emotion for one hour. Maybe for a lifetime.

Kurt Andres supported Micah to a pew. The two sat together. Arms around each other. Not speaking. Letting one-size-fits-all tears wash away years of separation. Eventually, Kurt rose and retrieved the manila envelopes. He shook the contents out onto Micah's lap.

Letters. Eighteen years' worth of letters. All marked "Undeliverable as addressed. Return to sender." All refused by the stone-cold warden of the mailbox. Kurt picked up a handful. "There are savings bonds in here. Some well past maturity. This should help you going forward."

Micah could do nothing but shake his head. "Why? Why would she… Why?"

"Your mother is a sick woman. I had assignments. Didn't always make it home in her idea of a 'timely fashion.' She resented it. Then she resented me. We agreed we would work it out when I got back from the last job. I didn't know she moved you and Paulus the next day. When I found you, she threatened to expose me and my people. She's still threatening. But we've finally figured out the work around."

Micah looked at his dad. "Paulus? Did you ever find him? He walked out…"

"It's his greatest regret, Micky…Mick. You have to understand. Everyone has a breaking point. He reached his."

Anger. Bitterness. Rage. Emptiness. Micah ran the gamut of emotions in a moment's time. "Where is he?"

"Some town in Canada—hard to pronounce and harder to spell. He'd like to see you when you decide the time is right. If you decide."

In the end, there remained one question. "What do I do now?"

Kurt emphasized, "*We* confront your mother." He stopped. "If you want. I'm assuming you want a relationship again. Do you?"

Micah hugged his dad. "Never doubt it. Never. I love you. I never stopped." *Which is why it still hurt so much.*

"We confront her. With the evidence. How she responds will tell us what to do next."

"Right." *She's not a widow.* The thought exploded in his mind. *I don't have to take care of her. I'm free!*

Micah smiled. Laughed. Giggled.

Pull it together, Andres. Micah sobered up. "Yes. We will

confront her together." He caught his dad's eyes. "I'm going to adopt Ben and BB." He touched the letters. "These will help."

Dad nodded. "From what Quinn tells me, they saved your life. I owe them for that. If you can't adopt them, I will."

Micah sighed. Drained. He was drained. There were no more emotions unless peace could be considered an emotion. Peace, he had in abundance. And gratitude.

It didn't replace the sorrow. Sorrow stayed locked in its own compartment. To be revisited soon. But for now, peace reigned.

* * *

HOME—TWO DAYS LATER

Micah drew a deep breath, trying to stop the jitters in his gut. Calm. He would be calm. He would be polite. He would be firm. He would be anything but the scared little boy about to confess doing something naughty to his mother.

Dad's warm hand on Micah's shoulder helped. "You can do this, Micky." Dad stopped, corrected himself. "Mick. I'll get it. I will."

Micah laughed. "If Micky is the worst you call me, I'll be happy." He settled his shoulders, pulled down his jacket, and stepped up to the porch.

His car sat in the driveway. His overused, beat-up twenty-year-old Honda Pilot. Why was it in the driveway? He'd left it on the street as his mother instructed. So the care workers would have a place to park. Luke picked him up the day they left. Someone moved it.

Not the chief worry. Too many other concerns right now. Except it may offer more proof of what went on. Of course, no care worker cars ever came. When he'd called the agency to figure the bill, they told him, "No charge." His mother canceled their service the day Micah left. Convenient.

Par for the course. Micah knocked. He'd lost his keys to the river when the raft flipped.

Mother came to the door. She wore a tailored jacket over a flowered silk blouse. Earrings adorned her ears. A matching gold choker completed the outfit. Obviously, she was headed out somewhere special.

She pulled the door open and stepped out onto the porch. "You're late, Iggy. The show starts…"

She trailed off. Her eyes swelled to twice their usual size. She gasped, spluttered, then stuttered, "Micah! What are you doing here?"

She ignored Dad as he stood behind Micah on a lower step. Micah moved aside so she could see him. Dad smiled. "Hello, Vera."

Mother's jaw dropped as Micah walked past her. "Thank you for opening the door. I lost my keys to the river. Dad, come in and have a seat."

Kurt followed Micah into the house and sat on the couch. Micah went to the refrigerator. "Drink?"

"Water, thanks."

Mother seethed as she stepped indoors. She glared at Kurt but addressed Micah. "How dare you bring a stranger into this house without my permission?"

Micah kept his hands from shaking. Challenging Mother was not something he dared do. Before now. But this was not the time to back down or show weakness. Strong. Be strong. "It's my house as well, Mother. I've been paying the mortgage for six years." He handed the glass with water and ice to Dad. His hand trembled only slightly. Dad smiled at him, and his eyes held his. *Be strong. Strong in You, Lord. Not my own strength. Give me Your words. No anger. Only truth. I can do this.*

Micah sat down at the dining table and held his mother's eyes. "And he's not a stranger. He's my father. You might remember him?"

Mother's face hardened. Micah saw the fire in her expression. "That man is not your father. Your father walked away from this family. You have no father."

Micah maintained the lead. He and Dad discussed it, and Micah would carry the conversation. "So, you always told me. Dad has a different story. He went on business, and you moved. And left no forwarding address."

"He lies. And he had no business to do. He chose to leave."

Micah shrugged. "We can argue the point until we're both blue. I'm more interested in why you felt it necessary to tell us we were abandoned when you left without telling him where you would be."

"Why would I? He abandoned us."

Micah felt his stomach tighten. "No, Mother. You moved. I have all the letters he wrote to me. To Paulus. All of them returned to sender."

She sneered. "Convenient. I'm sure they all—"

Micah cut her off. "Postmarked, Mother. Still sealed. You can't lie your way out of those."

"Lie?" Her voice grew cold. "You accuse me of lying? Your mother?"

"Did you?"

"Of course, I didn't lie. I protected you and your brother. This man abandoned—"

Micah cut her off again. "Not abandoned, Mother. You left. He tried to reestablish contact. You refused to let him. I've seen the police reports."

She snapped her head up. "What reports?"

"The missing persons reports he filed trying to find you. Us."

"He never—"

"So not only did Dad lie, the post office lied, and the police lied. Is there anyone else you'd like to accuse of falsehood in this?"

Mother crossed over and sat down at the table with Micah. "You don't know what it was like being the single mother of two young boys. There was no one to help me. I had to find work. I paid the bills. I managed the house. I —"

Micah stopped her. "Dad sent money for food and rent. He also sent money for child support. I saw those checks, too, Mother. Even after you moved. It took him six months to find you, but he did. He supplied for all your needs." Micah pointed to the gold jewelry his mother sported. "And many of your wants, apparently. When did you buy those, Mother?"

Mother went from fire to ice. "None of your business, boy. I don't have to answer to you. I provided for you. I gave you a roof over your head. Food to eat. Clothes to wear."

Micah corrected her. "All those provisions came from the money Dad sent you. While you lay sick in bed. Pretending to be sick, Mother."

Micah breathed in a prayer. *Help me. Please. No anger. No bitterness. Only truth.* "How long have you been able to walk on your own, Mother?"

She said nothing. Micah pushed the questions. "I worked part-time until high school to pay for your medicines and medical bills. I dropped out of high school to work full-time. And I slaved for you. Couldn't go anywhere or do anything because you needed someone to care for you. Bring you food and drink. Shop for you. Take you to doctors' appointments." His voice hardened. "Appointments I never attended. Only drove you, dropped you off, and came back. What did you actually do, Mother?"

"I was sick. I needed money for those doctors."

Micah wanted to keep his tone even. Needed to keep his tone even. Prayed, even. But he couldn't keep the tremor out of his words. "Where are the records for those visits, Mother? I want to see them."

"You have no right to demand anything from me. I am your mother."

"I paid for them. Six years I paid for them. I want to see the receipts. The records. If you deducted all those, that's tax fraud. I'm sure the IRS might be interested in seeing them, too."

Her tone switched. She became the wounded martyr. "Micah, why? Why are you doing this to me? I love you. I've done everything for you. I've been with you all of your life. This man walks in, and suddenly I'm the wicked witch? What happened to you on your trip? How did I lose the son I love?" She reached out and touched his hand. "Come back to me, Micky."

Micah closed his eyes. "You want to know what happened to me on my trip? I lost my best friend. I made friends with two boys I'm going to adopt. I got my father back. And I found out who I am." He opened his eyes. "All this despite you stealing my medicines."

Micah drew in a deep breath, let it out, and continued. "Whatever happened in the past is over. I am adopting two young boys. I'll be their guardian until we work out the formalities between the counties. But they will come live here with us."

Mother's eyes widened. "Adopt? Bring boys here? You will not! Never. This is my house. I will not share it with some stragglers you met while you neglected me."

"Neglected you? I took out a loan so you could have 24/7 care, Mother. And you discharged them before they ever came."

"Who told you such a lie?"

"The agency. I called to see what additional charges there might be. They said you sent the caregivers home and canceled the order."

"They had no right to tell you."

"I'm the one that placed the orders, Mother. They had every right."

"I'll sue them. They can't tell—"

"You do what you think you have to. I'm bringing Ben and BB home to live here."

"With what money? You're a self-employed drop-out. You have nothing to give anyone."

Peace flowed through Micah. Acceptance. Love. He smiled at his mother. "I have love, Mother. Which is more than you've shown me in years. I love these boys. I'm going to provide for them."

"Not here, you're not. Not in my house."

Micah nodded. "As you say. I'll buy my own place."

"With what? Who's going to loan you money enough to buy a house? Your father?" She made the word as much an insult as she could.

Micah glanced over at Dad. "No. I won't need his money. He offered, and I turned him down. I'm going to buy a house where he can live when he's in town. And maybe for when he retires."

Dad lowered his head. "You didn't tell me that part."

"Will you, Dad? Come when you can?"

"Of course." Dad lifted his head. "I love you, Mick." He smiled. "Got it right, finally."

Mother snarled. "So sweet. So endearing. And all of it is a lie. You have nothing. Everything here belongs to me. Leave if you choose, but you'll take nothing with you."

Micah stood. "I'll take what's mine." He headed to his bedroom. Mother jumped to her feet and slashed him across the face with her nails. "You'll take nothing! I own you!"

Micah felt the blood trickle down his face. He smiled. He laughed. "I got shot, I got burned, I got mugged. And you think a slap is going to stop me?" He stepped away, shaking his head.

Never turn your back on a crazy woman. Mother grabbed him from behind. She pommeled and pummeled and kicked and bit and slashed Micah. She swung her fists doubled into his head.

Micah refused to hit back. He ducked his head to avoid as many blows as possible, stepping away from her feet, but Mother would not stop.

Dad stepped in and grabbed Mother from behind. He held her arms at her sides and stayed clear of her kicks. She screamed, "I'll have you both arrested! This is battery! I'll have you thrown in jail."

Micah reminded her, "You attacked me."

She sneered, "No one will believe you. They always believe the woman."

"Unless there are witnesses."

"Who? Where?"

Micah motioned to the front window. Three neighbors stood in the yard watching the proceedings. Mr. Wilson, the neighbor on the left, waved. Sheepishly.

Iggy, Mother's friend, glared at Mother. She offered a tight-lipped smile. The third neighbor looked at the ground and shook her head.

Dad released Mother. Mother seethed, "You set me up! You—" She went off on a tirade of foul language that would have made Quinn blush. She gathered her hands into fists and pummeled Micah again before Dad could catch her. He restrained her and held her until the police arrived. All the while, Mother poured out her opinions of Micah, of Dad, of the witnesses, and any and all other persons she could think of.

The police sorted out the disturbance in short order. The paramedics who came verified Mother broke Micah's nose. They patched the cut beneath his eye and gave him a tetanus shot for good measure. The police escorted Mother downtown, where she would be booked for battery. Much as Micah didn't want to press charges, it was the only way he could get her out of the house. He wanted to ensure a few personal items remained safely in his possession. High school yearbooks. His six-inch silver-plated knight statue. The certificate on the wall Tav gave him when he joined the Knights. And photos taken from their last summer together before their senior year. He stared at the one of the four of them. Arm-in-arm, four faces laughing and smiling. The school's brightest and best ready to take on the world.

Well, there were only three now. Three originals. Tav, Luke, and Micah. Micah reminded himself the Knights now numbered eight. The Magary team had grown their numbers with the addition of Grace, Chay, BB, Ben, and Quinn. He tucked the photo, the certificate, and the knight into a small case. These would be the foundations for his new life. Loyalty. Friendship. The Knights of the Octagon.

Except maybe he'd get a round table…

EPILOGUE

Micah pulled at the tie around his neck. It helped to know both Tav and Luke suffered from the same malady. Luke muttered, "I hate ties."

Tav loosened his a notch. "Ditto. But for this ceremony, we can all be presentable."

Micah chuckled. "You think they got a tie on Quinn?"

"Doubtful. Very doubtful. He'll be in his khakis. Bet."

"No bet." Micah sighed. But inwardly. He wished Jeremiah could be here for this. His folks were picking up his prize on behalf of Jere's sons. The boys had been placed in the permanent custody of Jeremiah's brother and wife, Isaiah and Ruth Acosta. Jere made those arrangements the week before the rafting trip. Just in case, you know. You'll never have to do it. But just in case…

Micah returned to the present. He scrutinized BB and Ben in their slacks and shirts and pronounced them fit to be in official company. Five Knights walked down the hall to the ceremony room.

Tav murmured, "I hope this is short, to the point, and we get to get out of here."

"Amen to that." Luke threw in his support.

The hallway seemed to grow as they passed office after office down to the very end, where the conference room waited. Plus, all the official dignitaries and responsible agents and who knew who else would be there.

Tav opened the door and stood without entering. The look on his face made Micah step back away from the door. "What is it? What's wrong?"

Tav's eyes grew wide as he pushed the door open. The five Knights stepped inside. Cameras began taking pictures. A crowd of people—some standing, some sitting, one in a wheelchair—began applauding as they entered.

From the opposite side of the room, another door opened, and Grace and Chay entered. Grace wore a smart pants and jacket outfit, Chay a midi dress. Both women looked stunning.

Applause greeted them as well. From the center of the room, a man in a black suit stepped forward and shook hands with all the Knights. Micah saw Dad, as well as all the Acostas, standing in a group against the wall. Dad, finally safe from Mother's threats. With her attack on Micah, her accusations could be dismissed as those of a woman with an unsound mind. Not to be believed. Unstable, even. Tav and Luke's parents were nowhere to be seen.

Everything blurred after that. Welcomes. Speeches. Interviews. Questions. A chance to meet Mr. Warren Q. Magary (the man in the wheelchair). Quinn came out in full parade Marine Regalia. As he shook hands with Micah, he muttered, "You tell those clown brothers of yours there better not be a word of this ever. Got that?"

Micah swallowed his grin. "I got, I got it. Sir."

Quinn side-eyed him. "Boy…"

Micah dropped his hand to his side and signed, *No comments re Quinn in uniform. On your life.*

Tav and Luke gave the okay sign.

Then it was time. Mr. Magary addressed the assemblage. "When I created this little game in the seventies, I never dreamed it would take fifty years for the treasure to be found. I actually worried I wouldn't see a winner in my lifetime. But here you are." He nodded to the Knights, Chay and Grace, BB and Ben. He added, "And I know you lost a member of your team on the hunt. I mourn his absence as well. We are arranging to pass his portion of the treasure to his heirs."

He continued, "I have always been drawn to teamwork. To a collection of people working together for a common goal, for the common good. The monitors have reported that you seven committed yourselves to one another in an exemplary fashion. Indeed, over and above what would be expected with the stakes as high as they were. You started as individuals. You ended up as a team. You are to be congratulated for your conduct and gamesmanship."

Applause echoed around the room. Mr. Magary motioned to Quinn. The monitor picked up seven envelopes. He handed them out to the team. Each packet had a name engraved on it, one for each team member.

Micah forced his hands to his side. No tearing open the paper to see the figure inside. Exercise restraint. Decorum. He'd wait until after the affair ended. Then he'd rip it open.

But first, the receiving line. Smile. Say, thank you. Nod. Shake hands. Smile. Wash, rinse, repeat. Repeat. Repeat. Repeat.

Ben stayed beside Quinn through the reception. Safety. Micah envied the little guy. He'd love to hide behind the monitor and let Quinn field the questions. *I'm the adult. Act like it.* Smile.

Next came the dinner. No MREs. No frogs, either. Meat. Actual beef. Tender, succulent. Micah watched BB devour his and half of Ben's main dish. Ben, of course, passed it to BB. The youngest Knight still maintained the smallest appetite. He'd put on a few pounds since coming to civilization but was still too light in Micah's mind. Dessert, however, Ben did not share. Touch his sweet, pull back a nub. Micah grinned to himself. Expressive? Oh, you bet the boy could express himself.

After dinner came the dancing and mingling. Micah sat out. So did Tav. Micah got a kick from watching Quinn and Grace enjoy each other's company. Luke and Chay spent time with each other on the floor as well. Several young women found BB intriguing and invited him to dance. He didn't turn them down, either. Ben danced with older women or by himself. He did occasionally come between Quinn and Grace, Luke and Chay, or BB and his partners. No one seemed to mind.

Micah watched Tav's eyes. The First Knight seemed more relaxed with his brother and a woman keeping company. But he did keep his eye on the couple.

Micah leaned in to be heard above the music. "Luke seems to be enjoying himself."

Tav nodded. "He is. Got his dorm assignment, filled out his class schedule, and is all set to start school next month. I'm proud of him."

"I think he knows you are."

"I've told him enough times. He should be."

"I've told him, too. What about you? When do you start?"

"Next semester. I'll be half a year behind him."

Micah grinned. "Still giving him a head start?"

Tav turned to face Micah. "Now, what gives you that idea?"

"History."

Tav shrugged. "Maybe. Moving took some logistics. And working out the actual finances. I know what we have coming, but convincing loan companies to act on it was something different."

"Tell me about it. Once Mr. Magary put the award in writing, they had no more objections."

Luke and Chay swirled over to the table where Micah and Tav sat. Chay plopped down unceremoniously. Luke joined her. BB managed to duck any further dance partners and raced to the shelter of the team table. "Safe! I'm not moving." Ben slid in beside him. Both youngsters sat down in their places.

Chay grinned. "What an evening." She picked up her envelope. "When do you think it will be proper to open these?"

Tav suggested, "When your mom and Quinn quit dancing."

Chay's eyes twinkled. "That might be at dawn."

"Fine. I'll pay the band to take a break. Then your mom and Quinn can sit, and we'll open them together. We know what's in them. Quinn told us the Magary Group paid the taxes, so we all received the full $125,000. BB's and Ben's are in trusts, as are Jere's kids'."

Luke shook his head. "Knowing and seeing are different. I want to see the numbers."

The band ended the selection, and Quinn and Grace returned to the table. Quinn raised an eyebrow. "I wondered when you would all reassemble over here."

Grace laughed, "About time, too. Quinn and I were getting tired of supervising." She smiled at Quinn. "Though that was the most enjoyable supervision duty I've ever experienced."

Chay's jaw dropped. "Supervising? Supervising who?"

Quinn smirked. "Some information comes on a need-to-know basis. And you have no need to know."

Chay frowned. "I see how it is."

Micah fingered his envelope. "Can we open these now?"

Quinn nodded. His face became solemn. "Of course. I'm surprised you haven't before now."

"We wanted to do it as a team. We did everything else as a group."

Quinn smiled a straight-lipped smile. "Yes, you did."

Everyone picked up the marked envelopes. A silent count of four, and they all ripped the seal.

Stunned silence. Micah saw the figure. His eyes flared. His soul—and all the rest of him—went perfectly still.

Micah Andres. Awarded $125 000 for the finding of the Magary Treasure. All taxes paid.

Additional award: $500,000 for being a team player. Being willing to lay your life down for others. No greater love… Signed, Warren Quincy Magary.

P.S. This additional award is between you and your team. The IRS already knows about it. Beyond those parameters, it never happened. This is a figment of your imagination. Let your imagination guide how to use it well. Q.

Micah looked up at his team. All eyes reflected the same disbelief, awe, wonder, and amazement. All faces turned to Quinn. He raised a glass. Everyone followed suit. A silent four count and everyone drank.

If you enjoyed *Knights of the Octagon,* sign up for Colleen Snyder's newsletter to keep up with new books and projects. It will also give you a place to talk to the author directly. And she loves to talk to her readers. Trust me!
Emails will NOT be sold, shared, or used for any other purpose. Promise.
Go to: colleensnyderauthor.com and leave your email to sign up.
Also connect with her at Facebook, Colleen K. Snyder, Author.

Please enjoy this excerpt from Knights of the Octagon: MIA, coming soon from Winged Publications.

Micah's soul stilled as he stared hard at the email from his dad. *Practicing ASL. How do the letters look?*

Pictures of the hand gestures for the letters followed.

L. M. N. O. P. R. S. T. U. V…

No Q? The Q was missing.

Q was missing? Quinn was missing.

And Dad wasn't going through official channels to report it.

He emailed back *How long?*

Ten days. Lunch at Sadie's? One. Sending rep. Wendell Smothers. Green suit. Blue tie.

Micah looked at the clock. Ten o'clock. That gave him three hours to round up the Knights and assemble them at…who was Sadie this week? Micah gazed at the calendar. Fifth month, second week. He was. Three hours denoted urgency. Three hours meant drop what you're doing, cancel your plans, and gather. A Knight needed help. One for all, all for one. Right down to the dog.

Micah nudged Alabama. The oversized black lab sleeping under the desk came to life. She snorted, sneezed, stretched, and rose. Micah emailed back. *K. Love you.*

Maybe it seemed less than manly to end his emails with "Love you." The murder of Jeremiah Acosta, one of the founding Knights and Micah's best friend, was still too close to ignore. Tell your people you love them. Every chance you get. Because you never know when it might be the last chance.

Micah patted Alabama on the head. "Let's go, girl. I gotta round up the troops." The dog yawned and climbed up on the couch. She would wait for the command to follow him out the door.

Micah sent a group text to Tav and Luke. *Sadie's. One pm. N-O-P-R-S-T.*

Luke texted back. *K.*

Tav's response came moments later. *K. Final. Will be there when I'm done.*

Micah's eyes narrowed. That's not how the game was played. When one called, the group came together. Quinn was missing. Quinn needed help. None of them would be where they were if not for Quinn. They *owed* Quinn…

And Quinn would say, "I don't need help from a bunch of college boys. And girls. Stay in school. I'm fine."

Micah closed his eyes and prayed. *Lord, we formed the Knights under You. Show us what You want in this. You know where Quinn is and what he's doing. Direct my thoughts and my steps. And especially my words. Everything from You, Father. All from You. Amen.*

* * *

Micah watched the young man approach the house. Casual attire. Jeans, pullover shirt. Black suit jacket. Maybe Micah's age, maybe a year younger. Shaggy dark hair below his collar. Walked with purpose. Micah watched the man's face. Eyes sharp, focused. Scowling. Not happy to be here? Micah would see soon enough.

Micah pulled open the door before the man could knock. "Welcome. Micah."

"Wendell." *Who names their kid Wendell? Old family tradition?*

Micah motioned for Wendell to come inside. "Nice jacket."

Wendell nodded. "The green goes well with the blue tie. Are we done playing spy games?"

Micah didn't react. Externally. "I suppose. My father

insisted on the formality. We'll take it up with him when he gets here."

Wendell's face drew down. "Kurt Andres is coming?"

"Kurt Andres lives here. Yeah, he's coming." He wasn't, a detail Wendell didn't need to know right now. Micah waved him in. "Have a seat. Luke will be here at one. Tav will come when he's done with his final."

Wendell took a chair across from the window. Micah noted the man's features were small. His hands…his hands. Micah moved to shake Wendell's hand. Wendell reached out and grasped Micah's. Strong grasp. But thin fingers. Small nails.

Micah asked, "Drink? Cola, citrus, water, tea, coffee?"

Alabama wandered in from the bedroom. The dog ambled to Wendell, stuck her nose in his lap, and bumped his fist. Wendell reached out and scratched her ears. Alabama went belly-up and wiggled. *The Alabama seal of approval. Except she only asks for belly rubs from certain people. Certain kinds of people.*

"Water." Wendell looked at the clock. "Done with a final? I thought you guys were tight. Drop everything and come running."

"How long have you been with Quinn?" Micah handed Wendell a glass of water with ice, then sat across from the young man.

"What does that have to do with it?"

"Answer the question. How long have you worked with Quinn?"

"About eight months."

"How well do you know him?"

Wendell's eyes narrowed. "Well enough to know he's missing."

"Right. What has he told you about us?"

Wendell sniffed. "That you're two over-aged college kids and a slacker."

Micah grimaced. *I hear you, Quinn. I'll start school. Soon. I promise.*

Wendell continued. "You think as individuals but work as a team. You can navigate your way out of a paper bag."

Micah smiled. Quinn's favorite phrase.

Wendell continued. "He's called on you to help him in the past. None of that answers why your other guy isn't coming."

"Quinn repeatedly told us, 'I don't need help from college kids. If I do, I'll call you. Until then, stay in school.' He's missing. We'll help."

Wendell drank from his glass. His eyes narrowed, but he reached down and scratched Alabama's tummy. "We'll see."

Micah debated. *Go for it.* "Are you undercover?"

Wendell didn't look up. "Why do you ask?"

"Observation. Intuition. Spirit inspiration."

"What spirit?"

"Holy Spirit."

Wendell shook his head. "Bible thumper."

"Christ follower. But you didn't answer the question."

"What's it matter?"

"It matters because I need to know who I'm working with."

"You're working with Wendell Smothers. That's all you—
"

"—need to know. Heard it before. Not true. I need to know if you're more invested in protecting a secret identity than finding Quinn."

"I'm here."

"Didn't answer the question."

Wendell looked up. "Persistent bugger, aren't you?"

Micah smiled a straight-lipped smile. "That's me. The persistent one."

"And the slacker."

Micah nodded. "That's what Quinn calls me. And will until I get registered for college. But he knows what's kept me from enrolling."

"Care to share? Since we're getting to know each other?"

"Quinn should have told you if he's told you anything about us."

"The boys you found, right?"

Micah shifted in his seat. "Quinn would never say that."

Wendell nodded. "Fine. The boys that found you. Ben and BB. What kind of name is BB?"

"Quinn would have told you that as well. Is this a test or a diversion to keep from answering my question? Are you undercover?"

Wendell sat up and eyed Micah. "Yes. Why does it matter?"

"If we're working together, we may travel together. I have…principles…about arrangements."

"Meaning?"

Spell it out. "If you're a woman, we can't room together."

Wendell's eyes twinkled. "Is that what's bothering you? I assure you, it won't be a problem."

"It would be for me." Micah sat back in his chair. "But we'll have to deal with that when we come to it, right?"

"If we come to it."

"Right."

The back door opened. Alabama gave a happy "Woof" and jumped to her feet to greet the intruder. Luke called from the kitchen, "Honey, I'm home."

The lanky man walked into the living room. His eyes widened as he saw Wendell. "Oops. Sorry, bro." He extended his hand. "Luke Vaughn."

"Wendell Smothers." The agent returned the handshake. "You're the youngster of the group, right?"

Luke grimaced. "That's what Quinn always reminds me." He jerked his head to Micah. "As if him telling me isn't enough."

Micah grinned. "Speaking the truth in love, Luke."

Luke popped back into the kitchen, grabbed a soda from the fridge, and joined Micah and Wendell in the living room. He looked around. "Boys still in school?"

"BB has tutoring after school. Ben will be with the therapists until four. We've got time."

Wendell set his glass down. "You still haven't explained the name BB. And no, Quinn didn't explain it. Used it as if it was a matter of fact."

"BB stands for 'Ben's brother.' When we first met up, that's what he said to call him. His official name is Louis, but he wants to change it when he's old enough. Until then, we call him BB."

"Not many kids want their identity tied to their siblings."

"True. BB's not many kids."

Luke looked around. "Tav here yet?"

"Finishing up finals."

"Yeah, I know. Just thought he'd be done by now. He's aced everything in class so far."

Wendell raised an eyebrow. "What's he studying? What are you studying?"

"Tav is an engineering major. I'm still undecided. Going for psychology right now, but it may change."

Wendell looked to Micah. "If you go, what will you study?"

Micah bristled. "When I go, I'll study tax accounting. I'm a tax preparer now and want to be able to become a consultant eventually."

Wendell smiled. "Actually work in your field? What a concept."

Micah snorted. "It happens. What about you? What's your background?"

Wendell hesitated, then took a drink of water. He set it down. "Majored in criminology."

"Working in your field. Nice concept."

The front door flew open, jarring against the wall. Tav banged it shut and rolled into the living room. He peered out the front window, then closed the blinds.

Micah's eyes widened. "What's going on?"

Tav breathed hard. He took a moment to catch his breath. Luke came to his feet and moved to his brother's side. "What's the matter? What happened?"

Tav sighed, sat, and admitted, "Someone was following me."

Wendell cocked his head, skepticism on his face. "What?"

Tav nodded. "They picked me up coming out of the

garage at school. White sedan. No logo or front license. I watched them for about two miles, then did a four-corner right turn. They followed me all the way. I beat them at the light, but they caught me at the next one. Doubled back and lost them."

Micah sensed the group exhale. Until Tav continued, "Then, about three miles down the road, there's another sedan. Dusty brown. Same no logo, same no license. They tailed me for a mile or more. I jumped on the freeway, got off at Seventh. Got back on the same exit, and they stayed with me. Got off on Tenth. Doubled back, got off at Third, swung around the traffic circle, and hit Fifth. By then, they knew they were made and raced off. I didn't see anyone else, but I sure made the scenic route getting here."

Wendell leaned forward. "Lone driver?"

"Passenger in front. Both cars. Males, all of them. Caucasians. Dark hair. Passenger in one car wore a hat. No logo on it, either."

Wendell grimaced. "You seem pretty sure of your identification."

"If being with Quinn has taught us anything, it's to be observant. Pay attention to the details."

Luke nodded. "That's how we won the Magary game. Paying attention to details."

Micah added, "That and the Lord's grace."

Tav slipped in an "Amen."

Wendell ignored the affirmation and pressed Tav, "Why would anyone follow you?"

"I don't know."

"Do you expect to be followed?"

"No."

"Then why did you even notice?"

Tav turned to Micah. "Who is this?"

Micah swallowed a chuckled. "Wendell Smothers. He's the one Dad sent. Quinn's intern."

"Then you know Quinn insists we always be aware of our surroundings."

"Why does Quinn even know any of you?" Wendell's

voice carried incredulity.

Tav eyed Wendell. "Why does Quinn know you? You work for him. So do we. Sometimes. You tell us he's missing. Let's get to that. Then we can see if someone following me is connected." Tav leaned forward.

So Tav was taking control. Good enough. Micah sat back to listen.

Wendell tapped the table. "Quinn left ten days ago. Said he'd be gone about three days. Had an assignment in Hanford. Be there and back by Monday."

"And he never made it back."

Wendell nodded. "Right. I spoke to the powers that be, and they all said the same thing. When he's missing a month, they'll consider looking into it. But until then, this is standard operating procedure."

"But you're not satisfied with it."

"Quinn's never late, never gone without reason. This isn't right."

"And Kurt Andres, Micah's father, agrees with you." Tav motioned to Micah.

Wendell nodded. "He's the only one who did."

"And he directed you to us."

Wendell corrected, "He said you could help. I thought it was worth a shot. Now I'm not sure I shouldn't go this alone."

"Except what does Quinn say?"

"'Never go alone.'"

Tav leaned back on the couch. "Right. Hanford. Any idea what his business was there? Not exactly a booming town."

"Not exactly a hotbed of crime, either."

Tav looked across the room at his brother. "Luke?"

Luke typed into his phone, then came back. "Hanford. Central Valley. 2022 population 58,470. 18K households, 3.09 persons per house. Median income $68K. Per capita income $27K. Poverty rate is about 15%. Population density of 3300 per square mile, encompassing 17 square miles. What else do you want to know?"

"What do they do for a living there?"

"Top three are healthcare and social assistance, public admin, and retail trade. Top wage earners are, wait for it, public admin, finance and insurance, and transportation and warehousing."

"Crime?"

"It gets a D- for safety. But most of it is your assault, theft/burglary, vandalism, and drug variety. Nothing a major crime team would be looking at."

Tav shrugged. "That doesn't narrow it down." He looked at Wendell. "Give us something to start with. Something. Any phone calls? Suspicious packages? He win any lotteries?"

Wendell shook his head. "Nothing. 'I'm leaving. I'll be back in three days.' That's what I've got."

"Then I guess we take a field trip to Hanford."

Wendell's skepticism returned. "All of you?"

"All of us."

Wendell shook his head. "Who do you people think you are? Spies?"

Tav smiled, straight lipped. "No. We're Knights of the Octagon. We're ready for anything."

Micah added, "Because we get into most anything since meeting Quinn."

Luke's eyes narrowed. "Remember at the award ceremony, how Quinn wore his dress uniform? Marine, right?"

"Yeah, so?"

"So, Lemore Naval Air Station is not far from Hanford. The Navy and the Marines are part of the same branch."

Wendell chuckled. "Do not let Quinn, or any Marine for that matter, ever hear you say that."

Luke ducked his head. "Forgive me. But it could give us something to go on. Does he have any old shipmates or brothers-in-arms in the area he might want to visit?"

Wendell's eyes took a faraway glance. "There might be. I'll dig through his records and see what I can come up with. It still shouldn't make him ten days out and no communication."

"Granted. But we need to start somewhere. We could ask

those friends if they've seen or heard from him. Then take it from there."

Wendell nodded. "I can see that." He chewed his lip. "That's good thinking. I might not have come up with that idea. I've never seen him in uniform."

Micah added, "If you remember, he was very clear about us not commenting on his manner of dress."

Tav grinned, "Something about 'on your life,' right?"

Micah nodded. "That was it. He doesn't like to advertise his past."

Wendell snorted. "Or his present."

"That, too." Micah felt for Wendell. He couldn't imagine working for Quinn. Not full-time. It would be exhausting.

But would any of them have the chance to work with him again? They had to find him. One way or another. One for all...

* * *

ABOUT THE AUTHOR

Colleen K. Snyder has always had a passion for writing. She authored two previously published books: *Journey to Amanah: The Beginning* and *Return to Tebel-Ayr: The Journey Continues* (B&H Publishing). In 2020 she published the first book in the *Collin Walker* series: *Verdict at the River's Edge*. There are now seven books in the series. She lives on a "ranchette" in California and is the juniorest ranch hand. She serves on her church prayer team, and exercises a ministry of intercessory prayer. She has worked as a factory line worker, pharmacy technician, USAF missile systems analyst, janitor, nanny, teacher, accounting manager and anything else the Lord required. Her son, Bear and his wife Krystal, their two daughters, Mara and Kaylynn, and her daughter Katie all live in Ohio.

Colleen's story is for His glory, always.

Read on to learn more about Colleen's books in the *Collin Walker* series.

The Collin Walker Series

Six books of action and suspense for your reading enjoyment. Follow Collin Walker as she follows the Lord into murder, intrigue, mayhem…you know, Life.
Available on Kindle, KindleUnlimited, and in paperback.
(Also hardback, but why??)

www.ingramcontent.com/pod-product-compliance
Lightning Source LLC
Chambersburg PA
CBHW061205210726
48294CB00006B/1756